Praise for *The Art of Losing*

An ABA Indie Next Top 10 Book
A Goodreads Best Book of the Month

"You'll be obsessed." —***Cosmopolitan***

"*The Art of Losing* handles the themes of guilt and the cycle of addiction with grace and deftness." —***Entertainment Weekly***

"A riveting story about loss, addiction, and love, *The Art of Losing* is a poignant novel readers young and old will be able to relate to." **—Bustle**

"A story of family and sisterhood, Lizzy Mason's debut novel is a story that tackles grief and pain with so much heart. It's a powerful read, so don't miss out on this one."**—Paste Magazine**

"*The Art of Losing* is a lyrical and moving exploration of the fraught bonds of family, the suffocating bonds of addiction, and the warm, embracing bonds of love. This is a book you won't soon forget." **—Jeff Zentner, Morris Award–winning author of *The Serpent King***

"A brave and beautiful story about sisters, addiction, and finding your place in the world—a book that belongs on every shelf." **—Kathleen Glasgow, *New York Times* bestselling author of *Girl in Pieces***

"An unflinchingly honest and touching dive into the ever-complex relationship between sisters, the reality of addiction, and the nature of love in all forms. I will never forget Harley or her story." **—Alexandra Bracken, *New York Times* bestselling author of *Darkest Minds***

"With prose that taps into the highest of highs and lowest of lows, *The Art of Losing* shows exactly what it means to have a sister, to be a sister, and—the scariest of all—to possibly lose a sister. As a big sister myself, this story rang so true."

—Susan Dennard, *New York Times* bestselling author of *Truthwitch*

"Lizzy Mason's powerful debut is about the bonds and betrayals of sisterhood and accepting flaws in those we love. Emotionally resonant and, at times, gut-wrenching, Harley's story is one that will stay with you long after turning the last page."

—Elizabeth Eulberg, bestselling author of *Better Off Friends*

"Driven by authentic and well-developed characters and relationships, this work presents a compelling exploration of responsibility and forgiveness . . . A relevant and engaging coming-of-age novel that highlights the accountability that comes with adulthood." ***—Kirkus Reviews***

"Carefully crafted . . . With its authentic treatment of addiction, it's an appealing cautionary tale with conviction." ***—Booklist***

"Real characters with real problems make Lizzy Mason's debut novel a show stopper. Harley is facing a family tragedy, a boyfriend crisis, and teen alcohol use in a novel that is sure to resonate with every teen, parent, and teacher. *The Art of Losing* is a punch to the gut that will resonate long after reading and may act as a wake-up call to teens facing tough choices. Put this one on every book shelf in America."

—Pamela Klinger-Horn, Excelsior Bay Books (Excelsior, MN)

THE ART OF LOSING

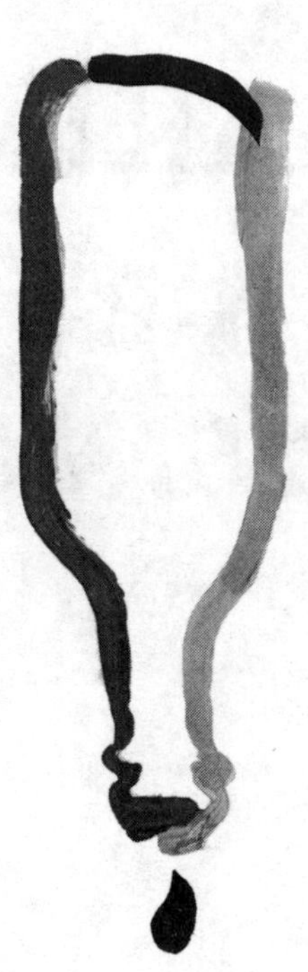

THE ART OF LOSING

LIZZY MASON

SOHO TEEN

Published in the United States by Soho Teen
an imprint of Soho Press, Inc.
227 W 17th Street
New York, NY 10011

Library of Congress Cataloging-in-Publication Data
Mason, Lizzy, author.
The art of losing / Lizzy Mason.
1. Sisters—Fiction. 2. Dating (Social customs)—Fiction. 3. Alcoholism—Fiction.
4. Drug abuse—Fiction. 5. Coma—Fiction.
PZ7.1.M37614 Art 2019 DDC [Fic]—dc23 2018030289

ISBN 978-1-64129-126-2
eISBN 978-1-61695-988-3
International paperback ISBN 978-1-64129-104-0

Interior design by Janine Agro, Soho Press, Inc.

Printed in the United States of America

10 9 8 7 6 5 4 3 2 1

For my sister, Anna, who loves stories with a happy ending
and didn't let me give up until I found mine

One Art
By Elizabeth Bishop

The art of losing isn't hard to master;
so many things seem filled with the intent
to be lost that their loss is no disaster.

Lose something every day. Accept the fluster
of lost door keys, the hour badly spent.
The art of losing isn't hard to master.

Then practice losing farther, losing faster:
places, and names, and where it was you meant
to travel. None of these will bring disaster.

I lost my mother's watch. And look! my last, or
next-to-last, of three loved houses went.
The art of losing isn't hard to master.

I lost two cities, lovely ones. And, vaster,
some realms I owned, two rivers, a continent.
I miss them, but it wasn't a disaster.

—Even losing you (the joking voice, a gesture
I love) I shan't have lied. It's evident
the art of losing's not too hard to master
though it may look like (*Write* it!) like disaster.

Sixteen Months Ago

When my little sister started high school, my family held its breath. With her late birthday, Audrey was always one of the youngest kids in her class. Her maturity level was never quite the same as that of her classmates.

But she had an unnerving ability to assume the best of people. It was annoying, really, the way she looked past people's outwardly obnoxious traits and found the good in them. I'd be bitching about someone, a teacher or a neighbor or whoever, and Audrey always, infuriatingly, had to point out something nice about them.

So none of us were surprised when she declared that she'd made valentines for all of her classmates in the ninth grade. But we were worried. I could practically hear the comments some of the girls would make. I could imagine the assumptions many of the guys would make. But Audrey wouldn't be deterred, no matter what I said.

"She's in high school now," Mom finally said to Dad and me while Audrey was upstairs gluing and cutting. "She can make her own decisions and deal with the consequences."

Dad and I disagreed.

"What if instead of cards, she gave out lattes?" Dad said, waiting expectantly.

Mom and I shared an eye roll and then she dutifully asked, "Why?"

"Because then they'd know she likes them a latte!"

I groaned. His puns made even Obama's "dad jokes" seem funny.

I think Mom had as much faith in the valentines as I did, but as usual, she pasted on a smile and busied herself with a crossword puzzle.

On Valentine's Day, I watched from my locker as Audrey passed out her cards. And, to be fair, they were pretty adorable, despite the glitter that showered down on her shoes with each one she pulled out of her backpack. She slipped some in people's lockers, and others she handed to the recipient directly.

People loved them, and not just her friends. I was stunned. If I'd done something like this, my classmates would have thought I was trying too hard or sucking up. But no one could accuse Audrey of being disingenuous. Her smile was too sincere, her delight in their reactions too contagious.

But I saw the nervousness on her face when she pulled out a slightly larger heart-shaped card that was more intricately decorated than the others. I watched as she slid it through the slats into a locker not far from mine. I'd never noticed who the locker belonged to, so I lingered for a little while before the first bell rang, hoping to catch a glimpse, wondering if all the other valentines were just to distract from the one person she really wanted to give one to.

My jaw went slack when Jason Raymond opened the locker and the heart-shaped card fell out and landed at his feet. He was a freshman who had been in my class the year before but was held back. When he smiled at the card, I couldn't help noticing the stubble on his chin. He was practically a man. Audrey had only quit sleeping with her favorite stuffed animal a year ago.

It felt like my sisterly duty to protect her.

So when Audrey told us about her crush matter-of-factly at dinner that night—something that I would never have even considered doing—I wasn't surprised. I was ready with about ten reasons why Jason was the wrong choice for her first date.

"He's so dumb," I interrupted her mid-sentence. "He got held back last year! You can't go out with a guy who's my age and still a freshman. That's just embarrassing."

Audrey's face turned red. Her eyes were glassy with rage. "You don't know him," she said. "None of you do. You just don't see what I see in him."

"Like what, honey?" Mom said patiently, cutting me off with a sharp look.

"Last week, at lunch, I saw him give his sandwich to a kid whose lunch money was stolen. And the week before that, he volunteered to be my partner in class when everyone else had already picked groups and left me out."

"Did he volunteer because no one else had picked him, either?" I asked. "Because he's an idiot and no one wants to do his work for him?"

"Harley!" Mom scolded me.

I slouched against the back of my chair and offered a half-hearted apology.

"If you're saying he's dumb, then you're calling me dumb." Audrey's voice wobbled. "Because we're in the same classes."

"Yeah, but you've only had to take the classes once," I muttered. But I felt guilty before the words even left my

mouth. Her grades were a sensitive subject, but no one was more frustrated than Audrey.

"So far," she said quietly.

I felt even worse when Jason asked her out a few days later and Mom and Dad wouldn't let her go. It was my fault, even though they said it was because of the D she'd gotten on her history test. I could still picture her smile as she told Mom about how Jason had asked her to the winter dance, and how it fell as Mom said no.

Audrey didn't speak to me for almost a full week after that. I couldn't blame her.

CHAPTER ONE

The atmosphere in the hospital waiting room felt as thick as the summer night outside. My parents' silent questions and accusations competed for space in the air with tension and worry.

Why didn't I drive Audrey home from the party we went to? Who was driving the car that she was in? Why didn't I make sure she had a way home? How could I have let this happen?

Guilt warred with anger until an anxious, bitter stew simmered in my stomach. Audrey shouldn't get to be the victim when I was the one who'd been betrayed.

I hadn't even wanted to go to the party. If my best friend hadn't been hosting, if my boyfriend hadn't wanted to go, I wouldn't have been there . . . and I wouldn't have brought Audrey. And maybe what happened would have stayed an unspoken fear buried in my subconscious.

The vinyl chair squeaked beneath me as I shifted restlessly. Dad's shoes scuffed the linoleum as he paced. Mom cleared her throat and sniffed. We were a symphony of anxiety.

Most parents are left waiting and wondering alone while their child is in surgery, but because Dad was an orthopedic surgeon at the hospital, every few minutes someone would come in and tell us how sorry they were. But no one could tell us what was going on. Or maybe no one wanted to be the bearer of bad news.

I wondered if they'd start bringing us Jell-O cups, but I wouldn't have been able to eat one anyway. It would bring back the memories I'd been pushing away: of the party that night where I had left my sister, of the gelatinous shots my boyfriend had been taking, of the two of them together in my best friend's bedroom.

Dad suddenly turned mid-stride and pushed through the swinging door. I could only assume he'd lost patience and gone to check on Audrey's surgery. A few nurses trailed after him like sympathetic baby ducks.

I stood and traced Dad's path across the small room. When he pushed back through the door a few minutes later, I froze.

"I finally got an update," he said. He spoke in a monotone. "Audrey is still in the OR. She's got swelling in her brain and it's pressing against her skull. They're draining some of the fluid so they can see what kind of damage there may be. She also has a broken arm that needs to be set and a fractured sternum and cracked ribs from the seat belt, but that will heal."

That all sounded like good news, relatively speaking. The tightness in my chest eased slightly. But then he turned to me.

"Harley, there's something I have to tell you," he said softly, putting both hands on my shoulders in a classic *I've-got-bad-news* stance. Or maybe he was trying to restrain me in case I tried to run.

"Mike was driving Audrey home tonight. The police said he was drunk, well over the limit."

My knees wobbled. I dropped back into the chair.

"He ran a red light," Dad continued, "and another car hit the passenger side where Audrey was sitting." He squatted down to look me in the eye for this last part. He was too preoccupied to remember that he had no cartilage in one of his knees from a college baseball injury. I heard it crack as he went down.

"Is Mike okay?" I asked. For a hateful second, I hoped that the answer would be no.

Dad nodded. "I just checked on him. He's in the ER, conscious but still drunk." His voice hardened. "He has a few bruises, a possible concussion and whiplash, but he'll be fine. He won't even have much of a hangover after the IV fluids he's getting."

I glanced at Mom, who met my gaze over the magazine she held in one hand, a ballpoint BIC in the other. She was doing the crossword puzzle in *pen*. And it wasn't even an easy, celebrity-centric *People* crossword.

Mom loved a good puzzle. She was always so satisfied when numbers added up, whether in a spreadsheet or sudoku. You could see the joy on her face when she filled in the last letter of a crossword or snapped the last piece of a jigsaw puzzle into its place. Puzzling was where she found peace, she said.

It was half of the reason she loved her job as an accountant so much. Her main clients were a handful of local businesses—boutique stores, mostly, which was perfect for her. She did the books from home, but she got serious discounts in the stores. She had this amazing talent where she could take one expensive piece from a boutique, add some cheap basics and accessories from T.J. Maxx, and end up looking like she should be in a glossy magazine spread about chic suburban moms.

Even now, with minutes to get dressed in the middle of the

night, her long-sleeved striped cotton shirt and pressed khakis would look completely appropriate if she was posed on the deck of a sailboat. Not in the waiting room of a hospital while her youngest daughter fought for her life.

But her face was white with rage, her lips a tight, pale line across her face. For the first time I could remember, it was a reflection of mine.

Mike had called my phone that night just as the police called the landline. I ignored it because I thought he was calling to apologize—and I didn't want to hear it—but also because just after my phone went silent, Dad tore into my room and told me to get in the car. Now I had to wonder what Mike would have said if I'd answered.

I turned back to Dad. "So Audrey is in surgery, possibly brain-damaged, because my boyfriend drove drunk and nearly got her killed?" I asked him.

My hands were suddenly fists. My heart throbbed so hard that a rushing noise filled my ears. How dare Mike even *think* of getting into a car with my sister when he'd been drinking? Like he hadn't done enough damage for one night?

Dad nodded once, his jaw clenched.

"And he's going to be *fine*?" I didn't wait for his response. "That asshole," I said. My fingernails pressed into the palms of my hands. "How drunk is he right now?"

"Why?" Dad asked warily.

"Because I want to scream at him. I want to punch him in the fucking teeth," I said. "But I want him to remember it."

"I don't think that's such a good idea," Dad said, even though he looked like he wanted to do the same. "The police are there now, talking to him about the accident."

Even through my anger, I couldn't suppress an innate flicker of worry. I hated Mike even more for that.

Just then, Aunt Tilly shoved through the door to the waiting room. Before she could say anything, my mom stood to meet her and collapsed into her arms, sobbing. She'd been keeping it together as much as she could up until that point, but somehow seeing her older sister gave Mom the permission to release her fear and worry and rage.

Aunt Tilly was a therapist who specialized in patients with agoraphobia, so unlike my mom, who was constantly pushing me to get out of the house and take an "active role in society," Tilly let me be who I was: a comics-obsessed girl who rarely left the comfort of her bedroom.

I felt sorry for my thirteen-year-old cousin Spencer, though. Aunt Tilly could spot a lie before it even came out of my mouth. His teen years were going to be hell.

But she was handy in a crisis, especially when my mom—and I—needed her.

It was Mom's sobs that finally cracked my shell of anger. I choked on the words I wanted to scream. Tilly reached out for me and smoothed my hair, brushing my overgrown bangs out of my eyes with one hand while rubbing Mom's back with the other.

"Let it out, chicken," she said.

I was gulping air like it was water and I'd just run through the desert as Aunt Tilly pulled me into the hug. Mom wrapped her arm around me. Inside the huddle, the therapist replaced the grieving aunt.

"Try to breathe," Aunt Tilly said. Her temple pressed against mine, and her hand was a reassuring pressure on the middle of my back. "In through your nose, okay?"

I took a shuddering breath in and Mom followed. Aunt Tilly counted to four.

"Good, now out through your mouth."

We followed orders, breathing in and out for eight seconds several more times. My tears wouldn't stop, but my heartbeat slowed a little, and I didn't feel like I was running anymore. Aunt Tilly finally released us from her grip, and we sat down in a soggy, red-faced row, passing a box of tissues.

Dad had slipped out the door, but by the time he came back from wherever he had gone, we'd dried our tears. I wondered briefly if he had been waiting outside the door to avoid us—or me.

"Is the other driver okay?" I asked him.

Dad nodded. "He's fine. He was wearing his seat belt and his airbags deployed. He's lucky."

I closed my eyes and took a deep breath, relieved that at least one person's life hadn't been destroyed by this. But as Dad pulled me into a hug, I felt sick. I knew I didn't deserve to be comforted by my father, who may have lost his baby daughter tonight and instead had his long arms wrapped around me.

I should have brought Audrey home with me. She's my sister. No matter what she did, I should have watched out for her.

When I opened my eyes, Aunt Tilly was looking at me.

"Harley, why don't we go get some coffee downstairs?" she said.

I nodded, even though I knew what was coming. She wanted to know what had happened.

AUNT TILLY FOLLOWED me to the elevator, but once inside, she hit the button for the ground floor instead.

"Where are we going?" I asked.

"I need a cigarette," she said, meeting my gaze with a guilty look.

I shrugged, thinking, *Me, too.* Aunt Tilly had supposedly quit smoking a year ago, but I wasn't disappointed in her failure to follow through this time. I had an only-when-drinking policy about smoking, and I hardly ever drank, but little-sister-in-peril seemed like a perfectly reasonable time to break my own smoking rule.

I followed her out of the elevator, through the chaos of the Emergency Room entrance, and across the parking lot to the farthest possible corner from the hospital so no one would glare at us. The stagnant humid air made me feel like I was breathing through a wet washcloth, but that didn't stop me from pointing at her pack until she reluctantly handed me a cigarette.

"So what really happened tonight?" she asked. "Why was Mike driving your sister home?" She let me light it before staring me down. Aunt Tilly was never one to hold back, but she wasn't afraid of a little silence, either.

After the first satisfying lungful of smoke, I opened my mouth to answer, but no words came. I couldn't tell her the truth about why I'd left Audrey behind at the party. I didn't want her feeling even one ounce of pity for me when her focus should be on Audrey.

I shrugged again instead, willing my traitorous tear ducts to stay dry. "I don't know," I said. "I thought her friend Neema was going to drive her."

She narrowed her eyes. I felt my pulse speed up. She knew I was lying. But she didn't ask me any more questions.

Instead, she changed the subject to Spencer, my cousin.

"He's supposed to go to camp this summer," Aunt Tilly said, "but I'm not sure how he'll handle it. You know how he can be with kids his age. Or anyone really."

I nodded. Spencer lacked some social skills, but he was

better with statistics than most graduate-level math students. He'd picked the winner of the World Series every year for as long as I could remember.

"If he hates it, I'll just figure something else out," she said. "Next year, he'll be old enough for that math camp at George Mason."

"Aunt Tilly, do you think my parents hate me?" I interrupted. I couldn't think about Spencer's math camp when I was spiraling through a tornado of guilt. Maybe she'd known that I'd cave out of boredom and start talking to her.

"Oh, chicken." She reached out to tuck my shoulder under her arm. "They don't blame you for this."

"Maybe not yet," I said darkly. But they would.

ONCE WE WERE back in the chilly air of the hospital, I steered Aunt Tilly toward the cafeteria. I really did want coffee, but I knew Dad needed a cup, too. He was used to late nights, but there's a big difference between doing surgery at 2 A.M. and waiting for your child to come out of it.

When we walked back into the waiting room, Mom gave Aunt Tilly a withering look. She sighed a soft "Mathilda" and shook her head. No doubt she could smell the smoke on us. But for once, I didn't care. I hadn't even bothered with gum.

"Has anyone come in to tell you what's going on?" I asked Dad as I handed him the cup of coffee. The chair sighed as I sat, as if unhappy about my return.

"No," he said. I tried not to read too much from the bags under his eyes. I didn't ask if he'd gone to check on Mike again. I preferred to pretend he no longer existed.

After what felt like days, a doctor I recognized—I think he'd been to our house for dinner—opened the door and motioned for my parents to step out into the hallway. I couldn't read his expression, but he wasn't beaming with joy.

I could just see the side of Dad's face through the glass as the doctor spoke, but Dad betrayed nothing. I clamped a hand over my mouth and gripped my necklace with the other. The pendant was a silver *H* that Audrey had given me for Christmas the year before. The sharp edges cut into my fingers.

When Dad opened the door, Aunt Tilly and I were already standing.

"She's resting comfortably," he said. "They set her arm—the humerus needed a few pins—and they repaired her fractured sternum. Her ribs will just take time. And they were able to relieve some of the intracranial pressure by inserting a shunt to drain some of the fluid from the swelling around her brain." He took a deep breath. "That's good news."

"Is there bad news?" Aunt Tilly asked cautiously.

Dad shook his head. "Even though she has a traumatic brain injury, there was no bleeding."

He sounded positive, but I could hear the strain and uncertainty. I'd watched enough TV to know that brain injuries *are* bad news. And he didn't make a "humerus" pun. He was too stressed even for that.

"So what now?" I asked.

He avoided looking at any of us. Even Mom, who'd followed him through the door and taken Tilly's hand. She was squeezing so tightly, her knuckles were white with the effort.

"Now they keep an eye on her and wait for her to wake up."

Aunt Tilly put her hand over her heart and whispered, "When will that be?"

"They've given her steroids to try to reduce the swelling in her brain, but Dr. Martinez said she needs to be put into a medically induced coma so that she can heal—" Dad's composure fractured, and he let out a choked cry. Tears filled his eyes. Mine filled in response. "So I don't know," he said softly. "It could be days . . . or weeks . . ."

Or not at all, I finished in my head.

Twelve Years Ago

"Hurry up, Audy!" I yelled, dragging our red plastic wagon down the hallway. Inside, two of our stuffed animals were wrapped in gauze like mummies. "This is an ambulance, and it has to go fast!"

Audrey caught up to me as I reached the stairs.

"Ready?" I asked her.

She nodded, sucking on her bottom lip as she climbed into the wagon. We'd padded the bottom of the staircase with blankets and a few couch cushions to catch the wagon when it landed.

"Okay," I said from behind. "I'll make the siren noise while you drive the patients."

Audrey's chin started to tremble. "I want to make the siren noise," she said.

I almost said no, almost insisted that I had to be the one to do the siren, but I didn't want her to cry and get me in trouble before I'd even done anything wrong. So I told her to hold on to the sides of the wagon.

"Now!" I yelled and gave the wagon a push. Her siren noise quickly morphed into a scream.

Audrey plunged down the stairs without flipping out of the wagon—which was amazing enough—but it was nothing short of a miracle that she didn't crack her head open on the hardwood floor when she landed. She had a goose egg on her forehead and had scraped one elbow and both knees. The padding we'd arranged had done almost nothing to break her fall.

Her cries were so much worse than they would have been if I hadn't let her make the siren noise. I should have told her to keep her mouth shut.

Mom came running, her face a wild mask of terror. She scooped Audrey into her arms and started firing off questions: "What hurts and where?"

When Audrey pointed to her head, Mom whisked her into the car, leaving me behind with Dad. He sat me down on the stairs, the scene of the crime.

"Do you have any idea how dangerous that was?" he yelled, looming above me.

I nodded, my lower lip trembling. "I'm sorry," I whispered.

"You can apologize to your sister," he said. "You could have killed her."

Audrey was okay, no concussion or broken bones, but those words—I "could have killed her"—stuck with me. Stuck inside me.

I got grounded for a week with no TV, but I punished myself much more harshly. I slept with Audrey every night until her scabs peeled off to reveal pink skin underneath, and I let her have whatever she wanted—the bigger slice of pizza, the red popsicle, the choice of what to watch on TV.

I gave myself the task of being Audrey's protector from then on.

CHAPTER TWO

As the sun began to rise, I turned my phone back on and watched as the texts, emails, and even voicemails poured in. Mostly friends wanting to know what was happening, but Mike had also texted me about a dozen times, asking me to call him. And even though I answered none of them, they all made me want to throw my phone out the window. So did the silence when it wasn't buzzing.

Aunt Tilly was stationed outside Audrey's room to usher away anyone who came by, probably less politely than Mom would have liked, but none of us had gotten any sleep the night before and I doubted Mom had the energy to argue. Plus, it did the job.

The only person Tilly let in was my best friend, Cassidy, who had spent more time with my family than her own over the last ten years. With three younger siblings, I think she liked the quiet of our house as much as she liked that Mom stocked her favorite snacks and cereal alongside mine and Audrey's.

Cassidy's parents weren't neglectful or anything; they were just distracted. Her grandmother had broken a hip two days ago, so her mom took her two younger brothers, Loren and Kelly, to Richmond to stay with her. Cassidy's father had a business trip that couldn't be rescheduled, so the Finches left her in charge of her fourteen-year-old sister, Morgan.

It wasn't like Cassidy to throw a party while her parents were away, but it was too good an opportunity to pass up. Still, she'd been nervous about it. Nervous they'd find out, nervous that no one would come, nervous that too many people would come. Nervous that Morgan would rat her out. I promised I'd be there to make her feel better if no one showed up. And I was.

So when I texted Cassidy, she answered right away, saying she'd come as soon as she could. She added a dozen *x*'s and *o*'s.

She opened the hospital room door an hour later. Mom gave her a long look, hugged her, then took Dad's hand and left the room.

I knew what Cassidy was thinking when her eyes settled on Audrey's inert body because I'd thought it, too. My sister was unrecognizable.

Tubes were shoved down her throat. Swollen bruises under her eyes squeezed the lids shut. She hardly looked human. Not to mention that her head was wrapped in gauze, her arm set in a contraption and propped up at her side, and her body was hooked up to so many machines that there were wires snaking out from under every available opening in her hospital gown. Her right cheek and her chin were burned from the airbag, and her chest was bruised from the seat belt. Purple, red, blue, and black cut angry swaths across her skin.

She wasn't sleeping, but she clearly wasn't dead either. She was in some horrible purgatory where no one could reach her.

Cassidy didn't comment; she just hugged me.

I closed my eyes and leaned into the warmth of her

embrace and the lavender scent of her shampoo. But even though her hair was still wet from her shower, she exuded the slight tang of alcohol, and I couldn't help but wonder how hungover she was.

"I'm so sorry," she finally whispered. "I wish I could've been here sooner, but I was up all night trying to find someone to cover for me at work and you'd turned your phone off, so I couldn't call you." She was trembling.

"It's okay," I said, squeezing her harder. "Did you find someone to work for you?"

She released me and sat in the chair Mom had vacated. "Yeah, reluctantly. The Flakey Pastry customers will have their coffee and croissants."

I tried to smile, but both of our expressions were pained.

"I'm sorry," she said again, her eyes flicking toward Audrey.

"Thanks," I said.

But Cassidy shook her head. "No, I'm *really* sorry. It was my party. At my house. I'm responsible for what happened."

"This is not your fault," I grumbled. "Mike didn't have to drink last night just because you had a party." But when my eyes met hers, I saw what she didn't need to say aloud. Mike wouldn't have been able to keep himself from drinking, even if he had bothered to try. "Okay, fine, but he didn't need you to have a party to get drunk."

She sighed and leaned back in her seat. "No, I guess not."

"Trust me."

"Have you talked to Mike since . . . it happened?" she asked.

"No," I said brusquely. "I haven't talked to him and I don't plan to, ever again."

Cassidy raised her eyebrows. She had never been Mike's

biggest fan, and she knew that I had wanted to break up with him for weeks. But she didn't know what happened. She didn't know what he'd done or what shape he was in now.

"How can I, Cass? He could have killed Audrey. And yet *he's* fine. He's going to walk out of this hospital with barely a scratch."

"Okay, but . . ." Her voice trailed off when she saw the tears welling in my eyes. "Harley, is there something you aren't telling me?"

I didn't want to tell her. For Audrey's sake, and for my own. It was humiliating.

But Cassidy was the one who knew all my secrets. And she had never broken my trust.

She knew about the time I kissed Harrison Sanders on a dare at a party in middle school, even though he was the scrawniest kid in our class, and I made a big deal about wiping my mouth off afterward. I felt bad about it every time I saw him after that. She knew about the time I threw up in a Ziploc bag in the back of the bus on a field trip in third grade and left it there, telling no one that I was feverish and nauseated, because I wanted to see the new baby panda at the zoo. She knew about the time Rafael Juarez, my next-door neighbor, asked me to sneak out to meet him one night the summer before eighth grade. How I waited for him for an hour and how he never showed.

She'd never told anyone any of it.

I steeled myself. "Mike cheated on me," I confessed. "With Audrey."

Cassidy's eyes went wide with disbelief. "What? *When*?"

"Last night, at the party. And then I walked out and left them behind to . . ." I let my voice trail off and gestured at Audrey's inert body in front of us. "My *sister*, Cass," I said.

"She said they didn't have sex, but still. How could they do that?"

She shook her head slowly, genuinely shocked.

"You can't tell anyone," I warned her. "Even my parents don't know."

Cassidy pressed her hand over her heart. "I would *never*," she said. "And I'm so sorry that he did that. That they did that. But she glanced away guiltily as she chewed her lip. "Okay, don't hate me, but . . ."

"What?" I asked.

"Exactly *where* did they hook up?" she asked. At least she had the decency to look sheepish.

I had forgotten about that part.

"No, wait, I changed my mind. I don't want to know," she said, covering her ears.

But it was too late. I'd gone this far; I needed to unburden myself of this one last piece of awfulness. "Sorry, Cass," I said. "You may want to wash your sheets."

Disgust flickered across her face, but she took a deep breath and squared her shoulders. "It's fine."

"Are you in trouble?" I asked her. "Do your parents know?"

"Oh yeah, they know. Mom's on her way home now. I may not be allowed out of the house for a while."

As I studied her face, I realized the circles under her eyes were as dark as mine. "How did they find out?" Her frown told me she'd been hoping I wouldn't ask.

"Your mom called my mom," she said.

Of course she had.

Rage boiled inside me. I could hear Mom justifying it in my head already. She'd tell me it was "her job as a parent."

But Cassidy was already shaking her head, preempting my

apologies. "Don't worry about it. I got Ryan and those guys to take the keg with them and nothing was broken. As soon as word got out about what had happened, everyone quit drinking and cleared out fast."

Ryan was Mike's best friend. He had more patience for Mike's drunken antics than I did and covered for him as much as he could. I bet Mike called him as soon as he got to the hospital, before he even called his mom. Not because Ryan meant more to him, but because Ryan could start smoothing over any potential fallout right away.

Mike would ask Ryan to find out who knew what and what people were saying, so he'd know what he could lie about and what he could cover up. I was surprised Ryan hadn't called me to gauge my mood, but then I remembered I'd turned my phone off.

"So everyone knows what happened?" I said.

Cassidy nodded slowly, as if trying to ease me into it. "Yeah," she said. "A few people texted when they saw the accident. The . . . aftermath. Mike's car is so recognizable with that happy face sticker on it. As soon as someone snapped a picture, it just spread. You know how it is."

I did indeed know. Ryan's job got a lot harder then.

But I cared more about how many people knew about what had happened between Mike and Audrey. How many of them had seen me running down the stairs, out of the house? How many had seen me leave my sister and my boyfriend alone together in Cassidy's room?

"I shouldn't have left Audrey there with Mike," I choked out. The brick reappeared, the one that seemed to have taken up residence in my throat. "It should have been me in that car—"

"Shut up," Cassidy interrupted.

I blinked at her. She kept her eyes on mine as she turned

her chair, facing me, wrapping my hands up in hers. Her thin fingers were chilly from the hospital air-conditioning. Every part of her seemed to be trembling.

"I know that you're hurting right now. But if you say anything like that ever again, I will punch you. Hard." A faint smile crossed her lips. "Harder than Batman would punch . . . um, the Joker?"

I couldn't help letting out a small laugh. Cassidy had always been confused by my love of comics. Real life was her escape, including our friendship. Cassidy preferred being a force in student government and debate and Model UN. Not physically, though. In our kickboxing segment in gym class, sophomore year, the heavy bag barely moved when she hit it.

"Batman is probably one of the weakest superheroes, comparatively speaking," I couldn't help saying. "A better threat would be to punch me harder than the Hulk or Superman. Just scientifically, they both have super-strength. Batman just has gadgets and human muscles."

Cassidy rolled her eyes. "Fine. I'll hit you harder than Superman would hit the Hulk or whatever you just said."

I snorted.

"Okay?" she pressed.

"Okay, okay, I won't. I swear," I said, pulling my hands from hers. "But I need you to do me a favor."

She narrowed her eyes. "What?"

I held out my phone to her. "I need you to erase all of Mike's messages. I don't want to see or hear his apologies."

She took it. "I'm deleting his number, too."

I nodded. "Good idea."

"I do have good ideas occasionally," she said, glancing up from my phone with a wry grin. "You should listen to me more often."

"You're going to say you told me so, aren't you? About dating Mike?"

She shrugged. "Can you blame me?"

"No." I sighed. "But try not to blame yourself either, okay?"

Cassidy handed me my phone and scrubbed her hands across her face. Her eyelids were heavy.

"Go get some sleep before your parents get home," I said. But I grabbed her hand as she stood. "It was a good party. Before the drama."

Cassidy leaned down and hugged me. "You're sweet for lying to me. Thanks for coming even though you hated it."

"I only hated it a little . . . until I hated it a lot."

Cassidy paused at the door. "That's how I know you love me. Because you stayed anyway. Until you couldn't."

AUDREY AND I were finally alone. I felt awkward and uncomfortable in the silence. I kept waiting for her to open her eyes and yell at me for watching her sleep.

Mom had turned into a semi-hysterical fountain of tidbits and facts, poring over articles about head trauma and car accidents, until Tilly finally convinced her to join her outside for a very long smoke. Meanwhile, Dad fidgeted, paced around, left the room, and returned so often that I had turned it into a game in my head. Every time he left, I would get the chance to win money (from myself) to spend at the vending machine. How many minutes it took him to come back equaled how many cents I got. I'd earned more than two dollars already, so I had big plans involving a Snickers bar and a bag of chips.

Party animal = me.

I leaned forward and smoothed Audrey's bangs flat on her forehead.

Two weeks after I cut my hair, she'd gone to the mall with her friends and had come back with a hairstyle that matched mine. I was so angry I wanted to cut her ponytail off in her sleep.

We'd always been the Langston Girls, a duo in everyone's minds and nearly interchangeable. Aside from the two additional inches and fifty extra pounds on my frame, we looked so much alike that I would answer to "Audrey," just in case they really meant "Harley." Sometimes I'd even pretend to be her when it was less awkward than correcting the mistake of our neighbors and family friends. I knew enough about her life to answer their generally surface-level questions. Or at least I thought I did.

I realized suddenly that I was staring at a bruise on her neck, a small reddish mark. It looked more like a hickey.

Mike was a fan of giving hickeys. I'd always pushed him away when he tried, but maybe Audrey hadn't known what he was doing. Or maybe she'd liked it.

I sat down next to her and took her small hand in mine.

"Hey, Audy," I said quietly. "I don't know if you can hear me, but I hope you can."

Only the rhythmic *whoosh-thump* of her ventilator answered. "So, listen, about this thing with you and Mike . . . I think we should just try to forget about it. For now. Don't you?"

She didn't respond, of course, but her familiar voice in my head said, *Yeah, sure, Harley. That seems likely.*

"I'm super pissed, and I want to scream and yell and beat the crap out of both of you. But, I mean, you're here and I don't plan to ever see him again . . . I think maybe we can deal with it when you wake up, okay?"

The Audrey in my mind turned skeptical. *Cool*, she said. *I'm definitely going to enjoy* that *conversation.*

"Don't let that be a reason not to wake up," I said, backpedaling. "You are going to wake up, right?"

Behind her eyelids, I saw her eyes move. Or maybe I imagined it. Maybe the stress and sleeplessness had finally caught up to me. But for the briefest instant, my heart lifted . . . and then just as quickly, the elation vanished. The doctors had warned us that we could see involuntary twitches.

"Just get better," I whispered as I put her hand back down on the bed and tucked the blankets up around her chest. "When you wake up, I swear I won't be mad. Just wake up."

She didn't respond, not even in my imagination. Maybe she thought I was lying. I couldn't really be sure myself.

LATER THAT MORNING, I awoke from a restless nap to the sound of a hushed conversation in the hallway.

Mom had gone home to shower and change; Aunt Tilly had gone to pick up Spencer; and Dad was in the cafeteria, getting lunch and making phone calls to his side of the family. Mom and Aunt Tilly were pretty much the only two left on their side.

I cracked an eyelid. The door was open a couple of inches, and a pair of dark brown eyes widened and disappeared behind the cover of straight black hair. *Neema*, I realized. Audrey's best friend. I shuffled on numb legs to the door and pulled it open, but Neema wasn't alone. Her dad lurked behind her in the hallway, his face grim.

"Hi," she said, her eyes not meeting mine.

Neema had been at the party, but I couldn't tell if the awkwardness was due to Audrey's hookup with Mike or because her best friend was lying comatose a few feet away. Maybe both.

"Do you want to come in?" I asked.

Neema nodded, so I stepped backward into the room and held the door open as she entered. She had spent plenty of time at our house, sleeping over and hanging out after school, but we weren't friends. I didn't like the way she bossed Audrey around, and I felt like Audrey gave in to her too much. But I knew that was probably just big-sister protectiveness.

She and Neema had fun together, and even though Neema wasn't as full of energy as Audrey was, she seemed to be the only one Audrey would sit still with. To watch movies or paint their nails or play video games or do homework. Neema and Audrey just kept up a steady stream of conversation even when they watched TV. I envied their easy comfort with each other.

So I tried to be friendly. I drove the two of them to the mall and let them hang out with me and Cassidy sometimes. I invited them to parties, including the one at Cassidy's house.

Neema approached Audrey's bed and picked up her limp hand. She had to curl Audrey's fingers around her own to hold it in place, otherwise it would drop back to the bed.

"Why did this happen?" she whispered. I didn't think she was looking for an answer, but then she spun around to look at me. "What was she doing in the car with your boyfriend? Why didn't you drive her home?"

My chest felt tight as I clutched at my necklace. "She didn't tell you?" I said.

Neema shook her head. "No, I left early. Before you did."

I felt her judgment like a slap. Audrey couldn't have gotten a ride home from Neema. When I left after walking in on her and Mike, he was her only option.

"I wanted to go home; she wanted to stay," I lied. It was sort of true. "So she found another ride." I pushed away the anger at Mike. I was used to doing that. But the anger at myself was too powerful to ignore.

Neema turned, staring down at her friend. "She can't die," she whispered. A tear slipped down her cheek and she swiped at it angrily. "We left her there alone." She leaned down and kissed my sister lightly on the forehead. "I'm sorry," Neema whispered.

A tear slid down my cheek. But I wasn't so much devastated as I was angry. At too many people to even keep track. Including myself. And now, Neema was apologizing for me, and in doing so, she was also blaming me.

I could feel my guilt beginning to simmer. I was a geyser and it was only a matter of time before I exploded.

"Don't apologize," I said.

Neema flinched slightly. My voice was louder than I'd intended.

"It's my fault that she's here," I added.

Neema's watery eyes were wide. Her lips quivered as she brushed past me toward the door.

"That doesn't make you feel better?" I snapped at her back. "That it's my fault? That I've thought that *every second* since it happened?" I was almost shouting now. "Did you think I *hadn't* apologized?"

Neema's father pushed the door open, his face a mask of disapproval.

"I think we should go," he said to Neema while glaring at me. "Clearly, this is a very stressful time."

He closed the door behind Neema before I could say another word. Not that it would have mattered. She was already halfway down the hall.

I sighed, flopping down in the chair next to Audrey's bed.

He was right. It was a "stressful time." My sister might die.

And yet Audrey's betrayal poisoned every second, no matter how hard I tried to forget. It reinforced every miserable, niggling suspicion I had always tried to push out of my thoughts: that Audrey was the more desirable Langston sister.

This was my proof.

I WAS SNEAKING out of thc hospital to smoke one of Aunt Tilly's cigarettes when I heard his voice.

"Harley?"

I froze. I should have known I'd bump into him.

Mike sat on the little brick wall outside the Emergency Room, hunched over in the bright mid-morning sun. The glare was too bright, but it highlighted how terrible he looked. His wavy blond hair was tousled on one side and matted with blood on the other. He had a bandage above one eyebrow and a burn like Audrey's on his cheek. He was wearing the same T-shirt I had last seen crumpled on the floor of my best friend's bedroom.

"What do you want?" I said through clenched teeth.

He stood and put out an arm to steady himself on the wall. He was wobbly, disoriented. *Good*, I thought.

"Can we talk?" he asked. His voice was hoarse.

I squinted at him. "No," I said. I turned to walk away, but he hustled up behind me, clearly in pain. I could see the strain on his face.

"Please, Harley?" he said. He reached out for me, but I yanked my arm away violently.

"Don't touch me," I spat. "The fact that you're walking out of here right now, and she's . . . she's . . ." The words got stuck in my throat.

He didn't move to follow me when I stepped out of his reach. I headed toward the shady side of the parking lot, catching a glimpse of his mom's car as she pulled under the awning that covered the ER entrance.

"I'm sorry," he shouted after me, his voice breaking.

I willed myself not to turn around. Instead, I ran, just like Neema had run from me. I shouted silently: *That's not enough.*

One Year Ago

Walking down the hallway at my school isn't like the scenes you see in movies. There are no girls tossing their hair while guys check them out. No one is slapping high fives about last night's big game. No nerds are being tripped or bullied. The social torture is much more subtle.

Audrey's English class was held next door to the AP English class during the same period. Her class was full of athletes and slackers, the kids who struggled, and the ones who had learning disabilities. And while no one would make fun of her publicly, everything felt deliberate to Audrey—her friends discussing the books they were reading in class that would take her months to get through, talking about the colleges they were planning to apply to that they knew she couldn't get into—and she ended up in tears a lot.

I was headed to lunch with a few of my friends one day when we passed by the freshman lockers. Audrey sat on the floor with her back against her locker, her head in her hands. A few papers lay shredded on the linoleum floor next to her.

"Go ahead, you guys," I told my friends and diverted my path toward Audrey.

I was still fifty feet away when I saw Mike walk out of the bathroom across from her. He did a double take and said, "Audrey? What's wrong?"

He eased down next to her and sat, quietly, waiting for her to talk. I stopped before they saw me and hid behind an open door. Audrey used to come to me with all her problems, but since starting high school, she was less interested in my opinion. But she liked Mike. She sought him out when he was over at our house, showing up wherever we were and putting a major crimp in our plans.

"You won't tell Harley?" I heard her say.

Mike drew an X over his heart. "I won't."

"I'm failing algebra," she said quietly. "I'm going to have to go to summer school."

"That's not such a big deal," Mike said. "Algebra is tough."

Audrey took her head out of her hands long enough to look at him skeptically. "You and Harley both got A's."

He shrugged. "We had each other's help," he said. "Maybe that's what you need, too."

"What, like a tutor?" she said with disdain. "Believe me, my parents have tried that."

"You haven't studied with me, though," he said. "Or Harley. Maybe we can help."

"There's no way Harley would do that. She hates me."

The words were a punch to the gut, but she was partly right. I didn't hate her, but I would have scoffed at the idea of helping her if she had asked.

"If you pass your final, will you pass the class?" Mike asked.

She nodded. "Barely."

"Then we'll do it. Leave Harley to me. She loves you. And

she loves me. So I think we can win her over, don't you?" When he flashed his straight-toothed smile at her, I knew she would agree. It was impossible to say no to that smile.

Audrey smiled back. "Do we have to?"

Mike laughed and nudged her with his elbow. "She's better at algebra than I am. Trust me, we need her."

Damn it, *I thought. Mike was right. I'd rather watch* Plan 9 from Outer Space*—arguably one of the worst movies in history—than help my sister with algebra, but she needed me.*

I ducked out from behind the door. "Hey, you two," I said, trying to act casual. "What's going on?" I dropped to the floor between Mike's legs. He slipped his arms around my waist.

"We have a job, or better yet, a duty," Mike said, "to get Audrey through her algebra final."

I patted her on the knee. "Don't worry, kid," I said. She wrinkled her nose at the moniker, but her tears had dried. "We got this."

Audrey heaved a relieved sigh while I fought back a wave of guilt that I hadn't helped her before now. I hugged Mike's knees and leaned against his chest, grateful that he was kinder to my sister than I was.

It never occurred to me to be suspicious of it.

CHAPTER THREE

The night air was humid and stale, like a wool blanket still damp from the dryer. I was almost done with the cigarette I'd bummed from Aunt Tilly, relishing the idea of getting back in the air-conditioning, when I heard the whisper of footsteps on grass. A telltale glowing ember—the orange tip of a cigarette—floated around the corner of the house next door. I considered putting mine out, but I figured if the person was also smoking, they couldn't give me too much grief.

He stepped into the dim light from the side porch. Definitely a "he." I could see that he was tall and broad-shouldered, but somewhat slim. So it wasn't Mr. Juarez, who had a belly that hung over his waistband.

My heart squeezed.

I recognized that sharp profile. It belonged to the person I'd spent every day with until I was seven. Before Cassidy, Rafael Juarez was my best friend.

Raf and I hadn't talked in years. But he didn't hesitate when our eyes met. He just walked up and sat down next to me on the low wall that surrounded our back garden. I tried to be discreet as I pulled my shorts down to cover more of my thighs and smoothed my humidity-frizzed hair.

"Hey, Harley," he said. "Long time."

"Hey," I answered. "Yeah."

I put out my cigarette and held the butt in my fingers, resisting the urge to cover my stomach with my arms. My T-shirt was tighter than what I would normally wear in public. It was one of Audrey's.

"I heard about Audrey," Raf said, as if I'd spoken out loud. "I'm sorry."

He and Audrey had also been friends when we were little. Sort of. We always forced Audrey to be the family dog or the baby when we played house. She didn't seem to mind; she was just happy to be included.

"Thanks," I managed to say.

I snuck another glance at him as he took a drag of his cigarette, the brief flare of the cherry illuminating his face. I could still see the six-year-old boy I'd pretend-married. His dark hair was longer and fell in soft waves across his forehead. But his face was harder-edged now, his cheekbones more defined, and there was a dark stubble across his sharp jaw. He was bigger, too. He used to be really scrawny as a kid.

"Is she, you know, doing okay?" he asked. "Sorry. I mean, I know she's not 'okay,' but . . ." He cringed. "Never mind."

I let him stew in silence for a few seconds before letting him off the hook. "Don't worry about it," I said.

He tapped me in the ribs lightly with his elbow. "But really. How is she?"

I took a breath. "She's . . . in a coma."

It was the first time I'd said those words out loud.

Earlier that day, her doctors had grown concerned about the continued swelling in her brain. After more than twenty-four hours on steroids and diuretics, the decision was made to allow her brain to heal as the swelling went down. Dad said they would keep her in the coma—and it was no different than being under heavy sedation—for a few days. Then, if her EEG and CT scan showed improvement, they would wake her.

"The doctors say the rest of her is healing," I added. "But it's so weird, Raf. She's just . . . not there."

Raf didn't say anything, but he didn't have to. He knew what I was feeling. He slid his hand over on the rough stone wall until his fingertips were so close to mine that I could almost feel their warmth.

"Thanks for asking," I said.

He nodded. "Of course," he said. "With Allie, people were always avoiding it. Like, they wanted to know how she was, how we were, but never wanted to come out and ask. They didn't want to remind us, but it's not like we could forget, you know?"

I nodded. I could feel his eyes on me as I stared into the dark.

"So how are *you*?" he asked.

"I've been better. I'm so numb and I just keep thinking, 'I wasn't expecting to spend my summer sitting at the hospital all day, hoping my sister wakes up.' How ridiculous is that?"

"I'm sorry," he said. "If it helps, I hear the hospital cafeteria food has really improved since the last time I spent *my* summer there. Mom says there's even a Subway now. The fact that that's an improvement is saying something about what it was like before."

I managed a smile. Of course Raf would remember the hospital food. Such a boy.

"It helps a little," I said. "But maybe not enough to make up for the fact that my boyfriend, the drunk asshole who almost killed her? He walked away with barely a scratch on him."

Raf inhaled sharply. I guess that part hadn't yet hit the neighborhood gossip circuit.

"But he's still your boyfriend?" he asked.

I shrugged. "Only because I haven't wanted to talk to him for long enough to break up with him."

"That sounds about right," he said. "The Harley I remember would have kicked him to the curb before he even got out of the car."

I turned and stared at him. Was that really what he thought of me? I found myself wishing that I was the girl he remembered, bossy and demanding of his time. Insisting that we play the games I wanted to play. Making him watch the movies I wanted to watch. He saw more *My Little Pony* than he'd probably ever admit.

Instead, I grew up to be Mike's girlfriend. I'd liked having a boyfriend so much that at first I'd pretended to be someone I wasn't. But when I was finally comfortable enough to stand up for myself, Mike saw it as some kind of betrayal. He'd made *me* feel guilty about it.

Suddenly I realized I'd been gazing at Raf for too long. It was getting awkward. I said the first thing that came into my head.

"So, speaking of drinking, how was rehab?"

He laughed softly. "You heard about that, huh?"

I found myself smiling, too. "You heard about Audrey, didn't you? Like, immediately after it happened? You know this neighborhood. I heard all about how your parents caught you with weed. How furious they were."

Raf's smile faltered. He took a deep drag from his cigarette and bowed his head, avoiding my eyes. He exhaled heavily.

"It was outpatient, more like group therapy with a urine test at the beginning of every session. Sometimes a Breathalyzer, too."

I swallowed. That sounded awful. Humiliating. "Did it work?" I asked.

"I don't know," he said with a sigh. "I guess so. I mean, I'm sober. I just don't want to keep being a disappointment to my parents, you know? Being a burnout. But I don't know if I'm actually an addict."

"How do you figure that out?"

He laughed again, softly. "I don't know that either. My therapist thinks I still need to 'come to terms with it.' But I think I'm just bored. Tired. Depressed. This city, this neighborhood, this house . . . it's stifling."

"But you're graduating, right? I can't wait to graduate, go to college, and get far away from here."

Raf was quiet for a moment. He eyed the glowing embers of the end of his cigarette.

"Yeah, I'm graduating, but barely," he said. Then softer, "And I didn't get into any of the colleges I applied to."

I blinked. "Oh," I said, fighting to hide my surprise. The Raf I knew—or had known—was brilliant. In middle school, my mom told me that he had taken the SATs as part of some gifted program and he had done better than some of the juniors. He could have skipped a grade if his parents had been willing to let him. But he'd just been through a pretty big trauma. His parents figured that he needed his friends around, so he stayed with his class.

"Did you apply to art schools?" I asked.

He took a last drag and then stubbed out his cigarette in the dirt between us. "No, my parents aren't exactly feeling my creativity lately."

"Why's that?"

"I've kind of gotten into street art. Like, graffiti-inspired?" he said with a crooked half-smile.

I barked a loud "Ha!" and then looked around guiltily, as though someone might accuse me of not being sad enough. But Raf's eyes glinted with amusement.

"So your bedroom walls are destroyed?" I asked.

"That depends on your definition of 'destroyed.'" He grinned, and I had a sudden memory of him telling me about how he had cut all the hair off his sister's Barbie doll. He'd thought Barbie looked great. His sister, Allie, had not agreed.

"Do you want to see it?" he asked, standing.

"Your bedroom?" I said. I couldn't be sure if that was weird. It wasn't weird when we were seven. But in that moment, I knew how lost I was. I'd convinced myself that I was comfortable around boys, but then I'd interact with one and realize my expertise was really just with the one boy. I was awkward as hell around the rest of them.

Raf put his hands up like a criminal who'd just walked into a police department in surrender. But he was still smiling.

"Not like that," he said. He started toward his house. "Maybe another time. See you later."

A little stab of disappointment took me by surprise. I opened my mouth to respond, but Raf had already faded into the dark.

INSTEAD OF GOING to bed, I went to Audrey's room. Her door was closed, as it nearly always was. Some of the stickers she'd slapped haphazardly all over it had started to peel. I tried to smooth their rebellious edges, but once a sticker has lost its stick, there's no going back.

The hinges squealed as I opened it. I froze, wincing. My

door did the same thing, and I'd always wondered if it was some Parenting Teenage Girls trick that my parents had adopted. Was there some substance—the opposite of grease—that *added* squeakiness to hinges? I made a mental note to pick up some WD-40 the next day. If I was going to keep sneaking out for cigarettes, I would need it.

Audrey's room looked exactly as it always had: chaos. Clothes littered the floor like fallen leaves. Her textbooks were stacked haphazardly on her desk, one open next to a notebook like she'd just stepped away to go to the bathroom or get a snack. Jewelry and makeup snaked and spilled out of their respective containers, as if attempting escape.

Her bed wasn't made, but the duvet was pulled up, at least.

I crawled on top of it and laid my head on the pillow next to hers—she would only sleep on the right side. The impression of her sleeping head was still visible. During the day, she barely stopped moving, but when she slept, she was like a mummy: hands at her sides, unmoving, blankets tucked neatly under her chin.

I leaned closer to her side of the bed and found myself caught off guard by the scent of her. It was hard to describe, but Audrey had this smell when she woke up in the morning that was a little bit sweet, a little bit like sweat, and somehow just . . . *Audrey*. Her sleep smell.

My throat burned as I curled my fingers back from her side, careful not to disturb what could be the last impression my baby sister would ever leave. I stood and fumbled my way through the clothes on the floor, my vision blurry.

If I was going to cry, I preferred to do that in my own bedroom.

Eleven Years Ago

I was six and Raf was seven when his sister dared us to kiss. We'd just left a birthday party for another kid in the neighborhood and, because Allie was with us, our moms let us walk home together after the party instead of coming to pick us up. Allie was two years older than Raf and she seemed so mature. She was tall and thin, with the longest, thickest black hair I'd ever seen. It nearly hit the top of her butt when she wore it down, but usually it was in a long braid that swung back and forth when she walked.

She stopped me at the corner and whispered in my ear, "Raf wants to kiss you. I dare you to do it."

I was torn. I wasn't sure if I wanted to kiss Raf. I was pretty sure I didn't want to kiss anyone. We played house and pretended we were married and sometimes we even fake-kissed, with our hands over our mouths, because we saw our parents kiss and thought that was just what you did when you got home from work. But real kissing was still gross then.

But I didn't want to disappoint Allie. She was older, and cooler, than me. I just wanted her to like me.

So I nodded and she skipped off to catch up with Raf, who

was holding Audrey's hand as they walked up ahead. Allie walked backward in front of Raf and Audrey, waving me over. I walked up to them slowly.

"You have to do it," Allie was saying. "Kiss her."

Raf looked at me uncertainly. I nodded. He glanced at Allie's taunting face and then stepped toward me. And I just planted my lips on his. It only lasted a second, but I still remember the feeling of his lips on mine, pursed and wet. I didn't get the appeal.

Allie let out a whoop when his lips met mine, and she applauded as we blushed. We didn't really talk afterward; he just took Audrey's hand again and walked the last block home. We had planned to hang out after the party, but he didn't really look at me. And then he just let go of Audrey's hand and followed Allie into his house. She looked at me over her shoulder before she went inside, but I couldn't tell if she was happy that she'd embarrassed us or mad that we had actually done it.

But I knew that I didn't like the way I felt. I didn't like that I'd kissed my friend and that he didn't want to hang out with me because of it. Years later, though, I would tell people Rafael Juarez was my first kiss and that we were early make-out adopters. By the time we started freshman year, by the time my friends were making out with boys while I watched movies at home with Audrey, I was desperate for a second kiss.

I met Mike later that fall and I soon lost count of the number of kisses I'd had.

But I never forgot the first one.

CHAPTER FOUR

I awoke on Monday morning with a heavy feeling of dread, the certainty that I had to go to school. Then a rare spark of joy hit me. School was over! Cassidy's party was the last one of our junior year; it was supposed to be a celebration . . . and as fast as the memory cascaded back, the spark fizzled.

I pulled the covers over my head and curled up with Floyd, our elderly black lab. He'd taken over half of my bed in the night. Somehow he always knew when I needed dog cuddles. But I couldn't go back to sleep. Not when Audrey's swollen face was the only image I could see when I closed my eyes.

I dragged myself out of bed and went to the one place that was as miserable as I felt: the hospital.

We'd been pretty quiet in the room, for the most part. I'd read every comic I could carry, plus most of the digital collection on my iPad. Mom had finished a ridiculous number of crossword puzzles. She also continued to read aloud bits of reassuring articles she'd found about head trauma recovery—for me, or for her, maybe for us both. She repeated them when Dad was able to stop by on a break. That was our new routine. But for the most part, we were letting Audrey rest in silence.

We were also getting to know the nurses. My favorite was the night nurse, Keisha, because she talked to Audrey instead of forcing small talk on me. She spoke as if she was sure Audrey could hear her and just wasn't ready to respond.

I spent most of that day and the next at the hospital by Audrey's side and tried Keisha's method. It helped. Talking to my sister kept me from constantly staring at her EEG monitor.

But I didn't know what to say. I'd told Audrey I wouldn't talk about Mike with her, but that didn't stop me from thinking about it. So instead, I bought every gossip magazine the gift shop had and read them aloud to her.

"Oh, look, Audy," I said. "Drew Barrymore is walking her dog! She's picking up dog poop, just like us!"

That would have made her laugh if she was awake. Audrey loved Drew Barrymore—and every single movie she'd ever been in—but she also found it hilarious that gossip magazines had whole photo spreads of celebrities doing things like picking up their dry cleaning.

Soon, though, I'd run through all the magazines and began reading her friends' social media updates aloud. They'd been posting messages to her nonstop. The barrage of notifications finally prompted Mom to turn Audrey's phone off. I read those to her, too. They were all basically the same. Her friends gushed about how wonderful Audrey was, how bubbly and kind and friendly, how she was the last person who deserved this. The notable exception was Neema, who hadn't posted anything. Odd. But to be fair, I didn't want to post anything, either. Audrey's friends knew her as someone who would go out of her way to help them, who would never hurt them. I wouldn't shatter their illusion, but I knew better now.

I would have read aloud one of the books I'd brought, but Audrey hated comics. And reading. Dad had never been able to convert Audrey the way he had converted me. Maybe because *she* wasn't named after a comic book character. (How he ever talked Mom into naming me Harley is a mystery, but I imagine it involved heavy drugs, a flood of postpartum hormones, and some kind of deal with the Devil. Or the Joker.)

Besides, Audrey had always been a romantic. She pretty much exclusively watched romantic comedies—and she would watch them over and over again, even the worst, most predictable ones. All she'd ever wanted was to find her Prince Charming. The One. True Love. Instead, I'd led her to Mike and he had almost killed her.

Later that afternoon, I decided to put on *The Princess Bride*, one of the few movies that Audrey and I had always been able to agree on. She liked the romance, I liked the action, and we both liked the comedy. It was a rare and perfect fit.

Taking a cue from Keisha, I even tilted my laptop toward Audrey. If she awoke, I wanted the first thing she saw to be something she would remember and love. But the movie ended without so much as a flicker of her eyelids.

MOM RETURNED THAT evening to find me staring out the window at the parking lot. I could see my sun-faded forest-green Honda out there baking in the heat. I'd been dreading sharing it with Audrey. She would be getting her license in a few months. Or she should be.

"Harley, you've been sitting in here for days," Mom said. She surveyed my cutoffs, Wonder Woman T-shirt, and flip-flops. "And I've seen you in that outfit three times."

She was somehow perfectly pulled together and appropriately dressed—if there was an appropriate outfit for visiting your comatose daughter in the hospital. For Mom, it was white linen shorts, a sleeveless button-down shirt in pale pink, and dark brown hair pulled into a low ponytail. She could have been going to play tennis later. Except I could see that her mascara was smudged from tears. She had no doubt cried privately in the car before coming inside.

Mom hadn't let her careful veneer crack in front of Dad or me since the first night at the hospital. Not that it really mattered when it came to Dad. He had basically disappeared since the accident. He would stop by Audrey's room because he was at the hospital, of course—but never for longer than five minutes at a time. He had always worked long hours—now he worked late every night. Though we weren't gathering at the table for dinner anyway.

"Have you showered lately?" Mom asked.

I shook my head. I could feel the weight of my greasy ponytail. She had a point.

"Or eaten?"

My stomach rumbled at the suggestion, even though I'd been steadily clearing out the vending machine down the hall all day. I stood up.

"You'll be here for a while?" I asked.

Mom nodded.

"Okay. Don't leave until I come back."

I took her silence as a complicit "yes." She was already propping Audrey up so she could brush her hair. The ministrations would take a while.

"Drive carefully," she said, her eyes focused on her task. An afterthought.

My chest tightened. I couldn't help walking over to Mom and wrapping my arms around her.

"Oh, baby duck," she said into my dirty hair. "I love you."

"I love you, too, Mom," I said. And then, after a moment I added, "She'll be okay."

Mom nodded and withdrew, gently steering me toward the door. I got the hint. I was a mess. And smelly. But I wanted to leave, anyway. I was looking forward to smoking a cigarette on the drive home with the windows rolled down.

As I turned down our street, I wondered if Raf was home. If he'd want to join me. I never would have imagined the two of us would become smokers.

He was so much the same kid as he was ten years ago—he had the same mischievous glint to his eye and the same smile that tilted a little lower on the right side—but he was so much more mature. I mean, of course he was, he was eighteen not eight, but he was kind of sexy now.

As soon as the thought occurred to me, I hated myself for it.

I hadn't even broken up with Mike yet. And he hadn't stopped trying to reach me, even going so far as to call the house phone. But Mom always screened his calls. She hadn't even had to ask.

THE NEXT MORNING-SHOWERED and changed, if not well-rested—I was parked in my usual spot in the chair next to Audrey's bed when Cassidy pushed the door open. Her eyes were searching and wide with hope. But I shook my head and her face fell. Audrey was the same as she'd been the day before. The only change was that the swelling in her eyes had subsided and she was starting to look like herself again.

Cassidy sat down in the chair across the bed and kicked off

her flip-flops, putting her feet up on the bed next to Audrey's legs. She tucked a stray blonde curl into her messy bun.

"How are you, Harley?" she asked.

I shrugged. "Same," I said. "You?"

She looked surprised that I remembered to ask. "I'm okay," she said. But her lips were pulled into a tight frown.

Cassidy, who had been the junior class vice president, got chewed out by the school administration for hosting a party with alcohol and without chaperones. She told me that the school was embarrassed by the "incident." The headmaster even left a message at our house. Mom erased it before I could listen, but she said he sounded upset. At least he and the rest of the faculty sent flowers to Audrey's hospital room. If this had happened during the school year, they would have been obligated to hold an assembly about drunk driving and offer counseling to students. They got off light, I think. And so had Cassidy. She might have been suspended—or worse—if school was in session. Unfortunately for Cassidy, her parents had taken over, and she was grounded for the foreseeable future. I knew she was allowed to drive to work, though. She must have left a little early to come here and see me . . . to see us.

I was surprised that I hadn't been grounded myself. I'd lied to Mom and Dad, a lie of omission anyway, since they weren't aware that Cassidy's parents weren't home during the party. But I guess they had bigger things to worry about. I had basically grounded myself anyway, tying myself to Audrey's bedside.

"Does anyone know about Mike and Audrey?" I asked quietly.

She shook her head. "No," she said. "No one knows why he was driving her home. They just assume you asked him to."

I nodded, relieved. I would much prefer that my friends and classmates blamed me than Audrey.

"So, um, speaking of Mike," Cassidy said, "he stopped by the coffee shop yesterday."

My eyes snapped up to her face. If he'd somehow found a way to hurt her or get between us, I would make him regret it. I'd march to his house and confront him at last. In front of his mom. Maybe steal his issue of *The New Mutants* #98. That would really piss him off.

"It's okay," Cassidy said, assuring me, "he just wanted me to ask you to call him. I didn't make him any promises."

"He shouldn't be asking favors from you," I said.

"The police charged him," she said, as if that were an explanation. "With a DUI and reckless driving to start with, so he'll lose his license."

Good. He deserved worse.

"What else did he say?" I asked.

Her lips were tight, as if she were keeping a secret.

"He's sorry," she said. "He just wanted you to know that."

"Why are you even relaying his messages?" I demanded, trying to shake off the flare of anger at Mike's apology. "You hate Mike. You wanted me to dump him over a year ago."

"I still do," she said defensively. "I'm not protecting him or advocating for him. I'm just the messenger." Her eyes were wide, innocent. And tired. The shadows under her eyes had only grown darker over the last few days. "And maybe I feel like you should just talk to him. Just once, to break up with him for good, and then I can stop deleting messages from your phone for you."

I sighed. "Fine." I pulled my phone from my bag and opened the string of unanswered text messages he'd sent since

I last had Cassidy do a purge. I didn't read them; I simply wrote: I'm coming over.

I FUMED ALL the way to Mike's house. My knuckles were stiff from squeezing the steering wheel. How dare he use Cassidy to get to me? My rage was at fever pitch when I pulled up in front of the town house, parking in the visitor's spot that I had always thought of as mine. Not anymore. A moment later, I was banging on the door.

Mike's mom opened it.

I hadn't been expecting her. Her nose and eyes were red, and her hair, normally cut into a tidy bob, was frizzy and mussed, as if she'd been running her fingers through it. Ms. Baker reached out for me, and I flinched away instinctively.

"Hi, Ms. Baker," I said.

"Oh, honey," she said. Her face crumpled.

I felt a little guilty that I couldn't be more sympathetic toward her. She worked hard and raised her son by herself, deliberately. She had gone to a sperm bank after breaking up with her girlfriend of ten years who hadn't wanted children. She told me it wasn't revenge; it was that she had finally decided she would rather have a child than a partner, if that was the choice she had to make. And as a result, she had doted on Mike, indulging his every desire. And maybe expecting a little too much from him, pinning her happiness on his.

"I'm so sorry," Ms. Baker said. Her voice trembled.

I stepped closer and let her pat my arm. That was the best I could do.

"Thank you," I managed to say. "It's been a tough few days."

"It hasn't been easy for Michael, either," she said.

Now I wanted to scream. He couldn't even *begin* to know

what I was feeling. But she was already crying again, so I bit my tongue.

"Is he here?" I asked, even though I knew he was.

Ms. Baker stepped back into the hallway to allow me to enter. "He's in his room. I've barely let him out except to use the bathroom and meet with our lawyer since Sunday."

I took a deep breath before climbing the stairs. Mike must have heard us because he was waiting for me in his bedroom doorway. His round face was in shadow, but I could see the dark bruise under his left eye. His hair was matted.

I stopped a few feet from him.

"Come inside," he whispered. "Please? I don't want to do this in the hallway with my mom listening downstairs."

I didn't especially care what he wanted, but I relented. I didn't want his mom listening in, either.

His bedroom was cleaner than I'd ever seen it. I guess he'd had time on his hands.

Mike sat on his bed while I hovered near the dresser across the room. I could see now that the shadows under his eyes weren't all bruises; his skin was dotted with acne. He was wearing a wrinkled lacrosse tournament T-shirt and mesh shorts. His socks were nearly falling off his feet.

"Just in case it's not clear," I said, "we're done. We're broken up."

"This wasn't—"

My glare stopped him.

He shook his head. "Never mind," he said. "I just want you to know that I'm sorry."

"I heard."

"Harley, I never wanted to hurt you." His voice was weak. His eyes were red-rimmed.

"I don't really care," I said, before he could go on. "You

could have killed my sister. She might never wake up and—" My voice caught in my throat. I put my hands up. "Stop calling me, stop texting me, stop reaching out to my friends. Just stop."

I turned to walk away.

"I'm going to rehab," he called after me. "For thirty days."

That stopped me.

"Good," I said, my eyes on the hallway carpet. "I hope it helps you realize what an ass you are."

I paused. I hated that I still felt sympathy for him. But I had lived my life around him, about him, for him, for so long. Seeing him so miserable was jarring.

"How much trouble are you in?" I asked.

"A lot," he said. "The rehab is court-mandated. It was that or thirty days in juvie. And I have to do community service. And my license is suspended."

And there it was: the familiar disappointment. I spun to face him. "I was hoping you'd actually made the choice to go to rehab on your own," I said.

"I'm not an alcoholic," he said. His jaw was set, his eyes narrowed. "I'm seventeen. How could I be?"

I shrugged. "I'm not saying you are, but I don't think there's an age restriction on being an alcoholic," I said. Audrey once told me that Drew Barrymore believes she was an alcoholic and an addict by the time she was twelve. She's been sober since she was a teenager. So clearly it's possible. "And I hope you quit drinking anyway, since you could have killed yourself and two other people."

"Do you think I don't hate myself for that?" Mike said. His voice was suddenly loud.

I took a step back.

"Not enough," I said.

He scowled. "My life is over, Harley," he said, quieter. "I lost my spot on the basketball and lacrosse teams, my friends aren't allowed to talk to me, and now my girlfriend is dumping me. That's not enough for you?"

"No," I said. "You deserve to be where Audrey is."

I left before he could reply. I ran down the hall, past his mom, who was listening at the bottom of the stairs, and out the door to my car. I had planned how I'd break up with Mike so many times, even before he'd cheated on me with Audrey. I hadn't ever imagined it would be like this. I should have expected that Mike would once again make everything about Mike.

But at least it was over.

One Week Ago

I was hiding from Cassidy's party, or I had been when I first escaped outside. Because I couldn't feel out of place if I wasn't in the place at all. But then I got caught up in an argument with a stranger on Twitter about what should happen in the next Marvel movie, and I finally started enjoying myself.

I didn't even notice Mike—not until he eased down behind me, wrapping his arms around my middle and kissing the side of my neck.

"Ugh, gross," he said, backhanding my sweat from his lips.

I leaned against him and rubbed my neck against his face. He scooted out of reach.

"Serves you right," I said. "Who tries to cuddle in a heat wave?"

"Can you blame me?" he said. "This party is boring and you're my favorite distraction."

"You're cute," I said. "But it's too hot. And I want to go home, where my air-conditioned bedroom is waiting." I sighed heavily. Dramatically. "But I'm here for Cassidy, so I'm going to stay. For a while at least."

"You wouldn't stay for me?" Mike said and pushed his full lips into a pout.

I shook my head. "Nope. But when I've known you for ten years, you can take precedence every now and then."

Mike rolled his eyes as he pushed up to his knees. He took a few extra seconds to steady himself, which is how I knew how many drinks he'd had. Somewhere around four. Wobbly, but not wasted.

He scoffed as he walked away, as if surprised that I wasn't stopping him. Or joining him. He should have been used to it by now, but he always seemed to hold on to the hope that I would suddenly transform into the type of person who'd join him when he played beer pong or flip cup. And he always expected me to jump at the chance to apologize when I didn't.

I picked up the plastic cup of beer he'd left behind for me and poured its contents over the side into the grass below. I was already planning my escape from the party, which meant driving and seeing my parents, neither of which I wanted to do drunk.

Unlike Mike, I actually cared about things like that.

I just hadn't realized I was steering him into the arms of my little sister. I wished I'd known to enjoy those last few minutes of ignorance.

CHAPTER FIVE

That evening I went back to the hospital and put on *Eternal Sunshine of the Spotless Mind*. Partly because I couldn't seem to keep my mind off Mike and wanted to fantasize about removing him from my memory entirely. But also because I kept imagining Audrey lying there with her eyes closed, unable to move, but able to hear every single word that anyone said. Or didn't say.

It was so quiet most of the time. She'd be so bored. And Audrey hated being bored. She was always asking me to do stuff with her, watch TV or a movie, play video games, go shopping. I snapped at her constantly, especially when she interrupted me while I was reading or hanging out with Cassidy.

By the end of the movie, I was crying. Again. Which Audrey would have loved. Well, mostly she would have been shocked that I was able to sit through it. But the fact that it had moved me to tears would have made her howl with delight.

I'D GOTTEN MYSELF together by the time Dad stopped by the room. I had moved on to *Breakfast at Tiffany's*, one of Audrey's favorites. She loved Audrey Hepburn even more than she loved Drew Barrymore. She'd even dressed as Holly Golightly for Halloween last fall. With her dark hair, pale skin, and lithe body, it was impossible not to see the resemblance.

"You should watch *The African Queen*," Dad said after watching over my shoulder for a minute. "Katharine Hepburn had something Audrey never did: range. I've been telling Audrey that for years."

I reached over my shoulder to grab his hand and gave it a squeeze. "I'll watch it with her when she wakes up," I said.

He squeezed my hand back and then silently left the room, closing the door behind him.

I SAT ON the driveway that night, the pavement still warm from the heat of the day. I'd finished a cigarette a few minutes before, but I couldn't go back inside yet. I smelled like smoke and Mom was still awake.

I looked up as Raf's Jeep Wrangler pulled around the cul-de-sac. He waved through the window. I didn't get up, but he walked toward me instead of going inside. Floyd's tail thumped loudly on the ground and he let out a little whine of anticipation.

"Well, get up and go to him, if you're that excited," I said, shoving Floyd in the side. He stood slowly, giving Raf an open-mouthed doggy grin. Raf reached out for Floyd's ears.

"You're a good boy," Raf cooed.

Floyd could stand it no longer. He stood on his hind legs, pressing against Raf's chest, until Raf collapsed on the grass next to him. Floyd stuck his nose in Raf's face, licking his chin and neck, his ears and eyes. Raf cracked up, loving every second of it.

"Would you two like some privacy?" I said after a minute.

Raf gave Floyd's ears one more rub, then stood, brushing grass from the back of his jeans.

"Give me a break," he said. "Floyd and I haven't seen each other for a while. We had some catching up to do."

This was true. When we were younger, before Audrey took over dog-walking duties, I used to take Floyd out after school. When Raf was outside playing basketball in his driveway, Floyd would start barking the minute he heard the ball bouncing. I'd get him outside, and he and Raf would run to each other like long-lost lovers. It would take me five minutes to break them up.

"Well, I hope you got it out of your system," I said, "because he's coming home with me." Raf's mom was allergic to dogs, so Floyd wasn't even allowed on the front porch.

"So, nice night to sit on hot asphalt and sweat," Raf said, easing down beside me and crossing his legs at the ankles. He leaned back on his elbows and gazed up at the sprinkling of stars in the sky. Floyd nudged his way between us and lay down with a heavy sigh.

"I just needed to get out of the house," I said.

"Everything okay?" he asked.

I shook my head. "My mom keeps trying to get me to do puzzles with her. She's got a five-hundred-piece one on the kitchen table and the picture is *Paris from Above*. Do you have any idea how much most of Paris looks exactly the same from above?"

Raf chuckled. "I think you made the right call."

"She's just trying to avoid talking to me about Mike. And the accident. She blames me for not driving Audrey home that night. I can see it in her eyes."

"Are you sure?" he asked. "Because I feel like it would make more sense for her to be blaming Audrey. Or Mike."

"No," I said, firm in my conviction that my mom thought I was an asshole. "I brought Audrey to that party; I should have taken her home, too."

"Why didn't you?" he asked quietly.

I hunched my shoulders, avoiding his eyes. I wanted to tell him, but I couldn't bear the embarrassment of Raf knowing that Mike had cheated on me with my sister. I didn't want to plant the idea in his head that she was the more desirable one of the two of us, if it wasn't there already.

"Because of reasons," I said finally.

"Oh, *reasons*," Raf said. "Why didn't you say so?" He leaned against me gently. "It's okay. You don't have to tell me."

I gave him a tight-lipped smile. "Thank you," I said. I paused for a beat and added, "I *did* break up with him, though."

"Atta girl," he said with a broader smile.

"He said he has to go to rehab. It's court-mandated."

"Interesting," Raf said. He even stroked his chin. "In residence?"

"What does that mean?"

"He has to stay there. He doesn't get to go home at night."

I nodded. "Yeah, that sounds right. But he only has to go for a month. Do you think that could be enough time to get him to realize what he did? To make him stop drinking?"

Raf shrugged. "It's hard to say. Some people never stop."

"Well, if you see him at an AA meeting, you have my permission to kick his ass. He's about six feet tall, with shaggy surfer-type blond hair, blue eyes, and a little beer belly. Usually wears a comic book or lacrosse T-shirt." I looked at him seriously. "Break his fucking legs."

Raf gazed back at me for a few seconds, then said, "Can I say something without you getting mad?"

I made a disgusted noise. "I hate that question. If you have something to say, just say it. Why do you care if I get mad?"

I knew I sounded like such a brat, but I was too drained to play games.

To my relief, Raf smiled. "Okay, fine. I've been thinking about it, and I just don't get why you stayed with him for so long."

I shrugged. "Why does anyone stay with someone?"

"But why would you feel like you deserved to put up with his bullshit?"

I stared at him for a few seconds and then said, "You've been in therapy too long."

He laughed, but his eyes were serious. "Maybe, but I don't think I'm wrong."

"Listen," I said. "You don't know what happened. And you might think you know me, but you don't. So just keep your opinions to yourself, okay?"

I stood, and Raf quickly sat up.

"Wait," he protested. "See? I knew you'd get mad."

"And yet you asked me not to. That seems a little unfair to me."

Raf smiled once more, frustrating me further. "You're right," he said. I turned to go inside, but he reached up a hand to stop me. "I want to show you something."

"What?" I asked warily.

"You don't have to be so suspicious," he said, pretending to be offended. "I'm not going to murder you. The boy next door is *such* an obvious suspect."

I couldn't help laughing. "Fine. Just let me put the dog inside."

Once Floyd was secured behind the storm door, I followed Raf into the woods behind our houses. About thirty feet past the property line, there was a nature preserve with a large pond. My dad had taught me how to skip stones here—Raf, too. We'd spent a lot of time by the pond together, playing hide-and-seek or tag, or sometimes Red Rover if we could round up more of the neighborhood kids.

I brushed a branch out of my way and stopped. "Raf, what are we doing back here? There's nothing I haven't seen down here a thousand times already."

He looked back at me. "Quit whining," he said. "Can't you just appreciate the mystery for two seconds?"

"I'm not whining!" I said. But he was smiling, so I couldn't smile back. "My sister is in a coma, and I just broke up with my boyfriend. I'm *fragile.*"

"I'm so sorry," he said, composing himself. "I didn't realize you were such a delicate flower. I must have mistaken your anger back there for tenacity."

My mouth dropped open.

"The Harley I used to know was feisty and confident."

"You want to see feisty?" I said in a threatening tone as I put a fist in his face.

I couldn't even tell if I was joking or not. I was reacting in the moment. Sure, I was a wreck, but I kind of liked that I didn't feel the need to please him.

He took hold of my fist and pressed it against his chest. "I just want to help you forget about everything that's going on for a few seconds, okay? Will you just trust me?"

I got a little lost in his dark brown eyes. He was so close and he smelled familiar. Sort of the way his house smelled, like warm bread, but I caught the faint scent of his cologne, too: sweet, inviting, and a little spicy. I found myself nodding, but I still managed to sound a little annoyed when I said, "Fine."

Just past the far side of the lake was a willow tree. Seeing it brought back a rush of memories: Raf and I used to pretend it was our house. It was quiet and spacious under the long branches. We'd say the canopy was our roof and the muddy grass was our living room, bedroom, and kitchen.

Raf held open a curtain of limp branches, and I walked through.

Suddenly it dawned on me what we were doing here.

I gasped. "It's not really still here, is it?"

Raf nodded. "I used to sneak out here to get stoned, sometimes with my friends, sometimes alone, and one night I ended up face-to-face with it."

He crept around the far side of the tree. At the base of two roots was the body of a mini My Little Pony, so entwined with the growth that it had almost become part of the tree—impossible to move without hacking the roots away.

"No way," I breathed, moving closer. The paint had worn off, and its eyes were now smooth turquoise spheres. Gone too were the bright polyester strands of hair. But the rest of the body was intact. "I can't believe this is still here."

"Imagine how surprised I was when I was high," he said with a grin.

I laughed as I bent down to stroke the nose of the Pony. We'd tied it to the tree with a shoelace almost a decade earlier. It was supposed to be a decoration for our "house." The shoelace was long gone.

"Do you miss it?" I asked after a minute.

"What? The Pony?" he said with a grin. "I'm pretty sure it was yours."

I hit him in the arm.

His smile faded. "Yeah, sometimes. It was a good escape. I just kind of floated along for a while there."

I wanted to hear more. "But . . . ?"

He sighed. "I mostly miss my friends. One of the things about rehab is you have to cut ties with all of your old friends from your 'using days.'"

"That seems a little unfair," I said. "You went to school with those people. It's not like you could just stop seeing them."

He nodded slowly. "Yeah, but . . . I get it. I mean, without those guys, it's a lot easier to stay sober."

I didn't really know what to say. If anyone told me I had to give up Cassidy, I'd fight like hell against them. She was the only person who really knew me. But she was *good* for me. My relationship with Mike was the biggest strain on our friendship. Especially after the first time we broke up because I found out he'd made out with another girl. Surprise: while he was drunk at a lacrosse party. Cassidy never understood why I got back together with him. And because of that, we saw a lot less of each other.

"Ow! Damn," Raf cried, pulling me out of the sinkhole of my thoughts. He swatted his calf. "Mosquito."

"Want to go back?" I asked.

He seemed hesitant. I studied his face in the moonlight. He avoided my eyes. "Are you hungry?"

I couldn't lie. "Yeah, I guess so," I said.

"How about the diner?" he suggested.

The diner held memories. Of my parents taking us there on Saturday mornings after sleepovers. Of Raf and me riding our bikes there for milkshakes when we were finally old enough to leave the neighborhood.

But also of Mike. Of eating there after lacrosse games and school dances. A few weeks ago, the morning after prom, he was so drunk, he knocked his whole plate of pancakes off the table. I tipped the waitress 60 percent to make up for the disgusting mess of syrup she had to clean up. But I took the money from Mike's wallet.

"Another time," I promised. "I should probably go see how Mom's progress on Paris is coming along."

Raf smiled, but it was strained. "Okay," he said. "Say hi for me."

I nodded but knew I wouldn't tell her I'd seen him. It would open the door to questions I didn't really know how to answer.

Two and a Half Years Ago

I first met Mike when he was still new at school. It was the end of October of our freshman year, and he walked into the cafeteria that first day alone. He was going to be on the lacrosse team. His reputation from his previous school team guaranteed him superstar status. He could have sat with his future teammates; he could have sat with anyone, really. But he happened to walk by my table, and when he saw that I had the first volume of Gail Simone's Birds of Prey, *he just sat down next to me and started talking about it, asking if he could borrow it when I was done.*

Cassidy didn't know what to make of this lacrosse star suddenly sitting at our table, completely ignoring everything around him except our conversation. But Mike didn't care. Neither did I.

It turned out Mike was also in my Life Sciences class (a.k.a. biology—snooty prep schools always feel the need to rename perfectly normal subjects) and because he was new, he didn't have a lab partner. Since we were supposed to dissect fetal pigs, Mr. Davidoff didn't think it was fair for Mike to do it alone. At the time, I believed it was fate: my lab partner, Sanjay Patel, happened to be out that day. So Mike was assigned to me. His gleeful expression as he took his seat next to me would have made anyone think Mike had engineered Sanjay's ear infection.

"Hey, Harley Quinn," he said.

I actually wasn't much of a Harley Quinn fan. She let the Joker treat her like garbage for so long. Plus, I couldn't even dress like her for Halloween because I'd never go out in public in a black-and-red bodysuit or short shorts. But I never told Mike. He was one of the only people who knew I wasn't named after the motorcycle company. I liked that.

His blue eyes were focused only on me, despite the handful of girls who were more popular, with shinier hair and thinner thighs under their uniform kilts. Their eyes were on me, too. The room was full of death glares.

"I didn't realize we were at a point in our relationship where we were using nicknames," I told him.

He grinned. "Would you prefer Harley Elaine Langston?"

I shook my head. "No way. I hate my middle name."

"Okay," he said with a laugh. "I just wanted to show you that I remember it."

I leaned over, partly to get close to him, partly so no one else heard. "Don't worry. I know how memorable I am."

I don't know where that confidence came from, except maybe from him. His attention made me fluff up like a peacock. But my confidence took a nosedive when the time came to pin the fetal pig's feet belly up inside its tray.

"Harley Quinn, your hands are shaking like a junkie's," Mike said.

He took the pin from me and sat me down on the stool. Then he took both my hands in one of his and tilted my chin back so I could look at him. His fingers were warm, and his eyes were kind and concerned. And beautiful.

"You don't have to do anything, okay? I'll do the whole thing. You just sit here."

I nodded, trying not to look at the shriveled body of the fetal pig.

Mike did exactly what he said he'd do: he completed the entire dissection—which took about a week—by himself.

When Sanjay came back to school, Mike told him to find a new lab partner. Even Mr. Davidoff didn't argue with him.

That was the day I fell for him. I never stood a chance.

CHAPTER SIX

A little more than a week after the accident, Audrey's doctor announced that he'd seen enough positive results from the steroids that they were going to try to bring her out of the medically induced coma. Mom practically fell to her knees while Dad and I listened to the practicalities of what would happen. We had to fill her in after the doctor left the room.

"It's going to take a while to ease her off the anesthetics," Dad said. "And there's no guarantee she'll wake up. But Dr. Martinez is very hopeful. The swelling in Audrey's brain has gone down, and her last CT scan showed that the damage from the brain injury was minimal."

I nodded, smiling for Mom's sake. Dad's tone was calm and even. I got the hint. If Audrey didn't wake up relatively soon, the chances of a full recovery just kept decreasing.

Mom must have known, too, because she began to cry. With his arm around Mom, Dad told me to go home and get some rest. Instead, I just drove around for a couple of hours. When I got back to the hospital, I could see on their faces that it hadn't worked. She hadn't woken up yet.

For now, we would wait. Again.

THERE WAS A knock on my bedroom door late Saturday morning. I was already awake. I'd gone to the bathroom and brushed my teeth even. But that didn't mean I had to leave the comfort of my bed. Besides, Floyd was snuggled up next to me. I kept quiet, but the door opened anyway. Cassidy walked in. She carried a tray with two coffees and paper bags from The Flakey Pastry.

"Hey, lady," she said. "That's quite a nest you've created there." She gestured to the tangle of blankets, the pile of pillows, and the lump of dog.

"Oh, I thought you meant my hair," I said.

She laughed. "That, too," she said, motioning for me to move over.

I scooted sideways as she set the coffee tray on my bedside table. Floyd shifted, too, but not without a heavy sigh. You gotta love dogs for their honesty.

"Your mom said to tell you that if you don't get up, she's going to send your dad in with a bucket of ice water," Cassidy informed me. "She also said you needed to find a job."

I sighed through my nose, in a pretty decent imitation of Floyd. "If you're playing messenger, would you be willing to tell her I said 'Bite me'?"

Cassidy snorted. She slipped off her flip-flops and slid onto the bed, leaning against the headboard, drinking her coffee. "You doing any better?" she asked.

"Does it look like I am?"

"Then let's do something today," she said. "A movie or a mani-pedi or something."

"Aren't you grounded?" I asked.

She shrugged. "They tried, bless their hearts. But with the three terrors at home, grounding me is really more of a hassle than my parents want to deal with. Getting out of the house and out of their way is a blessing for them."

Cassidy's brothers, Loren and Kelly, were five and eight. They didn't stop moving from six in the morning until nine at night. Her younger sister, Morgan, a.k.a. "The Nuisance," just added a moody haze to any situation.

I could see her point.

"So? What do you want to do?"

I turned my face back into the pillow. "I want to go see my sister," I said, "and hate my ex-boyfriend some more." I glanced back at Cassidy, knowing her exasperation would motivate me, and then sat up. "Fine. Hate Mike, see Audrey, *then* mani-pedi."

Cassidy's face lit up. "Super. But while you do the first one, take a shower."

I tried to act offended, and I *was* annoyed that people kept feeling like they could dictate my sanitary habits, but she was right.

"Fine, but keep Floyd company while I'm gone. He misses Audrey."

WHEN I GOT back from the nail salon, I went to the hospital for a few hours, where I watched *Mad Love* and *Boys on the Side* with Audrey (two of her Drew Barrymore favorites, both of which ended with me in tears—what was *happening* to me?), and then I grabbed a fast food meal on my way home and settled in for a night of reading. I'd finally gotten that week's pull list of comics—the new books Dad and I had the store put aside to make sure we got them every week—and while I tried to space them out, I ended up reading them all in one binge, as always.

It was nearly one in the morning when I finally came up

for air. Or, more accurately, food. I almost wasn't surprised when, after finishing a bowl of cereal, I saw the side-porch light from next door cast a glow across the corner of the lawn. I headed outside to find Raf.

"Are you stalking me, Juarez?" I joked. "And can I bum one of those?"

Raf smiled, but it was small and forced, not his usual crooked grin. "Not a stalker," he said as he pulled another out of his pack for me. "Just an addict."

I tilted my head curiously. "You okay?"

He shrugged. "Bored, I guess. As usual." He took a drag. The cigarette's cherry glowed, spotlighting the crease between his brows. "Now that school's over, I don't do anything all day, and I have no one to hang out with." He sighed a stream of smoke. "I've met some people at the NA and AA meetings I go to, but it's not the same. My old friends had known me for years. They knew all the good and bad and I didn't have to do this whole 'getting to know you' thing. It's just . . ."

"Exhausting," I heard myself say. I knew exactly how he felt. Making friends had never been easy for me. I wasn't a recluse or anything, but I just couldn't expend the energy to be "on" all the time, especially when I was thrown into Mike's social scene. It was always easier to just hang out with Cassidy.

Raf nodded, his expression softening. "Do you want to hang out?" he asked.

I found myself nodding back, even though I was already in my pajamas: yoga pants and a T-shirt that said EAT NUTS, KICK BUTTS. I'd been wearing them for three nights (and some of the days). The yoga pants clung to my thighs tighter than I was comfortable with. Dusting myself off, I also found a Froot Loop stuck to my butt that I couldn't be sure was from tonight.

Mom and Cassidy were on the same page, for once. I needed to snap out of this hygiene slump.

I followed Raf in through his basement door and found myself in a room I didn't recognize. It was no longer the brown-carpeted playroom with a plastic kitchen in thc corner where I'd played as a kid. There was a crisp white carpet and a sectional sofa in the center facing a flat-screen TV. It was smaller, too. Raf led me to the other side of the new wall, to his bedroom.

His door was covered with tags written in black Sharpie, most of which read "Cheech." Or at least I thought they did. They were hard to read. But I didn't bother to try to decipher them further because my eyes were drawn to the huge paintings on his bedroom walls. They were life-size cartoonish images: a piece of bacon frying in a pan that was saying, "I smell delicious," a blonde girl with a ponytail and bangs in a Catholic school uniform kilt giving the finger, and a puppy sniffing a kitten's butt.

"When did you move down here?" I asked. Last time I'd been in his bedroom, it was on the second floor, next to his sister's.

"A couple years ago," he said. "I couldn't stand living next door to the mausoleum that was Allie's bedroom anymore. It was too quiet, too empty."

I was beginning to know exactly how that felt.

Looking closer, I could see that someone had installed frames around the art. The frames were just pieces of decorative wood painted to contrast the walls, but it looked nice.

"Did you frame these?" I asked.

He shook his head. "Nah, it was my mom. She thought it would make it look less like graffiti."

It did. It looked deliberate, almost like she approved of the paintings. If I'd done something like this in my room, my mom's version of support would have been to hold the paint can while I repainted the walls a pristine white.

"She hates this part, though," he said, pointing to the smaller wall next to the door. "The 'Wall of Fame.'"

A poster board hung here, smothered in tags written in permanent marker. Not all were Raf's.

"These are my friends'," he said pointing out a few. He paused for a second, as if to grieve their loss. "It's not like we could go out and tag the houses on the block or anything. The best we could do was write our tags on stickers and put them on lampposts and mailboxes all over town. So, instead, we ended up tagging our own walls," he explained. "Or we used to anyway."

"I can kind of see why your mom hates it," I said. It looked like just a big mess of ink. Raf's tags were pretty good, actually, and so were some of the others. But most were essentially scribbles.

"You wound me," Raf said, clutching his chest in mock pain.

"What does 'Cheech' mean?" I asked, ignoring his histrionics.

"It's short for Chicharrón."

"That's you?"

He nodded. "I'm Latino and Southern. And chicharrón is like the Latin American version of bacon or pork rinds. And I'm just as salty and delicious."

I raised a suspicious eyebrow. "Virginia's not *really* the south."

His smile slid. "Okay, fine. My friends came up with it. Typical white boys, nicknamed me after the only Latino stoner they knew, Cheech Marin. So I looked up where he got his nickname and started telling people the Chicharrón thing."

"Oh," I said. I was glad he wasn't hanging out with those friends anymore. "We should come up with a new nickname for you to deface your walls with."

Raf's smile returned. "Yeah. Maybe." But he didn't seem over it.

"Do you do regular art anymore?" I asked to change the subject, then suddenly realized how insulting that sounded. "I mean like sketches, portraits, oil paintings of fruit bowls, whatever . . . I'm not an artist."

Raf was laughing now, too. He bent down to rifle through one of his desk drawers, pulling out a couple of sketchbooks and handing them to me.

The first one was completely full, cover to cover, with pieces that read "Chicharrón" and "Cheech." They were colorful, with multiple outlines and 3-D effects. They looked like they should have been spray-painted on a wall.

Interspersed with those were more of his cartoonish drawings of people, all equally as skilled as the ones on his walls, though some were obviously rough sketches.

The second book, however, was full of realistic sketches of people. Sometimes close-ups, of their eyes or their hands. A few featured several people in a scene of some kind. A grandfather holding an ice cream cone for his grandson. A little boy and girl kissing under a willow tree. This was a completely different side to his art. The sentimental side, I guess.

"Wow," I said. I could feel Raf's eyes on me, watching my reactions as I flipped the pages. But I didn't care that he could see how in awe of his talent I was. He deserved the praise. Still, I wasn't expecting the pain that sliced through me when I turned the page and saw an incredible rendering of his sister, Allie. She was bald from the chemo, with a scarf wrapped around her head and dark circles under her eyes. But she was laughing at something, and her grin was the same as it always had been.

"You make me feel inadequate. I'm not good at anything like this."

"You don't have hobbies?" Raf asked. It wasn't a judgment, just surprise. But it was also a way to brush aside my compliment. Calling his incredible talent a "hobby" was like calling a lion a "kitty cat."

I gave it some real thought before I answered. I'd never really considered my hobbies. Well, I had, but only when Mom asked me about college applications and what I was going to say about how I'd spent the last three years of high school. Sometimes I wrote poetry for the literary magazine, but I didn't want to be part of the club. I just wasn't big on joining activities. I only went to parties when Mike or Cassidy made me and that was a commitment of mere hours.

"No, I guess not," I said finally. "Except reading comics. But my mom doesn't think that's going to help me get into college."

"Comics?" he said, quirking an eyebrow. "I remember now that your dad used to bring us *Archie* and *Tiny Titans* and things like that."

"I've since moved on to slightly more sophisticated fare," I said. I could feel the scowl that formed any time I felt challenged about reading comics.

He held up his hands. "I'm not making fun of you, Harley," he said.

"Sorry," I said, trying to force my face to relax. "I get a little defensive about it."

"Why? Did Mike make fun of it or something?"

"No," I said, suppressing a smile at Raf's protective tone. "It was one of the only things he and I had in common actually. But his friends were less enthusiastic. So are mine."

"I get it. I was lucky that my passion was something I could study at school. At least part-time. But that didn't mean everyone respected it."

I glimpsed the small flicker of sadness behind his smile, but he shook it off.

"At least the things you're good at are tangible," I said. "You end up with a piece of art. But what does reading comics get me? Sharp reading comprehension skills and a superhero complex? How do the hours I spend bingeing shows that aired years ago help with my social skills? I'm a waste of space. You create beauty."

Raf was grinning at me, this time with no tinge of sadness or pain at all. "So what else do you do? Aside from comics and TV?"

I shrugged, legitimately stumped. "I don't know. I hang out with Cassidy. Mostly, I just did whatever Mike wanted to do." A whirlpool of guilt swirled in my stomach. "I wasted three years of high school doing whatever he wanted, hanging out with his friends, being who he wanted me to be."

A lump had risen in my throat, and tears were now burning in my eyes. I took a deep breath and tried to will them away.

"It's okay to be upset," Raf said, laying a hand on my shoulder. "Although, in the program, they say that 'upset' isn't actually an emotion. They want you to say you're angry or anxious or resentful. Mostly powerless. That's the big one."

"I'm not any of those things," I managed to say. But my voice was tight. "I'm fine." I sat down on the bed next to him.

"They also say that 'fine' stands for 'fucked up, insecure, neurotic, and emotional.'"

"Yeah, well, 'they' can bite me," I said. "Because that spells FUINE."

Raf burst out laughing.

I turned to face him, frowning at first, then fixating on his eyes. His lashes were still so long, the way they'd been when he was a kid. But I'd never noticed the golden flecks in his irises.

"You know what I find surprising about your lack of interests," Raf said, snapping me back into the moment. "You've always seemed so sure of yourself. I feel like you could do anything you want."

I turned away. "Yeah, right. You've obviously never seen me in gym class."

"Very few people look good in gym," he said. "But don't worry. We'll figure out what would make you happy."

"We?"

"You and me."

"Why would you want to figure that out?"

"Why not? What else do I have going on right now?"

"Okay," I said skeptically. "But not tonight. I should go." It was late and I didn't want Mom and Dad to worry.

"Hang on," he said, standing. "I'll walk you home."

A smile tugged at my lips. "Remember how we used to walk each other home, back and forth, for as long as we could? We kept doing it until our parents practically dragged us away from each other."

Raf grinned. "Yeah, they really had their hands full with the two of us schemers."

"It's probably a good thing we stopped hanging out," I said, as I opened his bedroom door. "You were a bad influence. Still are."

Once again, Raf made a show of being offended. "Me? I am pure as the driven snow! How dare you imply that I would ever try to corrupt you?"

I pointed at the unlit cigarette he held between his thumb and forefinger.

"If I recall correctly, *you* were the one who was smoking first that night," he said.

For some reason, it pleased me that he remembered. I turned away to hide my smile. But when we stopped at my front porch, I asked, "Are you going to smoke that?"

He nodded. "Yeah, but I'll wait until you go inside. I wouldn't want to be a bad influence."

Now I didn't feel the need to hide it when I smiled at him. "You're a good friend. I take back what I said."

"We go way back," he said with a shrug. Then he pulled out his phone. "Hey, give me your number. Friends have each other's numbers."

"Fair point," I said, adding my number. A few seconds later, my phone buzzed with an incoming text: Sleep tight, xo Raf

"You, too," I said and then closed the door behind me.

Floyd wasn't waiting at the door, so I assumed, gratefully, that my parents must be asleep, but Dad was in the kitchen when I rounded the corner on tiptoes. He glanced over at me and then went back to spooning out one of the omnipresent neighbor-provided casseroles onto a plate. Floyd, the traitor, was staring eagerly at the spoon in his hand.

"Did you just get home?" I asked.

"Yeah, I got called in for a pretty nasty compound fracture of the tibia," Dad said.

I sidled up next to him.

"Come on, kid," he said, sniffing near me. "Smoking?"

I shrugged. "Sorry," I said. "It's just . . ." But there wasn't anything to say.

"Who were you talking to out there?" he asked.

I looked up from the Post-it note I was shredding. "Raf," I said. "He bummed me a cigarette."

"Rafael?" Dad said, raising his eyebrows in the direction of the dish. "What's he up to?"

"I think he's just figuring that out," I said.

"I remember those days," Dad said wistfully. "Before college and bills and kids who made my hair turn gray."

"Totally worth it, though, right?" I asked as I hopped up on the counter next to him.

"Hm, that depends on your definition of 'worth it.'" Dad put his plate in the microwave and turned to me. "Did you pick up this week's issue of *The Walking Dead* yet? Your dear old dad is waiting to find out what happens."

"Yeah, do you want me to tell you?" I said, trying to look innocent. Dad hated spoilers and would run from me if I tried to talk to him about something he hadn't read yet.

"Do it and you'll get a plate of hot chicken divan to the face," he said. He took his plate out of the microwave menacingly.

"Your loss," I said, jumping down from the counter. I stole a piece of chicken from his plate before heading for the stairs.

"Leave it for me in the hallway, will you? And wash your hands and face before you go upstairs," Dad said. "Your mother is still awake, and if she smells that smoke on you, she'll put *you* in a coma."

"Boo," I said, deadpan. "Too soon." But we were both smiling.

I took it as a good sign that Dad was joking again. The man never met a pun or a joke he didn't like, but he hadn't been particularly funny (or unfunny) since the accident. Progress.

One Year Ago

Mike and I were in the basement watching a movie when Audrey and Neema came downstairs. They were lucky we were clothed, since "watching a movie" was usually a euphemism for "having sex." But it was early and Mike didn't have to leave for a while and, frankly, I hadn't felt like it that night, so Audrey and Neema were more welcome than they normally would have been.

We were watching a horror movie, one of those ones where people get killed in the goriest ways, which at any other time would have sent Audrey running for her bedroom. But this time, she and Neema settled in on the love seat next to the couch Mike and I were cuddled on. They whispered to each other occasionally, sneaking glances at us every now and then.

Finally, I grew tired of their furtive looks. "Is there something you guys wanted?" I asked.

Color bloomed in Audrey's cheeks. "No, we just wanted to watch the movie with you," she answered.

I rolled my eyes. "Audy, you're totally lying. It's because that guy you like is in this movie, right? What's-his-name from that movie you made me watch a few months ago."

"Bradley Cooper," Audrey and Mike answered in unison.

I snapped my head back to look at Mike. "How on earth do you know that?"

He only looked mildly embarrassed. "It's a decent movie," he said. "I watched it with my mom."

"You saw Silver Linings Playbook*?" Audrey asked.*

Mike nodded. "Yeah, I liked it."

"Even the dancing?" Neema chimed in.

Mike sat up, nearly pushing me off the couch as he extricated himself from being the big spoon.

"Totally the dancing. My mom made me take cotillion when I was in middle school in Atlanta, so I can do the waltz, the fox-trot, the jitterbug, even a little cha-cha." Mike stood and demonstrated his cha-cha, sending Audrey and Neema into fits of giggles. They were freshmen, after all, and neither had even kissed a boy.

"There were so few guys there that I had to dance constantly," he said. "I got pretty good."

After a few cha-cha-chas, Mike pulled me up off the couch and tried to get me to dance with him. I tried to keep up, but I wasn't a dancer. I wasn't much of anything that required coordination.

He gave up quickly and pulled Audrey up instead. She actually was a dancer. Not ballroom, but ballet, tap dance, jazz, hip-hop. She was the type of kid who had to be perpetually in motion, and dance got some of that energy out.

For a second, when Mike held her waist, I wished my stomach were as flat as hers and wondered if he thought the same thing. But it didn't matter because I was absolutely not the exercising type. I'd take my muffin top with a side of muffins, thank you very much.

Audrey looked so happy and graceful, even while doing

the jitterbug with Mike that I almost didn't feel jealous of her. She laughed out loud when he spun her out and pulled her back in against his chest. And I laughed with them.

That might have been the first time Mike saw her as more than my little sister. She was more fun than me, prettier than me, thinner than me. How could I blame him?

CHAPTER SEVEN

Very early the next morning, the faint ring of the landline pulled me out of bed and sent me running for my parents' bedroom all over again. I stood at the foot of the bed watching Dad's face. Mom sat close to him, squeezing his shoulder. As his features relaxed, my heart leapt. He put the phone down and turned to us.

"Audrey is awake," he said. His voice was so quiet, I could barely hear him. "She opened her eyes a few minutes ago."

His attempt to hold in his emotions faltered. He reached out for Mom, opening up his free arm to me. I ran toward him and fell against his shoulder. But the teary family hug was over almost as quickly as it started; Dad "the doctor" started trying to be rational, to talk us out of being too hopeful.

Yes, Audrey had awakened once, but it didn't necessarily mean she would wake up again if she slipped into unconsciousness. The key to managing the situation was to have realistic expectations. If she did wake up, she might have difficulty walking and speaking, she could have amnesia, or a number of other potential issues.

"Just let us have this moment of hope, okay?" I told him. "You don't have to always be the voice of realism."

"Why do you think I read those articles about recovery *out loud*?" Mom added, getting out of bed. "I'm just trying to counteract your dad's practicality. I've given up on making up for the bad jokes."

"Hey!" he protested, but he was smiling. "I'm hilarious."

I allowed myself a hopeful smile as I ran to my room to get dressed.

AUDREY WAS ASLEEP again by the time we got to the hospital, but lucky for us, Keisha was waiting. She'd been on duty when Audrey opened her eyes; her EEG had tracked the change and alerted Keisha at the nurses' station.

"I rushed to the room," Keisha told us. "And I took her hand and told her she was in the hospital. I told her she was going to be fine, but that there'd been an accident."

Mom huffed through her nose. No doubt she'd wanted to tell Audrey that herself.

"I told her that her family was on their way. That you all were going to be so happy to see her," Keisha added. She dabbed at her eyes with the sleeve of her shirt. I got the feeling that she didn't see people waking up from comas very often.

The doctor arrived then, so we moved to the hallway while he explained what was going to happen next. Which was, essentially, "wait and see."

I stayed with Audrey all morning watching movies while Mom and Dad went to work. They made me promise I would call as soon as Audrey did anything, but Mom stopped by the hospital near lunchtime anyway.

I caught a whiff of her perfume—spicy, with a hint of money—when she bent to kiss Audrey's forehead.

"Since so far you have thwarted my attempts to find you gainful employment for the summer, can you watch Spencer tomorrow?" Mom asked. "Aunt Tilly needs to go to see a client out of town, and he keeps refusing to go to his day camp."

My aunt visited her agoraphobic clients in their homes. A few times a week, she traveled as far as a couple hundred miles away from northern Virginia. So Spencer spent a lot of time with us or with babysitters or, now, at camp.

I couldn't blame Spencer for not wanting to go to camp. I may have had fun, but Audrey had trouble with it when she was his age, and I remembered how homesick she was at first. And unlike Audrey, who had little trouble making friends, Spencer could barely speak to other kids his age.

"Yeah, sure," I said. "Can I take him to a baseball game?"

"Okay," she said, but not without raising her eyebrows in surprise. Her idea of fun did not include baking in the sun watching the Nationals while the humidity made it feel like an overpriced steam bath you could eat in. But Mom recorded the nightly news, so clearly there are many definitions of fun.

When her eyes locked on mine, though, I could tell this was not the end of the conversation.

"While your sister is recovering," she said, "she'll need help around the house and someone to take her to physical therapy and things like that. But in the meantime, I really do think you should get a job. At least do some babysitting or volunteer somewhere. Something you can put on your college applications."

In my head, I added a notch to the "College Application Mentions by Mom" list I'd started on the last day of school. This was number seventeen. But what stood out in Mom's statement was what she hadn't said. In her insistence that I be available to help Audrey recover was a message: "This is your fault. You owe her this."

"I'll talk to Tracey at the White Magnolia. I heard she needed a new part-time salesperson," Mom added.

I couldn't keep the sneer off my face. I was absolutely not going to spend all summer helping middle-aged women try on boring clothes that cost more than my entire lifetime's wardrobe.

"Please don't," I said. "I'll start looking, I swear."

She leaned down to kiss me on her way out but paused a couple inches away and sniffed. Her face transformed immediately.

"Harley. Please don't make me tell you to stop smoking," she said. "Don't I have enough to worry about?" She gestured needlessly to Audrey's inert body next to us.

Damn it. Well played, Mom.

I wanted to roll my eyes. But I couldn't. She wasn't *wrong*. I mean, I didn't even like smoking that much; I just needed something to keep my hands busy and my mouth from screaming. But now, on top of being soothing and a nice distraction, it was also an excuse to see Raf.

"Okay," I whispered, ashamed.

"And the job?" she prompted, clearly not convinced by my half-hearted appeal.

"I'll see what I can find," I said, trying to sound more sincere this time. I even gestured to my open laptop.

She kissed me on the cheek and left, saying, "I'll be back soon, baby duck."

I wanted to tell her she was a pain in the ass. I also wanted to run after her and give her a hug and tell her that I loved her. It was only after a few seconds that I realized I had a smile on my face.

ABOUT AN HOUR later, when I was halfway through *Never Been Kissed* (which was equal parts terrible and adorable), there was a quick knock on the door, and then Neema poked her head in.

"Oh, hey," she said, walking in and standing by the side of the bed. She stroked the back of Audrey's hand with one finger.

"Hey," I said. "How are you?"

Neema's eyes slowly drifted over Audrey's body until they landed on me. "I'm fine. Has she woken up again?"

"No," I said. "But she's moved her fingers and toes a little. She twitches sometimes."

She didn't respond, so I took the hint and stood up. "I'll give you some privacy," I said.

She barely glanced at me as I walked out, but I saw tears pooled in her eyes.

I went down to the cafeteria for a soda and when I returned, Neema was gone. But somehow I could still feel a misty cloud of sadness hanging over the room. I moved my laptop off the chair and sat back down, putting my feet up on the bed and closing my eyes.

I wished I could talk to Audrey about what was going on. About Mom and Dad and how they were reacting to what was happening. About Raf and how weird it was that we'd reconnected. I wanted to tell her I was sorry for ever bringing Mike into her life and for not being strong enough to dump him. To be alone.

I'd been with Mike since I was a freshman, and I didn't remember what high school life was like without him. Aside from Cassidy, Mike and Audrey were the people I was closest to in the world. And Mike was the reason I had plans on weekends. Now, I wasn't really sure what to do with myself.

I thought of Raf telling me he felt alone.

Damn it. Maybe Mom was right. Maybe I did need a job.

THAT AFTERNOON, RAF texted to ask what I was doing. Mom and Dad were out and I was bored. And I wanted to see him. So I told him to come over.

Raf hadn't been in my room since the last time I'd been in his—the second-floor room, that is. It had been more than ten years. He took his time exploring while I fidgeted nervously, hovering near the door.

"I like the new color," he said. Now a soft dove gray, it had been a hideous bubblegum pink, which you could still find inside my closet. I opened the doors to show him and his jaw dropped. Not at the pink. At the sight of all the books, graphic novels, trade collections, plus the long boxes of bagged-and-boarded comics stacked on the shelves that were intended to be used to display shoes or purses.

"When you told me you liked comics, I don't think I understood the extent. This?" Raf spread his arms over the collection. "This is more than a hobby. This is an obsession."

I shrugged. "Dad and I used to take road trips to different comic book shops all over Virginia and Maryland, even Delaware and West Virginia a couple of times. New Jersey once, for a local comic con. I got most of these from dollar bins, but you should see my dad's collection. He's taken over half of the basement."

"What makes you think this isn't something to be proud of? That there's no future in this?" Raf asked. He leaned close, his gaze roving over the spines. "Who do you think makes these things? Robots?"

"No," I said quietly. "I've just always read comics, like,

my whole life. I never thought it was anything special. I mean, doesn't everyone read?"

He snorted. "Not everyone, no."

"You do," I said.

I distinctly remembered a shelf full of books that I'd snuck looks at. I'd taken note of the copy of *Slaughterhouse-Five* that had been sitting on his bedside table. I've always believed you can tell a lot about a person by their taste in reading material. Of course, not everyone kept reading material on hand. I went to school with people who refused to open a book, as if it was some kind of principle they were sticking to. Most days, I was the only person in the school's library who wasn't there just to study.

Raf glanced at me and then back at the shelves, as if he couldn't tear his eyes away for too long.

"Do you want to borrow something?" I asked. A number of books had been gifts from Mike, and I was more than happy to have them out of sight for a while.

"What do you recommend?" he asked. Keeping in mind the books on his own shelves, I figured he'd best start with something like *Watchmen*—a modern classic. I pulled it off the shelf and handed it to him.

"I expect a full report," I said.

Raf grinned as he took the book. "I want to see the movie of this," he said. "Would that ruin it?"

"Well, that's hard to say and it depends on who you ask," I said. I sounded like my dad before he started in on a rant.

"What?" Raf asked.

"Nothing." I sat down on the bed, and Raf sat next to me. "The movie followed a lot of it really closely, and they got a lot of details perfect, but they didn't change any of the super misogynistic storylines when they could have. Instead, they changed the end. But both are good, in different ways. I don't want to say more until you've read it. Then we'll watch the movie."

My cheeks flushed. I had just forced a movie date on him without even thinking about it. But Raf didn't seem to notice.

"Cool," he said, still engrossed in the first few pages.

I liked that he was enjoying something I'd given him for once, rather than giving me advice about what I needed to do to make myself better.

But as if he'd read my mind, he glanced up and asked, "Do you write at all?"

I turned away, embarrassed. "Not lately. My poems are terrible."

Raf shook his head. "I don't believe that. Your brain is built for words."

I could feel myself blushing. "I guess," I practically whispered. "But the literary magazine has only published a few of them."

He looked smug. "Well, at least think about it. Because someone has to write the comics, right?"

"Yeah . . ." I said.

"Why not you?"

I squirmed uncomfortably but didn't answer. Because I didn't *have* an answer.

"You used to write comics all the time when we were little. I'd be coloring, and you'd be scribbling away next to me, plotting out these intricate stories. And then you'd make me illustrate them for you in these tiny boxes that you'd drawn."

The memory made my lips tilt up at the corners. "They were pretty tiny."

"I started drawing because of you. So I guess my mom should thank you for all the destruction I've done to my bedroom."

I laughed, relieved we'd moved on from the subject of me. "Since you've now admitted that you owe me, I'll be expecting a commission when you become a famous artist."

Raf rolled his eyes playfully. "Only if you start writing things for me to illustrate again. Because your stories were good, even when you were seven."

My smile slipped. This was edging dangerously close to a conversation about my lack of ambition, and I already got more than enough of that from Mom.

"You want me to shut up now?" Raf said, bumping me lightly with his elbow.

I nodded.

"I have to get going anyway," he said. "I have to go to a meeting tonight."

"You're still going?" I was surprised. He was done with rehab, so it wasn't a requirement anymore. And I didn't think he thought of himself as an addict.

"Yeah," he said. "I kind of like going. It makes my parents feel secure that I'm not out using, for one, but mostly, I find it really inspiring to see people pull themselves up and dust themselves off after reaching bottom, and I mean *rock bottom* in some cases. It's encouraging. And it's making me think about what more I could be doing."

"Doing how?" I said.

"Like school, for one," he said. "I signed up for community college classes in the fall. I'm going to take some art classes, but also a psych course."

"That's great, Raf!" I said. I suddenly wanted to hug him, but I wasn't sure we were at that point in our friendship yet.

"So, have you met anyone at your AA meetings? I mean, like, have you made any friends?"

He shrugged. "Kind of," he said uncomfortably. "I mean, there are some people I hang out with at the meetings, but it's weird going to a party by yourself, you know? I need a wingman, but all my men are on the No Fly List."

I could see that even though he was making jokes, he really was sad. "Well, if you ever want a wingwoman, I'm a very good flier. I don't get airsick or anything."

I regretted saying it immediately because, truthfully, I wasn't great with strangers. Or parties. But even though he laughed, he also looked grateful, and I knew I'd go anywhere with him if it made him happier.

"Thanks," he said. "And I will report back on this," he added, gesturing to *Watchmen*.

I walked him downstairs and bummed a cigarette off of him before he left.

"Hey," I called to him before he reached the shadow at the corner of his house. "Do you want to go to a baseball game tomorrow with me and my cousin Spencer?"

It was getting dark, but I could see his smile in the porch light. "Yeah," he said. "I definitely do."

I couldn't keep the smile from my face, a goofy reflection of his. "Good. Come over at noon. And you're driving."

I turned around and went inside before he could argue. Spencer was going to love his Jeep.

Eight Months Ago

I was halfway through the latest issue of Batman *when I heard a car pull into the driveway. It was Mike. I hadn't been expecting him. I sighed as I closed the book, wishing I could finish it. But instead, I got up and headed downstairs to meet him.*

Audrey was at the door waiting for Mike as he came up the front walk. I saw her check her hair in the mirror before he reached the storm door.

She startled guiltily when she saw me and backed away. "Mike's here," she said.

"Yeah, I saw," I said. "So you can . . . leave." That came out harsher than I planned, but I couldn't figure out what she wanted. She shot me a dirty look before rounding the corner.

"Hey, Harley Quinn," Mike said as he opened the door.

I leaned in for a kiss, catching the lingering smell of alcohol from the night before. "How was the party last night?"

He shrugged, but I saw the dark shadows under his eyes, indicating that it had gone late and there had been plenty to drink.

"Same old, same old," he said. Then he reached for my waist and pulled me against him. "I missed you, though."

I smiled up at him. "I missed you," I said. And I had. I'd spent the night watching half of a season of Orphan Black, *which I'd already seen several times before. I hadn't been bored, but I did think about him. Maybe worried a little bit that I wasn't there to police him, to keep him from doing something stupid.*

I hadn't regretted skipping the party until just that moment, though. Now I longed for Mike's comforting embrace, his warm smile and his familiar kisses, I wished I'd been with him.

He herded me toward the basement stairs, and I smiled up at him. "How did you know my parents aren't home?" I asked.

"I saw them," he said. "They were leaving the neighborhood as I drove in. I don't think they saw me, though."

"What timing," I said as we headed down the stairs.

As we sat on the couch, Mike pulled something out of his pocket. It was a small navy-blue velvet box. A jewelry box.

"Michael, what is that?" I asked warily.

My stomach jumped into my throat as he got down on one knee in front of me.

"What are you doing?"

Mike just shushed me. "Harley Quinn," he said, "I have loved you for two years exactly as of today. And I plan to love you for many, many more. Will you continue being my girlfriend?"

My stomach dropped. I had forgotten our anniversary.

Part of me was thinking that I was a horrible, selfish girlfriend. Mike snapped open the box and held it in front of me, proudly displaying what was inside: a silver necklace with a pendant in the shape of the jester's hat. The original Harley Quinn's hat. I still hadn't told him I didn't like Harley; I liked his attachment to her, and me, too much. But another part of me was thinking that he should have realized by now that I didn't like Harley. He should have figured it out long ago.

"You are too sweet," I said, leaning forward to kiss him. "And I love you."

He slid into the seat beside me and put the necklace around my neck, kissing the nape lightly as he clasped it.

"Thank you," he said against my skin.

"For what?" I said, turning to look at him. "You're the one who bought me a present. I should be thanking you."

Mike shook his head, a serious firmness in his full lips and a hint of sadness in his eyes. "I'm lucky to have you," he said quietly. "I know that."

"Maybe we're lucky to have each other," I said. And tried to tell myself I believed it.

CHAPTER EIGHT

The next morning, I stopped by the hospital, but Mom was giving Audrey a sponge bath and washing her hair, which was a lengthy and embarrassing process for everyone present. Audrey would've hated it if she'd known what was happening. I guess it was the only upside to her not waking up.

I went to Cassidy's house instead. From the front steps, I could hear Morgan screaming, but I couldn't hear about what. So instead of knocking or ringing the doorbell, I texted Cassidy. She came outside a minute later, and we sat on the front porch. I wished I'd thought to bring coffee. We both looked pretty ragged.

"You have impeccable timing," she said as she threw a pointed look over her shoulder. Morgan was glaring out at us through the window next to the door.

I bared my teeth at her. She rolled her eyes and stormed away.

"So, that screaming was aimed at you?" I said.

Cassidy seemed a little reluctant to talk. She scrubbed her hands down her face.

"Remember when Audrey was about to be a freshman?"

she finally said. "She thought she was such hot shit, and we had to kindly teach her that, in fact, she was about to be dog shit on the bottom of the seniors' shoes."

I nodded, not really grasping what she was getting at.

"I was trying to explain this same principle to The Nuisance—for her own benefit—while she was attempting to borrow some of my clothes." Cassidy managed a wry grin. "She *really* took issue with it."

She and Morgan had never had the same relationship Audrey and I had. "The Nuisance" was not a term of endearment. There was too much distance between them. But I still felt a twinge in the center of my chest when I realized why Cassidy didn't want to talk about it with me. It was such normal sister stuff. And something I might never have again: a fight with my little sister.

"Do you feel like getting out of the house?" I offered.

She nodded enthusiastically.

"It involves baseball, though."

Her head stilled.

"And twelve-year-old and eighteen-year-old boys. Specifically, Spencer and Raf."

Cassidy's gaze turned stony. "Why, exactly?" she asked skeptically.

"I'm watching Spencer and so, obviously, baseball." Cassidy nodded again. "And Raf—"

"Out with it," she interrupted.

"We've kind of . . . reconnected," I said. "We've hung out a couple of times. For very short periods." I hesitated. "Just give him a chance, okay?"

Cassidy raised her eyebrows, still not convinced.

"You don't have to say it," I said. "I know that I said that about Mike. More than once. But Raf . . . I don't know. I like having him around. He's grown up and—I realize this does *not* help my case—rehab seems to have changed him."

To her credit, Cassidy didn't roll her eyes. But she didn't look convinced, either.

"Just come along and see for yourself, okay?"

She started to sigh but caught herself. "Okay, okay. I'll go steal my clothes back from Morgan's room and change, and then we can go. But I have to come home right after. I have to work opening tomorrow at five A.M. because God forbid Will ask Janine to risk her beauty sleep."

Cassidy's manager, Will, had a habit of dating his employees. Janine was the latest. I couldn't tell if Cassidy was jealous. He was flirtatious, and she thought he was cute, but as far as I knew, he hadn't made a move.

I didn't get the appeal—Will was tall and skinny, and he was always wearing beanies even when it was ninety degrees out. Not my type. Mike had been sturdy, an athlete, with a little belly and enough stretch marks to make me feel less self-conscious when naked in front of him. I still focused on my muffin top and double chin in photos of the two of us together, though.

Living a mostly sedentary life of reading comics and watching TV had left me with more padding than I wanted, but not enough motivation to actually do something about it. I'd rather read and lounge and eat carbs. Carbs are delicious.

But Will was Cassidy's type, so I supported her crush, even if she hadn't yet admitted it. But I found it suspicious just how often she complained that Janine got the best shifts while she was left working closing on Friday nights and opening on Sunday mornings.

I tried not to let on that, selfishly, I was happy about the situation. She now had Saturday off and could hang out with me. I'd wait until she was in a better mood to rub it in.

WE PULLED INTO the parking lot about a half hour before the opening pitch, but I could see that Spencer was anxious about getting inside to watch batting practice. I leaned forward and squeezed his bony shoulder. After his mom had slathered his gangly limbs with sunscreen and left with a warning not to let him eat anything with sugar, I'd let him sit in the front seat. It had made him smile so huge, his cheeks lifted his glasses. But that excitement had worn off, and now I could feel the tension even through the thick polyester of his Nationals jersey.

"We'll be inside in a few minutes, I promise," I whispered.

He didn't respond, but he turned enough to give me a tight-lipped nod.

Raf parked and let me and Cassidy out of the back seat. I paid for everyone's tickets, courtesy of my mom, and we wound our way through the stadium to our seats. Unlike most kids who immediately ask for food, Spencer made a beeline for the upper level. We were up in the nosebleeds, but he rushed to the edge and parked himself there.

Cassidy, Raf, and I found our seats, but Raf immediately turned around.

"Hot dog?" he asked, pointing at me and then Cassidy. "Hot dog?" We both nodded. "What about Spencer?"

"His mom only lets him eat organic, grass-fed, cage-free what-have-you," Cassidy said with disdain.

"So . . . yes?" Raf said, smiling at her.

"Exactly," she said, grinning back. "We need to pump him full of as much processed crap as possible before he has to go back to her."

Raf pointed at her. "You're my kind of girl."

Cassidy allowed herself a small smile. She was coming around to him.

When Raf got back, I offered to take Spencer's hot dog to him, but he waved me off.

"Don't be offended if he doesn't talk to you," I said as he turned away. "Spencer loves the stadium, but it's super overstimulating for him. He tends to stay quiet."

Raf just winked at me and kept walking.

Spencer ignored him at first, until Raf offered him the hot dog. He held it while Spencer put relish and ketchup on it, and then they sat in two free seats and talked. Or really, Raf talked while Spencer ate and listened, but I saw him nod and respond once or twice. By the time Raf and Spencer came back to our seats, the first inning had started. Spencer was talking, if not animatedly, at least with regularity. I tried to follow what they were saying, but it sounded a lot like gibberish. So instead, Cassidy and I focused on fanning ourselves with the magazines I'd brought in case we got bored.

Sometime in the top of the second inning, three guys took seats behind us. They were college-age frat types, each holding a beer—and judging from their loud voices, I doubted it was their first. They were immediately annoying, kicking the back of our seats and getting peanut shells in Cassidy's and my hair, and it didn't take long before I lost patience. But Cassidy gave me a look every time I shot a glare at them, or sighed loudly, or at one point called them assholes under my breath. They heard, though. And they just laughed. There was no point in doing anything but ignoring them. So I tried to restrain myself.

Until the Nationals got a home run in the bottom of the fourth. One of the players—I didn't know which—hit a home run over the wall in right field, and the guys behind us went wild. One of them kneed me in the back of the head when he stood to scream. I winced. When I spun around, he just flashed a drunken grin.

"Watch what you're doing!" I snapped.

He leaned down, grabbed the bill of my hat, and snatched if off my head. "Get up here and celebrate with me, fat ass," he said.

Without thinking, I batted his nearly empty beer cup from his hand.

"Don't fucking touch me," I spat.

Suddenly his smile was gone. He looked at his spilled beer on the ground, then at me. His bloodshot eyes were furious. I could see the moment he decided to slap me. Too bad for him my reflexes hadn't been muddled by alcohol. I shifted, and he caught my shoulder instead of my face and sent me slamming into Raf. The guy nearly fell on top of me, losing his balance from the force of his swinging arm. Raf and I were there to catch him from the front while one of his friends grabbed the back of his shorts and pulled him up.

"Asshole!" Raf yelled as he shoved the guy back up to his friends. "Are you fucking kidding me? Get the hell away from her!"

The guy reared back, looking like he was going to kick Raf in the face, but his friends held him back—one on either side. To their credit, they looked as shocked and pissed off at their friend as we were. As they pulled him out into the aisle, one of them muttered an apology. But it was too late. Two beefy security guards had appeared, and within seconds all three guys were being escorted from the stands.

We were standing now, even the people around us. They were all staring at me.

It had all happened so fast. I was shaking with rage, but I did my best impression of laughing it off for Spencer's sake, who looked as rattled as I felt.

"Nothing to see here," I joked lamely.

There was a smattering of sympathetic applause, and then everyone went back to watching the game. Everyone but Raf.

"Are you okay?" he asked, his eyes searching my face.

I nodded, but my hands were still trembling. I sat and tucked them between my legs, regretting my decision to wear shorts. I hoped Raf wasn't looking at the cellulite on my thighs.

"That was a nice dodge," he said as he settled back down into the seat next to me. "Maybe your hobby should be boxing."

I shrugged, trying to appear nonchalant. In reality, I was having trouble with the fact that I had wanted to punch that guy's face until his nose was a bloody pile of mush. I didn't know what to do with the aggression. It scared me. And it was still rolling off me in waves.

"He was drunk," I said, half to myself.

"Exactly. He could have hurt you."

"Yeah, well. I've spent years dodging Audrey when she tried to bait me into a fight by hitting me over and over again."

Raf bumped his shoulder against mine. "So modest," he said, lightening his tone. "Just consider me impressed."

I couldn't help smiling. But as the anger receded, I was left with something else: the embarrassment of being called "fat" in front of him.

"I wanted to punch that guy for what he said about your ass," Raf added, as if reading my mind.

"Let's not talk about that," I groaned. Besides, my butt

wasn't particularly fat; it was more flat and nondescript. But I don't think that guy was being literal. I knew I was overweight—I didn't have Cassidy's slim legs or Audrey's bikini-ready flat stomach—but I definitely did not want to discuss the particulars of my body here with Raf at a baseball game, in front of Cassidy and Spencer.

Raf held his hands up in defeat. "But let me just say this: I like it. It's a cute ass, just like the rest of you."

Blood rushed to my face. Definitely time to change the subject.

"Is Spencer okay?" I asked, craning my neck to peer past Raf. Spencer was engrossed in watching the game.

"He's fine," Raf said. He raised his voice a little so that Spencer could hear him. "He's about to owe me five bucks when Tejeda gets his second hit."

Spencer looked up at him and shook his head. "Tejeda hasn't had more than one hit in a game since July of last year."

"So you're giving away money now?" I joked to Raf. "Can I get in on this?"

He shrugged, grinning. "Let me think about it. I have to run to the boys' room."

I tried not to stare at his ass as he stepped over Spencer's short legs to the aisle.

The second he'd disappeared down the steps, Cassidy nudged me with her leg. "You are in trouble," she said, drawing out the last word.

I frowned, pretending to focus on the game. "What are you talking about?"

"He's smitten," she said.

When I shot her a glance, she smirked. At my blank look, she added, "With you. He's smitten with *you*."

I waved her off. "No way." But secretly, I kind of thought she was right. He wasn't exactly hiding it. "I mean . . . maybe. But I don't want him to be." My voice faded. Also not true.

Cassidy just stared at me, one eyebrow raised.

Now my cheeks felt flushed again. I pulled the brim of my cap lower to hide my smile. "Fine, I like the idea of him liking me. But I can't deal with it right now, Cass. I'm a freaking disaster. Look at me! I can't even go to a baseball game without getting into a fight with some douchebag."

She scoffed. "That was *not* your fault."

"No," I said, shaking my head. "It was." My jaw tightened. "I could have let it go. I didn't have to argue with him or antagonize him. But I'm just so tired of guys being complete dicks when they're drunk. I just . . . lost it."

"I know, sweetie," she said, stroking my arm. "But Raf's not drinking anymore. He might be one of the good ones."

"What if he starts drinking again, though?" I said. "I can't handle that. I can't fall for another drunk asshole. No matter how cute or sweet or nice he is."

Cassidy pursed her lips. She clearly wanted to say more but knew better when I was in this mood. "Good luck with that," was all she said.

She turned back to the game. But I couldn't help myself. I wanted to keep talking about this. About Raf. I needed to talk myself out of the way I was feeling about him.

"No, seriously," I said.

Cassidy's pursed lips widened into a smile.

"Come on, Cass. Think about Raf," I went on. "He's not what I'm looking for. Who I should be with. He barely graduated, he's going to *community* college, and he just got out of rehab! I can't be with a guy like that. He's a mess."

Cassidy lifted her shoulders. "Let me just say this: on

paper, Mike looked pretty good," she said in a flat voice. "Maybe you shouldn't be so quick to judge."

I opened my mouth, then closed it. She was right. Mike was from a middle-class family, went to my school (a private school), was a good athlete and better student, and was going to a four-year college, presumably. Good on paper. The type of guy who should appeal to me.

But she was right, and we both knew it.

Still, I had one rebuttal. "Are you actually defending *Rafael Juarez* as a legitimate relationship option? The guy we cursed with a voodoo doll after he stood me up the summer before eighth grade?"

She shrugged again, eyes glued to the field, even though she had zero interest in the game. "I'm not the one who kept thinking about him. Who never *stopped* thinking about him."

I was out of points to argue. Cassidy's smug smile meant she knew she'd won.

Rather than admitting it, I moved next to Spencer.

"Are you having fun?" I asked him. "Do you need anything?"

He didn't seem to notice I was there. His eyes were pinned to the pitcher from the Mets, who was about to throw the final pitch of the inning. If I'd been paying attention, I would have known to wait a few more seconds. But once the inning was over, Spencer relaxed his shoulders a little bit, finally turning toward me.

"Last time we came to a game, Audrey bought me this hat," he said, touching its brim.

I blinked a few times. "Oh yeah," I whispered. "I forgot about that." Or maybe I'd just blocked it out.

It shouldn't have surprised me that Audrey had used the money she'd earned babysitting on a gift for Spencer; she did stuff like that all the time. I teased her about her "random acts of kindness." That was the kind of person she was. But still, I didn't get it. When I asked her about it later, she just said it made her sad to think that Spencer didn't have a dad who would do stuff like that for him. And that, of course, made me feel like crap. There was a reason I didn't get it. I *never* thought about things like that.

She was the better one of us Langston girls. Even Spencer knew it.

"Do you miss her?" I asked him.

Spencer shrugged. Audrey's restlessness had never meshed well with his studious reticence. He and I, though, could sit next to each other and read for hours without saying a word and be perfectly happy. At Thanksgiving, we would do exactly that while Audrey bustled around the kitchen, peeling brussels sprouts and mashing potatoes, setting the table, and doing whatever she could to keep busy.

Spencer hadn't said a word about Audrey until now, but that wasn't unusual. He wasn't exactly the emotional type. So I let him be, since he seemed to be enjoying himself. Silently. No wonder I liked this kid. A quiet kid was my favorite kind.

The Nationals eventually won, so Spencer beamed the entire time that we walked to the car. Me . . . not so much.

We'd sweated buckets and spent exorbitant amounts of money stuffing ourselves with mediocre hot dogs and Cracker Jacks and ice cream. The hallways were mobbed. And loud. Lots of whoops and chants and the occasional person swooping out of nowhere to demand a high five. Almost everyone had stayed until the end of the game and the parking lot was, well, a parking lot. The lines of cars were barely moving.

Raf let Spencer ride shotgun again so he could dangle his

leg out the open door. He was fascinated with the idea that doors could actually be removed. Of course, his mom still made him sit in the back seat of her hybrid sedan with his seat belt fastened before she would even turn on the car.

Once we were finally on the road, I made Spencer put on his seat belt and promise to keep his arms and legs inside. I may not have thought of buying him a hat, but I'd at least keep him safe.

After dropping Cassidy off, Raf drove Spencer and me to our neighborhood. He pulled slowly around the cul-de-sac and parked on the street between our houses. Spencer leapt out as soon as the car stopped and ran inside to go to the bathroom, leaving me and Raf alone.

He offered me his hand to help me out of the back seat.

"So, tomorrow," he said.

"What about it?"

"A couple people from the program are having a party, and I wondered if you'd go with me?"

I tried not to look as surprised as I felt. "That . . . would be fun," I said, ignoring the nervous flutter in my stomach that awoke every time I had to be social.

"Since you offered the other day, I thought maybe you'd want to meet a few of them. Plus, get out of the house, away from the hospital . . . but you don't have to worry about anyone being drunk."

"You don't have to sell me on it," I assured him. "I already said yes."

He grinned and even pumped his fist before he suddenly got embarrassed and tried to pretend he was just stretching.

"Get some sleep," I told him. I couldn't hide my smile. "I think you're delirious from all the sun."

Raf laughed. "You're one to talk. I'd forgotten that you

had freckles, but now they're all over your face." He reached out and brushed a finger down the bridge of my nose, sending a shiver down my spine.

I could feel the tightness in my skin that told me I had gotten a sunburn. But that was pretty much to be expected when you spend all your time indoors. I could tell my shoulders were going to hurt tomorrow. I should have let Aunt Tilly put sunscreen on me while she was slathering up Spencer.

"I'll see you tomorrow, sunshine," Raf said. "Thanks for a great day."

One Year Ago

It was Sunday, two days after the last of our finals. Officially summer. So I woke up in a pretty good mood. I could hear Mom and Dad downstairs talking about their plans for the day. Neither one had decided to wake me, even though it was past ten. Next door, Audrey's bedroom was silent as I puttered around, showering and drying my hair, even though it was so humid outside that I would just end up pulling it back anyway.

I was tempted to get back in bed and watch TV, but the sun was out, and it wasn't blazing hot yet, so I called Cassidy.

"I'm coming to get you," I said when she answered. "We're going on a road trip."

She was quiet for a few seconds. "Why?" she asked suspiciously.

"What do you mean why? Because it's summer and we're sixteen and we can."

Cassidy was still skeptical. "Where are we going?"

"Where do you want to go?"

She was quiet again. "Is Mike coming?" she asked finally.

And suddenly I understood the reason for her resistance.

She and Mike tolerated each other's presence, at best. On bad days, they fought like a Republican and a Democrat discussing the economy. Except their arguments were about less important things, like which one of them was a better driver, who was the least likable character on a TV show they both watched (and loved spoiling for each other), and whether the local high school needed to change their mascot to be less offensive.

Cassidy was opinionated. But she wasn't argumentative. It was a rare combination and one reason why she was so good in student government. The truth is, outside of her family, I had never seen her fight with anyone but Mike. I didn't know what it was about him that made her so antagonistic, but it was clear to me by then, nearly two years into my relationship with Mike, that they needed to be kept apart.

"No Mike," I said. "This is just us and the open road."

"Okay," she said with a relieved sigh. "Then come get me."

"Be there in twenty. And wear pants."

"Um, I always wear pants?" she said.

I laughed. "No, I don't mean 'wear something to cover your butt.' I meant actually wear pants. Jeans. And sneakers or boots."

She was quiet. Suspicious.

"Just trust me, okay? I have a plan."

"Fine," she said with a sigh. "See you soon."

I texted Mike to let him know that I wasn't going to be around for the rest of the day and told him not to text me. He said he would try his best and then immediately texted me three more times before I'd even left the house.

I pulled up in front of Cassidy's house a half hour later. She opened the front door before I even honked.

I put on a song I knew she liked as she opened the door.

"Okay, what's going on?" she asked. "Am I dying or something? Have you been elected to be my one-woman Make-A-Wish Foundation?"

I laughed and turned the music down. "No, don't be ridiculous. I just woke up today and realized I hadn't spent a single day alone with you since Christmas break. That was six months ago."

She had been busy all spring with yearbook and government, but I hadn't made much effort to see her when she was free. Because the days she had off aligned with the days that Mike was free from his basketball and lacrosse commitments—he had practice on weekdays after school and games on Saturdays. Sundays were our day together, but before Will had changed Cassidy's schedule, it was also the only day she was free.

But this Sunday was ours.

I got on I-95 headed south toward Richmond and Cassidy raised an eyebrow. "Where, exactly, are you taking me?" she asked.

"If I told you, it'd ruin the surprise," I said.

"Kings Dominion?" she guessed. "Busch Gardens? Colonial Williamsburg?"

"Stop guessing," I demanded. "And no. Why the hell would I take you to Colonial Williamsburg? To make candles?"

Cassidy laughed. "Okay, fine. But don't mock those candles. I made them for my mom that time we went on a field trip, and she said she loved them."

I gave her a skeptical glance. "She's your mom. She had to say that."

Cassidy opened her mouth to retaliate but thought better of it. Because obviously I was right.

Instead, she turned up the radio. With the windows down, we sang along to her favorite band, screaming the words into the wind. And when we pulled up in front of a farm advertising a horse trail, a blueberry patch, and a petting zoo, my best friend grinned.

"We're going to pet baby animals, ride horses on a trail through the woods, pick blueberries, and then eat blueberry pie and ice cream until we puke purple," I announced.

She reached across the armrest between us and hugged me. Cassidy had ridden horses until eighth grade when her parents told her they couldn't afford it anymore and she had to quit. That's when she took up all the other activities that now filled her days. But I knew she missed it, even if I had never really understood the appeal. But I loved baby animals and blueberry pie. And I loved Cassidy. I reminded myself of that as I hoisted myself up onto the horse I was renting for the morning, and I immediately started sweating.

It was worth it, though—to see the joy on Cassidy's face when she leaned down to stroke the neck of her horse. I let her lead the way down the trail, through the sun-dappled forest, smiling at her ramrod-straight posture and the gleeful look in her eyes as she glanced back at me.

And I didn't think about Mike at all.

CHAPTER NINE

I regretted agreeing to the party before Raf even texted to say he would meet me at his car. Normally, I would have made an excuse to bail, but I couldn't do that to Raf. It was a big move for him to be going to this party, and I didn't want him to skip it just because I was presently a social disaster . . . if not a liability.

But when I saw Raf waiting in the driver's seat like Jake Ryan in *Sixteen Candles*, a movie I had finally watched in Audrey's hospital room that morning ("Delightfully eighties and perfectly captures first crush angst."—Audrey's spot-on review from two years ago), I couldn't stop myself from climbing into that Jeep. He'd even dressed up a little: he wore a collared shirt over his T-shirt, dark jeans, and a clean pair of sneakers. I appreciated the effort.

The party was at an apartment, Raf explained while we drove, of some older guys. My anxiety level rose. I'd never been to a party at a grown-up's place before. But I tried to convey enthusiasm as Raf went on.

Dave, Arjun, and Juan were roommates who met in AA and stayed sober together for years. And they hosted parties almost every Saturday, Raf said, but he had only been to one of these once before and didn't know who to talk to or what to do, so after embarrassing himself at a game of cards, he'd left. He thanked me for coming with him three times before we'd even reached the building.

"I have a confession," I said as he parked the car, trying my best not to sound too serious but failing.

"What?" he said. He cut the engine and turned to me, his brow furrowed with concern. He leaned closer.

"I'm probably not the best wingwoman," I admitted. My voice sounded weirdly high-pitched in my ears. "I'm terrible at parties. I spend most of them hiding and reading on my phone or talking to the same person, tailing them from room to room so I don't have to make small talk with other people. Until very recently, that person was Mike."

Raf just smiled. "That's okay," he said. "As long as we have each other to talk to, it won't be awkward. How about this? I promise not to leave you if you promise not to leave me."

I nodded. My heart was still racing, but it was best to keep my mouth shut. I didn't want to blurt out what I found myself hoping: that the sentiment didn't only apply to this party.

THE GUY WHO answered the door had several days' worth of beard growth and a flannel shirt that only made sense when I walked inside and felt how frigid it was. I immediately regretted my choice of a T-shirt and jeans with flip-flops.

"Hey, Raf," the guy said. He extended a hand to me. "I'm Dave."

"Harley," I said, shaking his hand.

As I shook his hand, I half-expected to smell beer on his breath, but his hands were cool and dry, his eyes clear and crinkled at the corners with his friendly smile. I was so conditioned to being greeted at parties with a blast of drunkenness by hosts much younger than this . . . adult. I felt such a wave of relief that my fingers tingled.

"Welcome!" Dave said, stepping aside.

Raf took me on a lap through the apartment, quietly pointing out various people. They all seemed to have nicknames. Like Hippie Jake, the guy who was a walking (well, sitting) stereotype with his Baja hoodie and soul patch, playing guitar in a corner of the living room. Then there was Animal, who had long, stringy hair and was so thin that his tiny T-shirt still billowed around him.

"He's a meth addict," Raf whispered when he saw the concern on my face. "He lost most of his teeth, so eating isn't exactly a favorite activity. He talks about how much he misses chewing sometimes in meetings."

I shook my head, speechless.

The next girl we ran into was closer to our age. Pretty. And normal-seeming. With her perfect posture and blonde hair, she could have been on our cheerleading squad. "Harley, this is Tina," Raf said.

I stuck my hand out, but she pulled me into a hug before I knew what was happening.

"It's so nice to meet you, Harley," she murmured. "Welcome." And then she skipped off, literally skipped, to Dave and an Indian guy in his twenties who I assumed was Arjun. Tina cuddled up next to him, and I caught him sneaking a look down her long-sleeved V-neck shirt. Tina didn't seem to mind. Maybe they were together. Besides, she wasn't showing much skin, so I figured she'd spent enough time in the apartment to know that it was freezing. But then she pulled up one of her sleeves to scratch her forearm, and I caught a glimpse of the dark veins that trailed from deep purple track marks. My stomach turned.

Raf turned toward the kitchen and I trailed behind, following our noses to the source of the scent of frying sausage. Thankfully, it was also about twenty degrees warmer in the kitchen. I sidled up to the stove instinctively. A thirty-something guy, with a grizzly beard and round belly, was transferring the sausage to a rice-based concoction in a second pan. He put the lid on it and wiped his brow with a paper towel.

"Rafael, my man," he said as he saw us.

"Cajun," Raf answered, doing that dude greeting thing that's half handshake, half hug. "What are you making tonight?"

Cajun lifted the lid off the pan. My mouth watered at the spicy, exotic aroma.

"That's jambalaya, my friend. It's going to be orgasmic." Cajun noticed me standing there and reddened slightly. "Sorry. But really, just wait."

"Believe me, I'll be first in line when you start doling it out," I answered. "But isn't jambalaya a little on the nose for someone whose name is Cajun?"

He laughed, a big, full-bodied laugh that filled the small kitchen and made me feel instantly relaxed. "I guess that's true, but I didn't get the nickname because I'm from New Orleans. I just like my food spicy. All of it. Pasta, tacos, vindaloo, fried chicken, Bloody Marys . . . well, I guess not that last one anymore. Virgin Marys just aren't the same, you know?"

I smiled and shrugged, not knowing how to answer, or if I should.

"Um, Cajun, this is Harley," Raf said, jumping in.

"Are you a friend of Bill's?" Cajun asked.

"No," I answered. "I'm a friend of Raf's."

Cajun laughed again, and I couldn't help smiling. His eyes met Raf's, who shook his head almost imperceptibly. I tilted my head, confused.

"He meant Bill W.," Raf said. "He's the guy who started Alcoholics Anonymous. Cajun's asking if you're an alcoholic."

"Oh, so 'friend of Bill's' is, like, code?" I asked.

Raf flashed a grin. "It helps us find each other out in the world," he said.

"That's cool! But no, I'm not."

"And that's cool, too," Cajun said with a wink. He took a couple of deep breaths. He seemed a little winded from laughing. "Listen, I have to let this sit for about thirty minutes. You guys up for a game of spades?"

I looked back at Raf. He grimaced. "Like I told you, I'm not very good," he warned me in a low voice. "But you can be my partner. That way, when we both suck, at least no one will get mad at *me*." Clearly, this was a sore spot.

"I'm in." I'd never been especially competitive—or good at card games—but it would give me something to do with my hands. Also, we wouldn't be wandering around the party aimlessly, which was a big plus for me. Being Raf's wingwoman, even at a completely sober party, didn't magically turn me into an extrovert.

Cajun grabbed Dave to be his partner. We sat down at a card table with four mismatched chairs as Cajun dealt the cards. He shuffled and tossed them out with the deftness of a pro. Raf didn't look particularly happy. We played a practice hand while Dave and Cajun taught me (and retaught Raf) the rules of the game. Or tried anyway. It was complicated. By the end of the practice hand, I was just staring at Raf, silently asking him what he had gotten me into. That prompted a laugh from him, at least.

When Dave cleared his throat, I realized we'd been gazing at each other for a little too long.

"We might be in trouble, Cajun," Dave said. "These two can talk to each other with their eyes."

Cajun sniffed. "Do I smell a hustle?"

"If I was here to hustle you, this would be a pretty long con, wouldn't it?" Raf said. "Getting myself sent to rehab, going to AA, getting invited to your party, bringing a pretty girl to distract you . . ." He let his voice trail off.

Cajun's lips twitched in a smile. "It was the girl that gave you away," he said. "No girl this beautiful would willingly hang out with a bunch of nut jobs like us."

"Speak for yourself," Dave said, pretending to be offended. "Harley and I are the normal ones here. It's you two I don't trust. Can we trade partners?"

I willed my cheeks not to blush. "I wouldn't be so quick to assume," I said. "Have you checked your wallet lately?"

When Dave reached for his back pocket, we all burst out laughing.

A HALF HOUR later, there was no longer any question about whether we were hustling anyone. Luckily, Raf and I had as much fun losing as Dave and Cajun did winning. And when the game was over, there was jambalaya, which was incredible—savory, with the perfect amount of spice—so it was a pretty excellent hour of my life. The best part: everyone seemed to be having fun. Genuinely. (Even the ones listening to Hippie Jake play "Stairway to Heaven" . . . again.) No one was faking it or forcing it, like at the parties I went to.

Without alcohol, there was a shocking absence of what I'd assumed *defined* parties: fighting, screaming, groping, burping . . . and probably regretting.

When Cajun and Dave went back to the kitchen to clean up, I noticed Arjun and Tina disappearing into a bedroom. I pulled Raf aside.

"How old is Tina?" I whispered.

"Sixteen."

I frowned. Maybe this party was like the others after all, just a sober version. "Don't you think she's a little young to be hooking up with someone who has his own apartment?"

"She's a sixteen-year-old emancipated minor. *She* has her own apartment. She's been through a lot." He didn't elaborate, but he didn't have to. She was a parentless heroin addict. What I could imagine probably wouldn't even cover half of it.

I hesitated, staring at the closed door. "Can we hang out and offer her a ride home?" It was literally the least I could do, but it made me feel slightly less bad for judging her.

He chuckled. "You might be waiting until the morning."

My shoulders sagged.

"When people quit drinking or doing drugs, it doesn't remove their other faults or insecurities," Raf said quietly. "Tina needs validation. Arjun does, too. They've found each other."

I was still frowning.

"Too much therapy, I know," he added. "But I'm not wrong. I'm just saying, some people can't change everything at once. Getting sober doesn't take away the things that made you use in the first place."

Only then did I realize he was talking about himself as much as he was Tina and Arjun.

"Come on," he said. "Let's say some goodbyes and see if anyone wants to go to the diner for dessert."

I groaned and wrapped my arms around my stomach full of jambalaya. "How can you think about eating right now?"

"Oh, that's easy," he said. "Another nice thing about not drinking? There's always room for pie."

AFTER OUR TRIP to the diner, Raf walked me home—well, the hundred feet between his driveway and mine. But he stopped me before I opened the door. He took my hand and pulled me off the bottom step so that I stood in front of him. His face was the most serious I'd seen it be all night.

"Tonight was more fun with you there," he said, looking me straight in the eye. "Thanks for coming."

I smiled, unsure what I was feeling. Shy? That didn't make sense. This was *Raf*. Happy? Yes, definitely. Maybe I shouldn't question it.

"Thank *you*," I said after a moment. "It was more fun and less scary than I thought it would be."

Raf's eyes glinted. "Why did you lie to me?" he asked. He knew; he just wanted to hear me say it.

"Because I wanted to hang out with you again, and it seemed like a good way to make that happen. Okay? Are you happy?"

He nodded, leaning close enough that I could feel his breath against my cheek when he said, "I couldn't be happier." And though I don't know which one of us closed the gap between us, suddenly his lips were on mine.

A tornado of thoughts whirled through my mind, but I didn't stop him. I didn't want to.

I didn't pull away when his tongue met mine. Or when his fingers wrapped around my hips, pulling me closer. Not even when they drifted under the hem of my T-shirt.

Raf was taller than me, but he was thinner. Not scrawny, but not thick. He had some muscle, but it wasn't defined. I felt small love handles when I put my hands on his waist. It made me less self-conscious about my own curves as his hands explored farther up my back.

I might have entirely forgotten my vow to keep my distance had Dad not pulled down the street just then. When I heard the familiar scrape of his rear bumper on the bottom of the driveway, I pushed Raf away and drew my fingers to my lips. They felt swollen.

"I'm sorry," Raf said. His eyes widened, following Dad's car.

I was still a little dazed. I couldn't figure out why he was apologizing at first.

"No," I whispered finally. "Don't be."

Raf nodded but still looked troubled. I was beyond trying to figure out my own feelings. I couldn't decide whether to be embarrassed or happy or ashamed.

I turned as Dad walked out of the garage. When I looked back, Raf was already headed toward his house.

"Good night, Dr. Langston," he called over his shoulder. Then he paused and shot me a smile. My stomach did a somersault. "'Night, Harley." And then he was gone.

Dad cleared his throat. I had no idea how much he'd seen.

"Hey, Daddy," I said, a little too loudly.

"Hey, kid," he said. His voice was gentle. "How was your night?"

"Seriously? That's all you have to say?"

"What?" he said, innocence plastered on his face. "It's not my fault I have impeccable timing. I should call myself 'The Cooler.'"

I turned and bolted for the front door. "I'm not hearing this."

"No, I mean it," Dad said. He raced after me. Luckily, once inside, he had to deal with Floyd, who had been waiting with his nose plastered to the window since I got home.

"Maybe I have special powers," he said once he'd given Floyd enough pets that he had rolled onto his back. "I'm like the Flash, except my power is keeping guys from kissing my daughters."

"I hate to say it, Dad, but if you have that power, you're really not using it right."

His smile faded.

"Hey, have you been to see Audrey today?" I asked, awkwardly changing the subject.

Dad crouched beside Floyd, stroking his ears. The crease between his eyebrows deepened. "Same as yesterday," he said.

I nodded. My throat tightened. "I saw Mom crying today," I blurted out. It felt a little bit like I was tattling on her, but Dad needed to know. Mom prided herself on responsibility and routine, but today, she'd skipped work and gone to the hospital all day. When I left for the party, she was lying on the couch with the lights off. The sun had almost set, casting the room into a slow darkness. She had barely acknowledged me when I told her I was going out.

Dad took a deep breath in through his nose and rose from the floor. "That's good," he said finally. "I think she needs to cry." Then all at once he pulled me into his warm chest and pounded me hard on the back twice before releasing me. "Let's go check on her, okay?"

I nodded, trying to hide my shock. So . . . he was letting me get away without discussing what he'd just witnessed?

He had never let me kiss Mike in front of him. He'd walk into the room, see us, and immediately start making an embarrassing siren or alarm sound, or just announce, "Father in the room!" It was all pretty effective. Maybe this was a test.

I turned to head up the stairs when he added, "You might want to clean off that smudge of lip gloss first, though."

And there it was. Best to just get it over with. I stopped on the first stair so that we were eye to eye.

"What you saw, that was just a mistake. I'm going to tell Raf that it was too soon and we need to be friends."

There was a flicker of relief on Dad's face. "Smart girl," he said.

My fists clenched at my sides. The anger was sudden and unexpected. I fought to keep it bottled up. Why was he so sure I was being smart? What did he really know about Raf, anyway? There was no need to get into it; I was only fighting with myself. Dad was just echoing what I'd told Cassidy. What I so desperately wanted to believe. That it *was* too soon. We *should* just be friends.

I hurried up the stairs and knocked on my parents' bedroom door.

"Mom?" I said.

Dad pushed the door open before she answered. "It's my room, too," he joked defensively.

I almost laughed, but then I saw Mom. She was curled on her side, in her nightgown, with a blanket tucked up under her armpit. She wasn't crying anymore. Her eyes were open, and she was glassily staring at the wall. The room was silent and smelled strongly of stale booze. Dad and I exchanged a nervous glance.

"Maureen?" Dad said. His tone reminded me of how he'd

talk to Audrey when we were younger, when Audrey was on the verge of a panic attack. "Honey, are you okay?"

I sat down on the edge of the bed and patted her foot. Her toes were tiny ice cubes. "Mom? What's going on?"

"Do you think she knows we're not there with her right now?" Mom replied. Her voice was unexpectedly calm and steady.

Dad and I exchanged another uneasy glance. I looked at him pointedly, and he knelt next to the bed so he was at eye level with Mom.

"No," he said. "I don't think she knows what day it is or what time it is. I think she can hear us sometimes, but other times, she's sleeping, healing. But I don't think Audrey would be upset that we aren't there every moment. I think she'd want us to try to live our lives as best we can. Don't you think so, Harley?"

"Yes," I heard myself say.

"She was moving a little more today," Mom remarked, not looking at either of us. "But she won't wake up. I just kept asking her to, over and over again . . ." Her voice trailed off as she squeezed her eyes shut. A tear leaked out. For once, maybe for the first time, her hair was matted and greasy. My eyes drifted to the glass on her bedside table; it was half full of brown liquor and stained with her lipstick.

She'd kept it together as long as she could, but now it was her turn to fall apart. Now it was my turn to take care of her.

I stood and walked to the other side of the bed. Mom tilted her head back to look at me as I reached for the top sheet and comforter, which were still crisp and neatly made. Dad took the other corner, and we eased them out from beneath her. She rolled onto her back and we tucked her in. Then I switched off the light and turned the TV on to distract her. Dad removed the glass of whiskey from her bedside table.

"Watch some *Friends*," I said over the soft laughter of the studio audience. "And get some sleep. We'll see Audy first thing in the morning."

I left Dad there. I imagined he would lie beside her after she passed out and stare at the ceiling all night. Not that I blamed him. In the end, I spent most of the night awake, doing the same thing. Mom was the bedrock on which this family was built. If she cracked, where did that leave us?

At midnight, I pulled out my phone to text Raf, but I ended up deleting draft after draft. Most began with "I'm sorry." But I wasn't sorry at all. I'd liked kissing him. He was a much gentler, softer kisser than Mike had been. I liked the feel of his unshaven chin against mine. His fingers in my hair. His warm breath on my neck.

But then the guilt came crashing back over me, a wave that dragged me under. I fought against its pull by tossing out rationalizations. Mike had cheated on me. We were broken up. I shouldn't be feeling guilty. And yet that didn't change the fact that Audrey was in a coma because I'd abandoned her. I shouldn't have been kissing Raf. I didn't deserve to feel happy when she was in peril.

I watched the phone until the backlight turned off and, finally, drifted into an uneasy sleep.

AS IF MOM had willed it in her stupor, the call came from the hospital around 4 A.M. Audrey had woken up again. Since the accident, I'd begun sleeping with the cordless house phone next to me, so I eavesdropped while Dad talked to Keisha. As soon as he hung up, I ran to my parents' room and flung open the door.

"It's just like her, the night owl," Dad croaked groggily as he swung his legs out from under the sheets. "She would wake up when we were all asleep."

He shook Mom. "Maureen, honey, Audrey's awake."

Mom's eyes popped open, but she winced at the light from Dad's bedside table.

"That's great," she said quietly. "Let me just . . . go take some ibuprofen and brush my teeth." She looked over at me. "Go put on something clean." Even hungover, Mom was still Mom.

By the time we arrived at the hospital, Audrey was unconscious again. Dr. Martinez was waiting for us in her room, so I figured that had to be a good sign. Or a bad one.

"She was more alert this time. And while she was conscious, she was fighting the ventilator," he said, ushering us into the hall. "She's trying to breathe on her own. So she's no longer comatose. She's too weak for it to be removed, but we'll do a trial soon to see if we can start trying to wean her off. We're very hopeful," he added, seeing Mom's anxious expression.

"When will you do that?" Dad asked.

"I'd like to try in a day if she's alert enough."

I tuned out the conversation and glanced back at her open door. I could just see the two lumps of blanket-covered feet.

I ducked back into the room. I was so nervous, my chest felt like it was full of bees. Or maybe it was hope, trying to lift the leaden feeling of guilt that had been weighing me down. I sat down on the chair closest to her pillow and leaned in, stroking the soft skin between her eyebrows. It used to help her sleep when we were little.

Her eyes blinked open a crack. My heart leapt and I nearly lost control of my hand and dropped it on her face. I pulled back just in time.

"Hey, Audy?" I gasped, trying to contain my excitement.

She made a soft noise in her throat.

"It's me." Remembering that she may have memory loss, I added, "Your sister, Harley."

Audrey moaned again quietly. She moved under the covers, pointing her toes.

My pulse began to race. "I missed you," I whispered. She blinked at me, her eyes unfocused. "I've been talking to you. And reading to you. Watching movies. Do you remember any of that?"

Her expression remained blank. But her stare was fixed now. Fixed on me. This was real. This was happening. I knew I'd start crying if I stopped, so I kept babbling.

"Mom and Dad are right outside, talking to your doctor and Keisha," I said. As if on cue, the door opened and Mom and Dad rushed in. I jumped out of the chair to hug them.

"Why didn't you tell us she'd woken up again?" Mom barked at me.

My jaw dropped. I froze mid-step.

"It literally just happened," I snapped back. But the tide of guilt lapped over me once more. I moved out of her way and mumbled, "I'm sorry."

Mom ignored my response anyway, falling into the chair where I'd been sitting, wrapping her hands around one of Audrey's.

"It's Mommy, sweetheart," she said, her voice quivering. "I'm here. I'm so sorry I left you."

I glanced over Dad's shoulder. Keisha and the doctor had followed my parents into the room. Suddenly it was feeling way too cramped.

"She may not remember waking up," Keisha said to

Mom. "So try not to be too hard on yourself. Audrey needs positivity."

Audrey's eyes fixed on the sound of Keisha's voice and she tried to turn her head. Keisha immediately brushed past Dad and me, kneeling beside Mom. Maybe Audrey didn't remember us, but she recognized the voice that had been there all along.

Mom's face fell as she watched Keisha interact with Audrey. My heart squeezed. Keisha chattered easily while she checked Audrey's pupils and took her pulse. Audrey didn't look away once. Mom's prayers had been answered, yes, but none of us had expected this.

Audrey's lips were cracked and dry from the ventilator, so Keisha ran a cotton swab coated with Vaseline across them. Mom's fingers unconsciously mirrored her actions, so consumed was she with the desire to do it herself. It was almost too painful to watch. Right now, honestly, I wanted to punch something.

Mike's face came immediately to mind.

A FEW HOURS after Audrey fell asleep again, I decided to go home. It was eight in the morning and I was exhausted. Mom still had plenty of energy to hover, and Dad wandered in and out, trying to find distractions. Both Keisha and Dr. Martinez had made it clear that returning to full consciousness would be a long process. The implication was that we could *all* use a break, but I was the only one who seemed to get it.

I called Cassidy and woke her up. I must have sounded as tired as I felt because she didn't even sound annoyed when I asked her to come pick me up. She even had coffee and a donut waiting for me in her car's cup holder.

"I don't deserve you," I said as I took a grateful sip. Liquid warmth spread through me. Sweet and milky, just the way I liked it.

"No, you don't," she deadpanned. "Luckily, I love you anyway."

I laughed sadly as I reached for the donut.

"So, do you want to talk about it?" she asked.

I shook my head. "Not really. But do you think you could get me a job at The Flakey Pastry? Mom told me to find 'gainful employment,' but I'm also thinking of emancipation. I'll need to pay rent."

Six Years Ago

I heard my friends grumble, the ones closest to the cabin door. I heard them even before I heard Audrey's voice. But I knew what was going on. She was back. Of course. This was the fourth time this week.

With a sigh, I climbed off my bunk and went to shoo her out of our cabin and herd her back to her own. It was nearly lights out. We'd both be in trouble if we were out after "Taps" had been played.

"Hey, Audy," I said quietly.

Her small, freckle-scattered face was red and streaked with tears.

I led her back outside, onto the cabin's small front porch. My counselor raised her eyebrows at me through the window. I held up my pointer finger, asking her for just a minute. She reached for her walkie-talkie anyway. I knew she was calling Audrey's counselor to come get her. I didn't have much time.

I sat Audrey down on the stairs and stood in front of her so we were eye level. Her chin trembled and fresh tears slid from her eyes.

"I want to go home," she said. It sounded like an

accusation, as if I was the one keeping her here at camp. Like she was a prisoner, being forced to make baskets and row canoes and play tennis.

"I know you do, but you can't," I said. I tried to be patient. "Even if you called Mom and Dad, they're in Italy. There's nothing they can do."

Mom and Dad had made it perfectly clear why we were at camp. They'd been planning a European vacation for years, before I was even born. Now they could finally do it.

I wondered if Audrey had gotten the same postcard I had—the one with the Roman Colosseum on the front. On the back was a hastily scrawled "Thinking of you and missing you in Rome!" I wondered if that was true. Because I didn't miss them that much. Yet. I had Cassidy with me, for one.

Audrey was having a tougher time. She had made friends, but at night, she couldn't sleep because she wasn't in her own bed. The exhaustion was catching up to her.

Her chest started to rise and fall rapidly. Her face was blotchy. I could hear her struggling to breathe.

A ball of dread formed in my stomach. She was panicking.

I knelt in front of her and grasped her shoulders. "Audy, you need to calm down, okay? Take a deep breath, in through your nose and out through your mouth."

This was how my dad handled her when she got this upset. Audrey tried—she took three deep breaths in a row—but she was still shaking in her nightgown.

I heard her counselor walking up the gravel behind me and Audrey's eyes grew wide. She started shaking her head rapidly.

"I don't want to go," she whispered. "I don't want to go! I want to stay with you!" She was shrieking by then and gripping me around the waist.

I looked back at her counselor and then at mine. She'd gotten out of bed and was now silhouetted in the screen door. She shook her head. I ignored her. I ignored both counselors.

"You can stay with me tonight," I said. I knew this could be the end of my new, easy friendships, but I tried not to care. My little sister could share my bed if it meant she would sleep. If it would get rid of the dark circles that had gathered under her eyes.

That night, spooned against my side, Audrey did sleep. I also got some shit for it, but most of the girls understood. They almost seemed jealous that I had my sister to cuddle with. I think maybe we were all a little homesick, even if we didn't admit it out loud.

The next day, I walked Audrey back to her cabin, and I hung out with her cabinmates for a while. I introduced them to Bear Bear, Audrey's stuffed bear, by way of a song-and-dance number I'd often perform for Audrey. And an hour later, Audrey was showing them her books and iPod, and they were giggling and listening to music, so I tapped her on the foot and waved goodbye.

"You can come sleep with me again tonight if you need to," I whispered as she hugged me. But she shook her head.

"It's okay, I have Bear Bear," she assured me.

By the end of our second week, I'd only seen her across the mess hall when she'd given me a wave and gone back to laughing with her friends. I walked to her cabin one night while the rest of my friends were getting ready for bed.

The girls in Audrey's cabin were already in bed as I snuck inside and crouched next to her on the bottom bunk.

"What are you doing here?" she asked, automatically scooching over to make room for me in bed next to her. I climbed into the narrow bed as best I could.

"I just wanted to make sure you were sleeping okay," I lied.

Audrey knew it, too. She pulled Bear Bear out from underneath her and made him look me in the eye.

"Okay, I'm homesick," I admitted. I missed my room, my comics, my privacy. A bathroom and shower that I didn't have to share with a hundred other girls.

She gave me a hug, with Bear Bear squished between us.

"Take Bear Bear," Audrey said. "He'll keep you company."

I was tempted to say no, but the shard in my chest made the decision for me. "Okay," I said. "But promise you'll come pick him up tomorrow so he doesn't get lonely?"

She stuck out her pinkie and linked it with mine. "Deal."

CHAPTER TEN

The Fourth of July snuck up on me. I hadn't made plans and a full day of doing nothing stretched ahead. I couldn't call Cassidy; she had agreed to take a shift at the coffee shop since Will and Janine planned to see the outdoor concert on the Mall downtown. I'd done that once with Mike. It was enough. Every summer it was the same: some band older than my parents and a bunch of angry protesters, coupled with stifling heat and hordes of sweaty tourists. Mike had brought a mini cooler full of beer. That had not helped the situation.

I'd gone to the hospital that morning with Dad and Mom. They'd brought miniature American flags and festive window clings to decorate Audrey's room, but when they left to get lunch, I left, too. By mid-afternoon, I was bored. I was even bored enough to take Floyd out into the muggy summer sun for an impromptu walk. He didn't seem enthusiastic about the idea.

We ambled slowly up the street. It was so hot I could see the heat shimmering in the air above the pavement. Floyd gave up a few minutes in, sighing as he lay down on the sidewalk under a tree three houses down from ours.

"Seriously?" I groaned.

There was laughter behind me.

I spun around to see Raf a few feet away. He wore shorts and a white undershirt, with flip-flops on his feet. It was the first time I'd seen him in days . . . since the kiss. The memory of it rushed back.

He'd texted, but I hadn't responded. I hadn't known what to say. I still didn't.

He stepped closer and bent down to scratch Floyd behind the ears.

"This dog is no fool," Raf said. "He knows when it's not worth being outside."

"I guess it makes me feel better about not having any big barbecue plans today," I said.

"Yeah," he answered, sounding wistful. "Instead of drinking on the Mall, in the sun, with my friends all day, eating mushrooms, and sneaking off to the Porta Potty to get stoned before the fireworks start like I did last year, I'm planning to sit in my basement bedroom and . . . I don't know, cry?" He laughed, but I didn't think he was kidding.

"Would you want to maybe do something with me instead?" I asked before considering whether it was a good idea. My lips formed words independent of my brain, as if they were desperate for another chance to be on his. *Traitors.*

He looked at me, squinting. "I was worried you were mad at me or something," he said. Floyd pawed at him, urging Raf to keep scratching his ears. It gave him an excuse to look away. "You didn't answer my text from a couple days ago."

I chewed my lip. "I'm sorry," I said. "Things got a little busy. With Audrey and everything."

My voice sounded weak and unconvincing. I was a coward

for using her as an excuse instead of just telling him the truth: that I was a mess.

Raf stood up. "I'm going to go to a meeting first, but what did you want to do?"

In the past, the Fourth of July had always meant a party at our house. A crab feast, with fresh July corn and hush puppies dipped in melted butter. I could almost taste the fresh sliced tomatoes on my tongue. But with Audrey in the hospital, the party was canceled this year. Mom and Dad were spending the evening watching the fireworks on TV in her room in the Neuro ICU.

"Do you want to go to the high school to watch the fireworks?" I asked. It just wouldn't feel like the Fourth of July without fireworks.

Raf's eyes brightened. "Absolutely. I'll meet you at the Jeep at eight thirty?"

I nodded, trying not to show the nerves I was suddenly feeling. "See you then."

BY THE TIME eight thirty rolled around, it was still muggy, but dusk was falling. Fireflies winked as they hovered in the sky.

I'd deliberately stayed casual, in cutoffs and a T-shirt, my hair in a ponytail. I leaned against his front bumper, already feeling beads of sweat prickling my scalp. Raf came around the side of the house a few minutes later. He'd changed into jeans and a different shirt, and his hair was still wet and combed neatly. As we got in the car, I could smell his shampoo—the same "No Tears" kind he used when we were little.

"What do you have in your bag there?" he asked, gesturing to the tote bag at my feet.

"Um, sparkling cider," I said. "And cookies with red, white, and blue sprinkles."

"Patriotic," he said dryly. "U-S-A . . . U-S-A . . ."

I smirked. "Don't get too excited. The sprinkles are already melting from this heat."

I didn't mention that I'd also brought a blanket, but a scratchy one so we wouldn't be too comfortable. I was determined to keep this friendly tonight.

But when Raf snuck a glance at me, his eyes roving over my bare legs before turning back to the road, my stomach fluttered, and I knew he didn't feel the same way. My plan to keep things platonic suddenly felt muddled as I wondered how committed I really was to it.

"So how is everything?" Raf asked over the rushing wind and the roar of the Jeep's engine. "With Audrey?"

"Actually, she's started waking up a little, opening her eyes and everything."

He smiled so wide and for so long I worried bugs might get stuck in his teeth.

"That's great!" he said. "How does she seem?"

I couldn't manage the same enthusiasm. "It's hard to say. She hasn't been awake long enough to be truly conscious of what's going on. She hasn't spoken yet, anyway."

He glanced at me for a second, but he nodded. "She will, soon," he said. "She's strong."

I nodded back, wishing I shared his certainty, and closed my eyes as he shifted into a higher gear, the wind blasting in my face. The night air had cooled at least.

A few minutes later, we pulled into the high school parking lot—the local public school where Raf went. The sun still hadn't set fully, and the twilight sky was like a countdown clock for when the fireworks would start. Raf and I got out and walked through a full lot of cars, out onto the football field. It was a neighborhood tradition, so hundreds of families sat with their picnic dinners spread around them, their kids running around, chasing each other and screaming.

I found a small empty patch and spread out the blanket. But once we were side by side, we fell silent for a few awkward moments. The memory of our kiss hung in the air between us like static electricity.

"Cookie?" I offered, opening the tote bag and taking out the container. Raf reached for the sparkling cider and poured two cups, then clinked his plastic cup against mine. At least now our mouths were full.

After draining his cup, Raf lay back on the blanket and looked up at me.

"Lie down," he said. "It's nice down here."

Holding my breath, I clumsily squeezed next to him on the blanket and crossed my arms over my chest to leave a few inches of space between us. Then I exhaled, trying to relax. It did feel a little quieter and more secluded, being so low to the ground. The sky above us was darkening quickly. It was a cloudless night, but there weren't any stars past the bright lights on the football field.

Raf opened his mouth to say something, but just then the floodlights over the field shut off, plunging the area into darkness. A hush fell as the first of the fireworks flew, releasing a high-pitched scream before it exploded in a shower of red sparks. The crowd "oohed." Another went off, and another, and soon the sky was full of light. Gradually, I felt my muscles loosen, and I let my arms fall to the blanket. I could feel the heat from Raf's arm next to mine.

I had always been a sucker for fireworks, and there's no better way to watch them than lying on the ground as they explode directly above. I glanced over at Raf a few times. He was smiling just as widely as I was.

After what felt like only a few minutes, the grand finale began, and I felt Raf's fingers lace through mine. My heart started beating double-time. But I didn't pull away until the show was over and the sky was thick with smoke. The crowd around us began to stand and disperse, and it would be weird to stay and keep lying there. But in the parking lot, Raf reached for my hand again and pulled me to a stop next to the Jeep.

"Close your eyes," he said, uncurling my fingers.

I looked at him skeptically. Still, I did as he asked. He placed something long, thin, and metallic in my open palm.

"Okay, open," he said.

I opened my eyes and looked down. "A sparkler?"

He nodded with an impish smile. "Who doesn't like to play with fire?"

I laughed, surprised and relieved. I'd assumed he was going to kiss me. Maybe I was hoping he would.

I watched as he pulled out a lighter and lit the end of my sparkler. Then he lit one of his own, and we stood in the parking lot, writing our names in light. My lips curled up when I saw him trace a heart in the instant before my sparkler died, followed by his. And all that remained were the streaks in my vision, remnants that faded quickly.

Suddenly I noticed that a crowd of kids had gathered around to watch, mesmerized. I turned toward the Jeep, assuming they'd scatter now that the show was over, but when I glanced back, Raf was distributing sparklers to them all.

"Stand in a line and put your arms out!" he called. Once they were spaced far enough apart, he walked down the line, lighting each sparkler. The kids squealed as the sparklers lit up their grinning faces. Raf grinned just as widely.

I couldn't help remembering the last time I'd seen Mike around kids. Cassidy was babysitting her brothers, who were three and six at the time. I'd gone over to help her study for our geometry test, but Mike and I had just been to the comic book shop. It had only taken Loren five minutes before he had torn the bag off of Mike's near-mint issue of *Superior Spider-Man* #1 and crumpled half of its pages. It had taken twenty minutes and a red popsicle to get Loren to stop crying after Mike had screamed at him.

I closed my eyes against the memory as Raf took the long way home to avoid the crowds. It had been a nice night. It wasn't supposed to be a date, but it felt like the best one that I'd ever been on. All that was missing was the good-night kiss. But I intended to keep it that way. So when he pulled into the driveway, I gathered my stuff and hopped out, making sure to stay one step ahead of him. And when Raf stopped at the scene of our last kiss, I held up a hand to stop him as he leaned in.

"I can't," I said.

He blinked, confused.

"I'm sorry. Mike and I just broke up . . ." He nodded, but I still felt like I needed to explain. "I spent a lot of time doing what Mike wanted. I need to figure out what *I* want."

Raf offered a reassuring smile. "I know," he said. "And I get it. I want you to figure things out. And to be happy."

I stared back at him. Why the hell was I turning down a guy who was so damn *nice* to me?

"Thanks," I managed. "And I'm sorry."

"Don't be. I'm not technically supposed to date until I have a year sober anyway," he added, and I momentarily felt less doubtful about my decision. "And the fact that I want to kiss you until I forget about that is probably not a good sign."

"Yeah, probably not," I said, blushing and doubting myself all over again. "Well, um, good night."

I forced myself to turn around. To walk away. Even though my heart was practically leaping out of my chest, as if trying to get back to him on its own.

ON THE MORNING of July 5, Audrey had a "successful breathing trial." By that afternoon, Dr. Martinez had agreed to take her off the ventilator. Mom left work early, picked me up, and rushed the two of us to the hospital to meet Dad.

With her face no longer obscured, the first thing that struck me was how young Audrey looked. How small and fragile. Not to mention pale. Her freckles stood out in stark relief against her chalky skin. But she was awake when Mom, Dad, and I were finally allowed into her room—*really* awake—though groggy. Keisha was at her side, moistening a small sponge on the end of a stick and running it across Audrey's lips. Audrey licked them greedily.

"Can't she have water?" Mom asked Keisha. She sounded annoyed. It was clear that she considered Keisha to be an interloper, that she saw caring for her daughter in this way as a mother's job. She so desperately wanted to do something, to be useful.

The nurse shook her head. "Soon," she said. "She's on IV fluids to keep her hydrated and with the feeding tube in, she's fine. But we don't know yet what her motor function is like, and we don't want her to aspirate while trying to swallow. Her injuries are still too severe."

By the time she'd finished, Mom's face appeared to have aged ten years. The crow's-feet were more prominent, the frown lines deeper. She pressed the back of Audrey's hand to her cheek, but Audrey had already started to fade back into sleep. She hadn't been "really awake" at all, I realized. I'd been fooling myself. We all had.

By dinnertime, I was ready to leave. I considered watching another movie, but Audrey was asleep, and I somehow couldn't muster up the same enthusiasm I'd had when she was in a coma. It was ridiculous, but romantic movies had lost some of the magic without Audrey's creative input. The *old* Audrey. The new Audrey wouldn't be able to stay awake for long enough to watch a full movie with me for weeks, most likely. And there was a very good chance she wouldn't be able to remember, understand, or process what she was seeing, anyway.

THE NEXT MORNING I came downstairs to find Mom poring over a small stack of framed photos. "Will you take these to the hospital for me?" she asked, without looking up. "I'm not sure if I'll make it. I have appointments at a few stores today, but I want to be sure Audrey has something to remind her of us."

I stepped closer and peered over her shoulder. Five photos in all: four of Mom and Dad, taken professionally in honor of their twentieth anniversary last fall—and one of Floyd and me, taken last summer, which had been hanging in the hallway until now.

"Feel free to bring some more pictures of yourself," Mom said absently. "I just couldn't find any good ones."

Gee, thanks, Mom, I replied silently. *You mean ones where I don't look fat?*

The truth was that I didn't feel like going back there today. I couldn't shake the kernel of resentment I'd felt that she still didn't even know who I was. After the way she'd betrayed me, I should have been foremost in her mind. My name should have been the first thing she'd uttered upon regaining consciousness, followed immediately by "Sorry." That night should have been burned into her memory.

It was irrational. And ugly. But that didn't stop me from feeling it.

Mom handed me the photos and stood, straightening and smoothing her skirt suit. "That nurse seems to think—"

"Keisha?" I interrupted.

Mom's eyes met mine. She was wearing more concealer than usual. It didn't help; there was no hiding how tired she looked. "Yes. Keisha. She seems to think that bringing familiar objects might help, too. So if you feel like it, maybe also grab Bear Bear?"

"Do I have to go today?" I asked.

"Weren't you planning on it?" Mom said sharply.

I lifted my head, my lips pressed into a tight line.

Mom opened her mouth and then sighed, her expression softening. "Harley . . . I—just do me this favor, please, okay?" she said. She looked at her watch. "I have to go."

OF ALL THE scenarios I'd imagined when I arrived at the hospital, not one included a flash of recognition. But that's what I saw on Audrey's face when I opened her door. It was there, and unmistakable, and it snapped me out of my funk in an instant.

"Harley," she said.

Her voice was hoarse, her speech slurred. Her mouth tilted lower on the left side than it did on the right. But her light blue eyes belonged to the old Audrey. Every mean thought and lousy feeling I'd had slipped away. I laughed and rushed toward her, dropping my bag in the chair and draping my arms around her thin shoulders.

"Hi, baby sister," I said into her messy hair. "How are you?"

"O-kay," she managed to say. She pulled away, her face twisted in frustration. Talking took effort, clearly.

"I brought you a friend," I said as a distraction, pulling Bear Bear out of the tote. Her eyes lit up and she tried to smile, but she didn't speak again. Instead, she reached out with her left arm; her right was still in a cast. I tucked him in the crook of her elbow, put the bag in my lap, and sat down next to her. She gazed down at her stuffed bear. I felt the need to fill the silence, but my mind was blank. I had no idea what to say.

"Do you need anything? Are you thirsty?" I asked.

Audrey nodded. I poured a small amount of water into the plastic cup on her table. I helped her sit up, tilting the bed up and propping pillows behind her head. As I fluffed them, I caught a whiff of that familiar Audrey sleep smell. Before I knew it, I was crying. She had smelled different while she was in the coma. I hadn't been able to pinpoint what exactly was different, but this clinched it. I knew for certain that she was back now.

Audrey noticed the tears and she knitted her eyebrows together. I shook my head and took a deep breath, then put the straw in her mouth so that she could drink.

"Sorry, I've just missed you," I said. I tried to smile, reaching for a Kleenex to dab my eyes. "It's been so weird and quiet in the house without you there." To busy myself, I started arranging Mom's framed photos on the bedside table. "I figured you were probably bored, so I brought your iPad, too. So you could watch Netflix. Well, so we could watch together. You'd be proud of me. I've been watching lots of your favorite—never mind. I'll tell you later."

She rewarded me with a small lopsided smile. "Thanks," she said, drawing out the *s*. "You . . . have to tell me."

"I will," I murmured. "I promise."

Fifteen Years Ago

I was almost two when Audrey was born. Experts say that's too young for most people to have memories, but I remember clearly how Audrey sounded through the wall when she cried. I remember the feel of the carpet against my cheek when I would lie down next to her crib and put my fingers through the bars. I remember the touch of her tiny fingernails as she stroked my finger.

Mom confirms that she would find me in there night after night. We'd both be asleep, and she would pick me up and take me back to my own bedroom. And in the morning, she'd find me back on the floor next to Audrey.

After a few weeks, they finally moved my toddler bed into Audrey's room. Mom says I would sing to her before I fell asleep, or try to anyway. Through the monitor, they'd hear me babbling things that sounded like "The Wheels on the Bus" and "You Are My Sunshine," and she would coo along with me.

When she got old enough to need her own bed, though, Mom and Dad put me back in my room. Audrey didn't wake up in the middle of the night anymore, so eventually I stopped my nightly visits. But I was attuned to the sounds of her next door like a mother with a newborn. If she so much as whimpered from a nightmare, I was there, pushing the sweaty hair from her forehead and singing to her.

Mom still found us sleeping beside each other in Audrey's bed from time to time.

I felt sorry for people who didn't have a sister. Audrey and I could be horrible to each other all day long, but at night, when the house was dark and Mom and Dad were asleep, we could lie in bed next to each other and share our secrets.

I told Audrey things I couldn't even tell Cassidy. Because Audrey was required to love me. Her love was a guarantee. So when I told her that I wanted to break up with Mike but was scared of what my life would be like without him, she told me to stop being an idiot and get it over with. Because sisters will also say the things you need to hear.

And then they'll make out with your boyfriend.

CHAPTER ELEVEN

Certain things became clear over the next few days. Audrey remembered her family—including Aunt Tilly and Spencer and Floyd—but she didn't remember last year. The gaps were strange. When the doctor asked how old she was, she said she was fourteen, that she was a freshman. (She also guessed it was spring because there were leaves on the trees she could see out of her hospital room window.) She remembered Neema and, oddly, her old locker combination, but couldn't remember Bear Bear's name.

The good news was that the doctors were optimistic. Dr. Martinez assured Mom and Dad that, given her test results, much of her past would return to her eventually. Her brain was functioning as it should, both in terms of long-term and short-term memory. But they doubted she'd have any recollection of the accident, or even the weeks or months leading up to it.

Once again, I felt that gnawing resentment I'd tried to suppress. I could still see a faint trace of the hickey Mike had given her, right next to the bruise from the seat belt. Hiding in plain sight. Everyone just assumed it was an injury from the accident. For me alone it was a constant reminder of the unfairness of it all, how I was left to live with those memories and the truth of what had happened between us—and she wasn't.

But I kept my mouth shut.

THE DAY AFTER Audrey's feeding tube was removed for good, Raf's mom stopped by the house. I was alone; we were back to our routine: Mom at work, Dad at the hospital. She was carrying two dishes. Most of the neighbors had long since stopped bringing casseroles, and our freezer was still stuffed full, but I'd never turn down Mrs. Juarez's cooking. I was salivating from just the sight of the steam condensing on the lids.

"Oh my God, are those nacatamales?" I said. I could smell the steamed corncakes through the plastic.

"And arroz con frijoles," she said, holding up the second container. "Rice and beans. And I put in your favorite part."

"Plátanos maduros?" I nearly shouted. I hoped I wasn't drooling.

Mrs. Juarez laughed and nodded as she handed me the containers. She lingered on the stoop for a moment.

"Do you want to come in?" I asked. "My parents are out, but . . ."

She reached out for me, pulling me against her chest in a tight hug. With the containers in my hands, I couldn't hug her back, but that didn't stop her. She held on for longer than I expected.

"Little Harley," she said as she released me, even though she wasn't much taller than me. "I'm so sorry about what happened to your sister. It's so good to see you."

"You, too," I said.

"How's Audrey doing?" she asked.

I nodded as reassuringly as I could manage. "Better. She's awake, and the doctors are pretty hopeful about her ability to recover completely."

"Thank God," she said. "Rafael told me she'd woken up and I'm just so relieved." Her eyes were darker, more creased than I remembered, her skin paler. She was a glimpse at what would have happened to my mom if Audrey hadn't awakened. Or still could.

"Have you seen Rafael lately?" Mrs. Juarez asked. "He's been gone so much that I haven't gotten much of a chance to talk to him."

"Not in a few days," I said. "With Audrey awake, it's been pretty busy . . ." My voice trailed off.

"Thank you for being his friend right now, Harley," she said. Her voice and eyes were pleading. "I hated taking away his friends, his whole life really. But you're a good girl, a good influence. He needs you."

No pressure or anything, I thought guiltily. "I'll keep an eye on him. But, um, I should go put this in the fridge," I said, holding up the food in my hands.

"Oh, sure," she said. "I just thought you guys might want something fresh. Not a frozen casserole. I remember how hard it was to cook when Allie was sick. Even just turning on the oven was too much some nights."

I managed a smile this time. "Thank you so much, really," I said. "I'll try to leave some for my parents, but I can't make any promises."

Mrs. Juarez almost seemed happy as she turned to leave. I couldn't say the same for myself, but at least now there was food. I wondered if Audrey would want some, now that her swallowing reflex was back and she could eat anything she wanted to again. Not that I had any intention of sharing.

THAT SATURDAY, AUNT Tilly and Spencer stopped by the hospital for the first time since Audrey had awakened. Mom called and asked me to come over, too. Aunt Tilly wasn't the type to bring sweets, but she arrived carrying a carrot cake, Audrey's favorite. To celebrate, Aunt Tilly even let Spencer have some. He sat in the corner, scooping the thick cream cheese frosting off and licking it from his plastic fork. I leaned against the windowsill next to him.

"You actually *like* carrot cake?" I whispered.

He shrugged. "It's better than no cake," he said.

"But it's made of carrot. That's not dessert," I said. I began smooshing up a corner of my slice on my plate.

That got a little smile. "Yes, but it's a sweet carrot, with sugar and raisins."

"And white flour," Aunt Tilly added from across the room. Clearly, I hadn't been talking quietly enough. "So you only get one piece, chicken."

I had to smirk. Tilly was such a hypocrite. After having spent her youth drinking, smoking—and being a "wild child," as my mom said—she got pregnant with Spencer. That prompted a drastic swing in the opposite direction. The only exception being the smoking. It was the one habit she couldn't kick, but to her credit, she never smoked in front of Spencer.

When he finished his piece of cake, I slid half of my slice onto his plate and winked at him. He tried to wink back but blinked both eyes instead. I tried not to laugh.

"So how are the Nationals doing?" I asked.

He launched into an explanation about their standing

within their division compared to the other divisions and the American League. I let him talk for a while without really listening.

"Okay, but bottom line: Who's going to the series?" I interrupted.

Spencer furrowed his brow. "It's way too early to say," he said.

"What good are you?" I said, smiling as I reached out to muss his hair. Spencer pulled out of my reach and looked at me seriously for a moment, trying to figure out whether I was joking or not. I forgot sometimes that he wasn't good with sarcasm. But Aunt Tilly also told us it was good for him to learn.

"I'm just kidding," I said. "You're the best cousin I could ask for, even if you can't tell me in July who'll win the World Series in October."

That got another smile. It felt like a victory. And given that I could barely look at Audrey at the moment, I'd take all the victories I could get.

ON THE WAY home, I got a text from Raf. It had been a week since the Fourth of July. He made a joke of it, asking if I was alive, if Floyd missed him, and if I wanted to meet him for a walk. I lied and told him I was at the hospital, and then instead of driving home, I drove in the direction of The Flakey Pastry. Cassidy had finally gotten me an interview for a job there. It wasn't for another hour, but I could get there early.

I desperately *wanted* to see Raf. I wanted to see him and touch him and talk to him. And kiss him. But when I thought about kissing him, it made me think of kissing Mike. Which led me down the dark rabbit hole of my bitterness toward Audrey.

I wondered if it was the first time anything had happened between them. I couldn't ask her, of course. And I'd never trust Mike to tell me the truth. So I spent long hours analyzing as many of Audrey and Mike's recent interactions as I could remember.

I knew if I saw Raf, he would sense something was wrong. I squirmed just thinking about all of his perceptive, probing questions. More than that, though, I couldn't bear to turn him down again. If he tried to kiss me, I didn't know if I would have the strength to say no. And then I wouldn't be the good influence, the good girl Mrs. Juarez had asked me to be.

I pulled up outside The Flakey Pastry and hung out in the parking lot in my car, letting the anemic air-conditioning in my ancient Honda dry the beads of nervous sweat on my nose and forehead. I knew Cassidy would be working, but it was still a relief to see a friendly face at the counter when I opened the swinging glass door.

"Hey," I said. "I feel perkier already just breathing in the smell of this place."

"Enjoy it while it lasts," she said. "If you get this job, you may never want to drink coffee again. I leave work every night swearing I'll never have another sip."

I gave her a long look, and she laughed. "I know, I break that oath as soon as my next opening shift rolls around. And for friends," she said, sliding an iced vanilla latte across the counter.

Samir—the other manager, the one who didn't date employees (he was married)—was expecting me. With one hand he waved me over to an empty table near the trash cans. He held a clipboard and pen in the other. Like Cassidy, he was wearing The Flakey Pastry uniform, a black apron. Another reason I liked the place: no forced polyester outfit.

"So, Harley, thanks for coming in," he said as we sat across from each other. He clicked open the pen but held the clipboard so I couldn't see what was printed or the notes he was taking. "I have your résumé here." He glanced up. "Have you ever worked in food service before?"

"Um . . . I . . . no," I said, faltering. I wasn't sure why I was so anxious. I knew this place as well as Cassidy did. "Not exactly. I've worked a couple of times at the bake sale for the literary magazine . . ." I let my voice trail off. That was not the kind of experience Samir was looking for.

I glanced up at the counter, hoping Cassidy could somehow help. But Will had appeared. They were behind the counter, laughing together. He wasn't dressed for work, so I wasn't sure what he was doing here. Maybe flirting with Cassidy behind Janine's back?

Samir cleared his throat, and I snapped my focus back to him.

"Sorry," I said. "Oh, I forgot to mention that I've worked for Cassidy's mom's catering company a few times." I just helped load and unload the van, did dishes in the kitchen, and put hors d'oeuvres on trays, but that still counted as work.

His face brightened a little, betraying some relief. "Listen, your timing is good because I just lost someone yesterday and I need to fill a few shifts a week. I'm going to give you a shot because you're Cassidy's friend, and you've spent a lot of time in here. But I expect you to do your job and learn quickly. It's three strikes and you're out."

That seemed a little extreme for a coffee shop where I

had never seen a line more than two people deep. I had no idea what qualified as a strike, either, but I nodded enthusiastically anyway.

"Thank you so much," I said. "I'm a coffee lover. I'll do my best to make it proud."

"The coffee?" Samir asked.

"Uh, yeah." I flushed, hoping Samir wasn't already regretting his decision to hire me. But I'd made the first step. Not toward anything like emancipation, but toward . . . something. Making Mom happy and getting her off my back. But more: Freedom. My own money. My own life, away from home and school. And the hospital.

AUDREY WAS AWAKE and sitting up when I came back later that afternoon. Neema had come to visit, and they were watching something on her iPad.

"Hi," I said.

Audrey smiled and pointed at the empty chair on the other side of the room. "We're watching TV," she said. Her words were slow, but her diction was clearer than it had been.

"It's a show about wedding dresses," Neema added. "You'd probably hate it."

"You're probably right," I said. I left the hooded sweatshirt and gossip magazines that I'd brought at the foot of the bed. "I'll come back later."

Audrey needed time with her best friend, I told myself. I knew I should feel guilty about not spending time with her, but I didn't. I was relieved that I didn't have to.

AS I TURNED the corner on our block, I spied Raf's maroon Jeep driving toward me. It was customary in our small neighborhood to slow down and chat for a minute, or at least shout a hello, so there was no avoiding him. These are the pitfalls of living next door to your crush.

Raf slowed to a stop in the middle of the block, and I pulled up next to him. We rolled down our windows at the same time.

"I always feel like a cop when I do this," he joked. "Like I should be telling you that we just had a big bust. Or that it's your turn to take over the surveillance."

I racked my brain for a witty cop joke but came up empty.

"So, how are you?" he asked.

I shrugged. "Busy. I got a job at The Flakey Pastry."

He smiled. "Oh yeah? Maybe I'll swing by and have you make me a cappuccino."

"I would hold off on that for at least a few shifts," I warned him. "Cappuccino is complicated."

"Damn," he said. "Well, maybe I can be satisfied with a chocolate croissant."

"That I can probably manage."

He nodded. "Okay, well, good luck. Gotta run. I'm already late for my meeting."

"Thanks," I said. I rolled up the window and watched him drive off with a quick wave goodbye. I'd managed to escape without either of us bringing up the fact that we hadn't spoken in more than a week. It was what I wanted, though, right?

Maybe we'd slipped into Cassidy-and-Will territory, flirting whenever we saw each other, and nothing more. I brushed the thought aside. It was too depressing.

MY FIRST DAY on the job, Cassidy tried to be patient. Maybe she was showing off for Will a little, too; we were the only three behind the counter. Apparently, Janine was the one who'd quit, which made me wonder if that meant she and Will had called it quits as well, but I couldn't ask while he was in earshot.

Cassidy spent a couple of hours teaching me how to use the register, brew coffee, make a shot of espresso, and a few other things. I was so distracted that I gave almost every customer the wrong change and burned myself three times by over-pouring the cup. The result: a scalding splash on my hand whenever I put the lid on. My skin had turned red in the crook between my thumb and forefinger.

When I spilled a full cup of coffee, I nearly lost it. My eyes began to water. Cassidy quickly waved Will over to cover for us and pulled me aside.

"What's going on?" she whispered. "You seem really off. Is Audrey okay?"

I nodded. "Yeah, she's fine. I'm sorry, I'm just nervous."

"Why? Wait, did Samir give you the 'three strikes' line?" Cassidy asked with a reassuring smirk.

"Yeah," I said. I hadn't talked about Raf with her lately and I didn't want to get into it, so this was a handy excuse. "You've heard it?"

Cassidy glanced at Will, who must have been eavesdropping, because they shared a laugh. "Samir is big on sports analogies. He hardly ever gets them right. But the point is, he's never actually fired anyone. He's a good guy."

I felt a little better, but I was still a little shaky. "Okay, but maybe you should still show me again how to make a shot of espresso."

"You should have Will show you," she said. "Now's a good time; there's no line. Besides, customers always look relieved to see him on the bar instead of me."

He shook his head. "Doubtful."

"You think I don't see it?" she teased. "I'm bad at making espresso, not blind."

"Are you sure?" he said dryly. "Because somehow you always overfill the filter and get dark, bitter shots."

"You can be on the bar the rest of the night then," Cassidy said, disappearing into the back room.

I tried not to groan at how obvious they were being. Best just to concentrate on not screwing up anymore. With Cassidy gone, Will showed me how much espresso should go in the filter, how to tamp it down hard enough, and what to do when the filter got stuck in the machine (which was: pull it harder).

"So, um, you know Janine quit, right?" he said. "That's why Samir needed a replacement so quickly."

"Yeah, Cassidy told me."

"We kind of broke up is why," he added quietly.

"Oh," I said, shooting daggers from my eyes in Cassidy's direction as she emerged through the swinging double doors. I'd figured as much, but leave it to her to omit the most important detail. "Well, I'm sorry."

Will shrugged off my apology. "All for the best. Refill the espresso beans in the grinders, okay?"

I got the hint. When Cassidy was within earshot, there was to be no talk of Janine.

By the end of my first shift, I had learned three other things: pulling those espresso filter things in and out was hard work, the steam wand was way hotter than you'd expect (and so was the steam), and I was going to need to buy black jeans and sneakers. Despite the apron, my jeans were streaked with brown drips, and the toes of my Converse were covered in a thin film of coffee grounds.

When I finally got into my car that night and sat down for the first time since my dinner break, my feet throbbed so hard I thought my shoes might pop right off. I pulled down the visor to look at myself in the mirror and was unsurprised to find that I had coffee grounds in my bangs, no doubt from wiping sweat from my brow, and there was a streak of mocha syrup down one cheek.

Cassidy was waiting in her car for me to follow her to her house. I was going to spend the night, away from the watchful eyes of my parents and the possibility of running into Raf. He had sent another text that afternoon saying that it was good to see me. And that he was holding my copy of *Watchmen* hostage until I hung out with him again. I didn't know how to respond, so I stuck to my policy of silence. It wasn't an easy policy to follow.

"Why don't you just go for it with Raf?" Cassidy asked me as we sat on her bed that night, staring at our phones.

"Why don't you just go for it with Will?" I shot back.

"I don't know," she said. She hid her face behind a curtain of blonde curls. "He acts like he doesn't care about me. Now that Janine's gone, he's making me work more closing shifts, and he's always there, like, watching over my shoulder. I know I'm not great at my job, but I don't need a babysitter. You know?"

I gave her a look that probably mirrored hers when she told me that Raf liked me. "He's making you stay late because he wants to get you alone at closing time."

"No way," she said. "He's my manager. And he's in college. He goes to UDC part-time. Actually, it's pretty cool. He's getting a degree in . . ." Her voice trailed off. "Jesus. I really sound like I have a crush on him, don't I?"

We both burst out laughing.

Morgan knocked loudly on the wall. "Stop talking so loud!" she yelled from her room.

Cassidy rolled her eyes and got up to go deal with The Nuisance, but I put a hand on her arm to stop her.

"Just let it go," I said. "Let's go drown our sorrows in ice cream."

Eight Months Ago

When Mike called that day, I could hear in his voice that something was wrong. He asked to come over for a little while, when normally he would have just texted me to say that he was already on his way.

My parents were playing golf, so I told him he could come over. When he got to the house, he rang the doorbell. He hadn't done that since the homecoming dance that fall. He'd brought me a corsage, but he knew Audrey didn't have a date, so he'd brought one for her, too. She'd kept it next to her mirror, dried and hanging upside down.

But that day, he came only with his guilt, his head hanging, his shoulders slumped. Full of shame, he asked me to sit next to him on the front stoop. I think it was easier for him to admit what he'd done when we weren't face-to-face.

"Last night, at the party, I kissed someone," he said.

My ears got hot first, as if they'd been burned by the information. The heat traveled to my cheeks, then down my neck to my chest. The tears that slid from my eyes should've turned to steam.

I didn't know what to say. I was so shocked that any words got stuck in my throat on the way out.

"Who?" I finally managed to whisper.

He didn't want to tell me at first, but I glared at him until he did. "Sofia," he said, adding quickly, "but it wasn't her fault."

"So it was yours?"

Mike's face turned pale. "No! It was just . . . we were drunk, and she was flirting, and I got confused. I don't know what I was thinking."

"How could you do this?" I said. "Do you want to break up?" My heart ached just saying those words.

"No!" he said, kneeling on the asphalt in front of me, his hands on my knees. "I don't want to break up. I just . . ." His voice trailed off as he slumped to the ground.

"What, Mike?" I said. Sobbed, really.

"You didn't know me before I came to DC, but I wasn't someone that girls wanted to hook up with. I was overweight and smart and I read comics. No one was interested . . . until I started playing lacrosse in seventh grade. You're the first girl I'd ever kissed."

He wasn't looking at me, and his eyes were glued to the concrete stairs, but I let my face register my shock anyway. He had never mentioned that, not in the many hours we had spent making out. But that didn't change the fact that he'd cheated.

"So what?" I said.

"So I love you," he practically shouted. He was on his knees in front of me, begging, but I had pride. I wasn't giving in. Yet.

My silence rankled him.

"This wouldn't have happened if you'd just come to the

party with me last night," he said resentfully as he sat back on his heels.

A flash of rage burned through me. "Are you kidding me?" I yelled. "Are you saying this is my fault?"

He winced and started to backtrack. "No! I just wish you would come out with me more. Can you blame me for wanting to be with you all the time?"

He was good, I'd give him that.

"I don't want to look at you," I said. I closed my eyes and dropped my head into my hands. "You should leave."

I should have screamed at him. I should have made a huge scene out there on the lawn. I should have dumped him right then.

But I didn't want to break up. I was in love, but more than that, I didn't want to go back to the way my life was before him. Before I had plans on the weekend—even if I didn't always go through with them. Before I had someone to tell me I was beautiful. The way Mike looked at me was intoxicating, like I was someone worth looking at.

But that didn't change the way the hurt had started to burrow a hole in my chest. Or how that hole widened when I looked at him.

He nodded and stood up, and we awkwardly stood around for a minute, unsure how to end this.

"I love you," he said again. And then he got in his car and drove away.

CHAPTER TWELVE

Over the next few days, I worked several more shifts and slept at Cassidy's after each one. Her house felt so normal—full of noise and the smells of dinner cooking—it was the ideal escape from my empty, silent house.

When I finally stopped by the hospital, the nurses greeted me like it had been weeks since I'd been there, not a few days. Mom and Audrey were working with the hospital's speech therapist, but I hesitated in the hall. I could hear Audrey struggling with certain sounds. I watched through the doorway as the therapist held up flashcards and Audrey tried to remember and pronounce each word.

Finally, I couldn't take it anymore. Watching her struggle was too painful. I pasted a big, fake smile on my face and cleared my throat. I felt like I was doing her a favor when I interrupted.

Audrey's face broke into a lopsided smile—a genuine one.

"Hi, Harley," she said slowly.

"Good work, honey," Mom said, as if she were talking to Floyd.

I couldn't help cringing. Luckily, Mom didn't notice.

"Hey, Audy. I just stopped by to bring you some clean clothes." I pulled her favorite sweatpants and a hoodie out of my bag, along with a few T-shirts. "Hope you don't mind that I went into your room."

Audrey looked relieved. Mom had bought her half a dozen new nightgowns to replace the gowns the hospital provided. Audrey had been hooked up to a catheter for a month, so the open bottom was necessary. But they were supposedly going to take out the catheter that afternoon, provided she could manage getting into a wheelchair and into the bathroom, or at least raise herself up enough to use a bedpan. No wonder this was the happiest I'd seen her. Not just about the catheter, but because the floral flannel nightgowns Mom had bought made her look about ten years old.

"I have to get to work," I said. "Fingers crossed you get to pee on your own today!"

Audrey grinned. The speech therapist stifled a laugh. Mom, on the other hand, looked annoyed. She followed me out to the hallway.

"Harley, this job at the coffee shop is taking up a lot of your time," she said. "I've barely seen you this last week."

"Mom, you *told* me to get a summer job, remember?" I said. I leaned against the wall and examined my fingernails so I wouldn't have to look at her. I was avoiding the hospital, and Audrey, and she knew it.

"Yes, but I wanted you to have something more flexible. Your sister is being moved to rehab soon. We'll all need to be there to help her and support her so that she can come home."

Steeling myself, I looked up. "She's stronger than you think. She'll be okay if I'm not there to watch her every minute."

"What's that supposed to mean?"

"That she might want to take care of herself again!" I said. My voice was louder than I intended. "That she might want *that* more than we know."

Mom blinked, as if I'd spoken to her in a foreign language. "I just don't understand," she said, reaching out for me. I shifted away from her hands. "You were here every day while she was unconscious, but now that she's awake, you can barely spend more than five minutes with her."

I tried to breathe past the knot forming in my chest. "I'm just busy, Mom." I didn't add the next thought, which was, *At least I didn't run for a bottle of whiskey.*

She eyed me wearily, but she knew my stubbornness better than anyone. Pushing wasn't going to help.

"Fine," she said. "But come right home tonight. No sleeping at Cassidy's again."

I sighed but nodded. Then I leaned forward and gave her a quick kiss on the cheek. "Pass that on to Audy for me," I said.

I WAS INTENTLY focused on the carafe I was wiping down when someone cleared his throat. I looked up into the wide, dark eyes of Ryan Carter, Mike's best friend. Weird: I'd spent a large chunk of the last two years with this guy, but I hadn't thought of him once since the accident. Maybe it was easier to break up with Mike—and his world—than I'd ever anticipated.

"Hey, Harley," he said. "I didn't know you were working here, too." He gave Cassidy a wave, and she smiled and waved back.

"Only for about a week," I said. My voice was tight.

An awkward silence followed. I wondered whether I was supposed to ask him what he wanted to order or keep making small talk. Ryan wasn't a jerk or anything. We'd even had fun together. Sometimes. Maybe I missed him a little.

"So, iced coffee?" I asked.

"Oh, right, um, large," he said. "Room for milk."

"Yeah, I remember," I said without thinking. I'd seen Ryan drink about three hundred iced coffees since I'd known him. It was his drink of choice whether it was ninety or nineteen degrees outside.

"Of course," he said. "Just don't ruin it with sugar the way you poison your own coffee."

All at once I remembered a lame inside joke we'd shared. Mike, Ryan, and I had always treated "coffee" like the fourth person in our group. Just so Ryan wouldn't feel like a third wheel. We were always a foursome, thanks to Ryan's date, Iced Coffee. Then he met Connie. How convenient: her name rhymed with coffee.

I smiled to myself as I put ice in his cup.

"How's your sister doing?" he asked.

The smile slid from my face. "She's good. She's awake, and they're talking about moving her to a rehab facility. So, as good as could be expected, I guess."

He nodded, his own face growing serious. "I'm really glad to hear it," he said. "I've always liked Audrey."

I swallowed. It was time to acknowledge the elephant in the room. "So, how's Mike? Have you seen him?"

He raised his eyebrows.

"What? One of us had to bring him up."

Ryan shook his head. "No, he's not really allowed to talk to me from rehab."

I nodded. That made sense. "But he told you . . ."

"Yeah, he told me that you dumped him. And honestly, I'm surprised it took you so long."

Right. There was that familiar stab of guilt in my gut.

"So, hey," Ryan said, "the guys and I are having a party tonight, if you want to come?" He added hastily, "No drinking or anything."

"Wait, really?" I said, turning my head so quickly that I almost spilled the pitcher of cold brew I was pouring. "You guys aren't drinking anymore?"

Ryan nodded. He looked me straight in the eye. "Yeah. Mike's accident was kind of a wake-up call for us all. Or most of us anyway."

I handed Ryan his coffee and waved off his attempt to pay for it. "It's on me," I said. He didn't need to know that I was trying to make up for not thinking about him once. For not even considering how he and his friends might have been affected by Mike's accident. "It was really good to see you," I added.

"So you're not going to come tonight?" Ryan actually looked disappointed.

"I can't," I said. "I'm working closing. But I really appreciate the offer." And I did.

He tipped his coffee in my direction and slid a dollar into the tip jar. "Thanks for the coffee," he said. "I'll see you around."

"I hope so," I answered honestly.

I almost expected to see him getting into Mike's car, his arm hanging out the passenger-side window, before I remembered that it was totaled.

THERE WAS A voicemail on my phone when I got it out of my locker in the break room at the end of the night, but I didn't recognize the number. I waited to listen to it until I was in my car, just in case it was something about Audrey and I needed the freedom to cry. The message, though not about Audrey, made me want to cry anyway.

It was from Ms. Baker, Mike's mom, telling me to call her back because she needed to ask me something. She wasn't specific about what, and though I didn't really want to talk about Mike, my curiosity got the better of me.

"Hello, Harley," she answered. "Thank you so much for returning my call." She sounded oddly formal for a woman who had made sure to keep my preferred brand of tampons in her guest bathroom.

"Hi, Ms. Baker," I responded, matching her tone. "What can I do for you?"

"Well," she said slowly, as though she was reluctant to continue, or maybe unsure of how to start. "As you know, Mike has been in rehab for a couple of weeks now. As he comes to the end of his stay, one of the steps that he is supposed to complete is to make amends for the things he did wrong."

Oh God, no. My stomach plummeted.

"Mike would really like to see you, Harley, and have the chance to talk about some things. I don't expect your parents to come, though he'd like to apologize to them, too, but I'd love it if you could be there. There's a family day on Saturday."

My mouth dropped open. Shock shifted to annoyance, then to anger. But there was a sliver of hope, too. I may have been furious with Mike, but as Ryan showed me, this was about much more than Mike himself. After going to that party with Raf and meeting real addicts, I didn't think Mike fit the bill of an alcoholic. Not yet. But if he kept going the direction he was headed, he could become one. And I didn't want to imagine the damage he could do along the way.

"Harley?" Ms. Baker said from the other end of the line. "Are you still there?"

"Yes. I'll go. Text me the address, please."

I hung up before I could second-guess myself.

BY THE NEXT afternoon, I was pacing the house anxiously, as much of a wreck as I'd been waiting for news about Audrey. I'd been up all night thinking about what I could say to Mike, what he'd say to me, how to keep my shit together in front of his mom and the other people at the rehab center. I was furious with myself for agreeing to go.

With Mom and Dad gone—first to the hospital, then to a dinner with friends—lonely hours stretched in front of me. I could only binge-watch TV shows for so long. And even though I could have gone to the coffee shop and talked to Cassidy, what I really wanted was to talk to Raf.

By six o'clock, I'd run out of excuses. I felt as if I were about to explode, so I finally caved and texted Raf, asking him to meet me outside.

I sat on the garden wall between my house and his, knowing that he'd see me on his way over. I heard the basement door open. Floyd trotted into the shadow of the house next door. Raf appeared and Floyd followed, his tongue lolling and tail wagging.

"Hey," Raf said, sitting down. He lit a cigarette and handed it to me before lighting one for himself. As I took a drag, I tried not to focus on the fact that his lips had touched the filter mere seconds before mine. *It's not like a kiss*, I reminded myself. Clearly, I had spent *way* too much time watching movies in Audrey's hospital room. They were turning me into a romantic.

"Hey, yourself," I said. I took a drag. Floyd ambled away,

but I whistled to get him to come to me so I could stroke his soft ears between my fingers.

"So . . . I'm glad you texted. It's been a while." Raf leaned forward to pet Floyd along with me. It was easier than looking at each other.

"Yeah, sorry." After I exhaled, I held the cigarette without smoking it. It wasn't as satisfying as I'd wanted it to be. Or as appealing.

"You've been busy, right?"

I looked at him out of the corner of my eye. Was he being serious, or did he know I was holding back? And when did he get his hair cut? Because it looked nice.

"Well, Audrey woke up," I said.

"Yeah, I know," he said. "You told me, remember?"

"Right," I said. "And I have a new job, working at The Flakey Pastry."

"You told me that, too." He sounded impatient.

What could I say? That I had finally allowed myself to text him so I could talk to him about going to see Mike in rehab, but that now that he was in front of me, I didn't want to bring it up? That I didn't want to talk about my ex-boyfriend when I couldn't stop thinking about kissing Raf?

If Audrey were here, she could give me advice. And right now those movies were of no help. I was too unsure of my own feelings. Maybe my attraction to him was just a reaction to my anger at Mike. Maybe it was a reaction to Raf's rejection of me when we were kids. Maybe it was the fear of putting my heart in the hands of someone else who could crush it and blame it on alcohol.

"My mom said Audrey's going to be moved to a rehab facility soon," Raf said, filling the silence between us.

I nodded.

"How does she feel about that?"

I took a moment before answering. "She still isn't talking much," I said finally. "Her memory of the last year is gone, you know, and I think it's freaking her out."

"Wow. Yeah, I can imagine how that would feel. But she is talking?"

"A little bit. Some words are still hard for her to remember. Doesn't seem to stop her from trying, though. She just deals with the struggle. Way better than I would."

Raf smiled a little. "That sounds like Audrey. Jump in; worry later."

"Yep, that's her," I said. I stubbed out my half-smoked cigarette in the grass. "It'll be interesting to see what happens when they let her start trying to walk."

"When will that happen?" Raf put out his cigarette and reached out to take the butt from my hand, like we'd been smoking side by side for years instead of a handful of times. He didn't comment on how I'd wasted it.

"This week. She's been asking about it, apparently."

I regretted the "apparently" as soon as it was out of my mouth. Raf's head tilted and he turned his body toward mine. I felt his gaze but couldn't meet it. He waited for thirty seconds or so, maybe to see if I would keep talking. I remained quiet.

"You haven't been going to see her," he said. It wasn't a question, but it wasn't an accusation, either. "Why?"

I shrugged, trying to curl inward. To avoid his questions.

"Why is it that you don't seem happier that Audrey is awake?" he pushed. "You spent more time with her when she was in a coma."

"You sound like my mother," I grumbled.

"Are you denying it?"

"No, but I find it creepy that you know where I've been."

"Stop trying to turn this back on me," he shot back. Now he sounded irritated.

I stared down at the grass. I was irritated myself. "Maybe it's none of your business," I said. I could hear the bitter edge in my voice.

He turned to face me even though I wasn't looking at him. "Harley, seriously. What are you so mad about?"

I drew a shaky breath, fighting to stave off angry tears. "I can't," I said.

"Okay," he said. "It's okay." He leaned back on his hands, sitting quietly. Waiting me out.

The longer we sat there, the more unnerving the quiet between us became. This wasn't what I wanted things to be like. I didn't want to keep pushing him away. I didn't want to keep avoiding him.

And I was so tired of keeping this secret.

I sighed, defeated. "Fine," I said. "But I don't really want to talk about what I'm about to say. So just hear it and shut up. Okay?"

"Deal," Raf said.

"Mike cheated on me that night of the accident. With Audrey. And she doesn't remember it. She doesn't remember anything that happened that night." The words tumbled out in a rush.

I'd been expecting to scream or vomit or run away when I'd finished. But something else happened. I actually felt a tiny bit of relief.

Raf's jaw dropped, and his eyes went wide. But true to his word, he didn't speak. For once, maybe he didn't know what to say. I knew the feeling. Unfortunately, it didn't last long. As soon as my guard was down, he spoke.

"Does anyone else know?" he asked.

"Just Cassidy," I said. "I don't want my parents to find out. I don't want them to think about her like that. Especially not now." I tried to swallow the lump in my burning throat.

"Yeah, but Harley, you've been holding on to this for weeks now. No one knows what really happened that night, except you, and you're carrying around this weight when she's the one who hurt you. How is that fair?"

"Shut up, Raf," I said.

"No. I'm serious." His voice was firm. "She slept with your boyfriend. Eventually, she could remember that."

"She said they didn't have sex," I countered lamely.

He shook his head. "That doesn't make it okay," he said. "Don't you think that at least your parents deserve to know the truth about what happened that night? I know you're worried they blame you for not driving her home. This proves that it's not your fault."

"It *is* my fault!" I yelled at him. "I knew he was drunk, they both were, and I just left her there with him anyway." I was breathing heavily now. I turned away, but Raf put a hand on my shoulder.

"It's not your fault," he said. "You don't have to protect him."

"It's humiliating enough that he cheated on me," I managed to say. "I don't want more people to know about it. Not that they would be surprised. I bet everyone thought it was just a matter of time before he fell for the prettier sister." I let out a harsh, humorless laugh.

"Harley, that's ridiculous," Raf murmured. "You're beautiful."

My cheeks heated, even though I instinctively dismissed his praise. The old reflex kicked in: I wondered if he thought Audrey was beautiful, too. Of course he did.

Raf shifted beside me. I knew he wanted to say something but was afraid he'd upset me further.

"What?" I demanded.

"I'm just wondering . . . well, are either you or Audrey talking to a therapist?"

I looked at him sharply. "Audrey is. It's part of her rehab. I'm not interested." I tried to relax; he was only trying to help. My eyes fell again to the grass. "Listen, I texted you because I have to go see Mike at rehab this weekend. It's family day or something and he wants to make amends. Or he has to, as part of his rehab. I'm not entirely clear."

Raf was quiet at first. "You're going to see him?" he said after a moment.

I could hear the anxiety in his voice, but I couldn't tell if it was concern for me or jealousy.

"Yeah. Do you think I'm making the wrong choice? Should I not go?"

"I don't know," he said cautiously. "That's not my call to make. But he sure as hell owes you an apology."

"Oh, he's apologized," I said. I glanced back at Raf. "But he can say he's sorry all he wants. I'll never forgive him."

Raf didn't seem happy to hear that. We sat quietly next to each other for a few minutes, the humid air thick with smoke and our unspoken thoughts.

"Listen, I have to get to a meeting," Raf said, offering me a hand to pull me up. "But if you want to talk about this, I'm willing to listen. It's important."

I didn't move. I couldn't bear to go back to the nervous quiet that had settled over the house since the accident. It was like standing on a frozen lake at the beginning of April. Any second the last thin layer was going to crack.

"Would it be weird if I asked to come?" I said to Raf's

waiting hand. "Maybe it'll help me be less nervous about going to see Mike in rehab this weekend."

"Uh, yeah . . . I mean, you can come," he said. A faint smile crossed his face. He was clearly taken aback. "It's an open meeting, but you know, it's still anonymous and all, so just remember that part. But . . . yeah, come."

I questioned whether he actually wanted me there, but tried to shake it off. If he didn't want me to come, he wouldn't have said yes. That was a mantra I'd had to adopt with Mike after he snapped at me for asking him one too many times if he was sure he wanted me at one of his friend's parties. So I ignored the hollow feeling in my chest that I would normally have filled with doubt and followed Raf to the car.

WHEN WE PULLED into the church parking lot, I looked at Raf, my mouth open.

"This is where the meeting is?" I said. "I went to preschool here!"

Raf laughed at my surprise.

"I never knew there were AA meetings here."

"This church holds so many suburban secrets," he said with a smile.

He slowed and waved to a man in his twenties, a good-looking guy with dark skin and a small frown on his full lips. He was on his way out. Raf eyed him with concern. The guy only nodded back, not stopping his determined stride. Looked like he wouldn't be attending.

Several people were hanging out front, including Cajun, Dave, Arjun, Tina, and a few others I recognized from the party. Raf stopped to smoke a cigarette with them before going inside. Not only were they happy to see him, but they seemed happy to see me, too.

"Hey there, hustler," Dave said with a smile.

"You liked us so much you became an alcoholic?" Cajun added, giving me a side hug that squeezed me up against his belly.

"No, I just needed to feel better about myself, so I figured I'd come hang out with you."

That got a half-laugh, half-groan from the group. I felt a flicker of relief that they didn't take it as an insult. Sometimes my sarcasm didn't come across as good-natured. Audrey had gotten her feelings hurt more times than I could count.

After putting their cigarette butts into a bucket of sand, the group led the way through a basement door and into the fluorescent light of a hallway. It looked the same as it had when I went there as a toddler: like an elementary school, with children's artwork lining the walls, the only difference being that the curriculum here was Jesus.

I followed them into one of the classrooms, where a circle of folding chairs was set up. Nearly every seat was filled, with a few people lingering by the coffee machine.

I'd been expecting something more formal, like rows of chairs lined up facing a podium and a silver carafe of coffee at the back. There were more people than I'd expected, too, some older than the people I'd met, but also a girl who looked no older than fourteen. She had the pale skin and dark circles under her eyes of a new mother. Or a drug addict. Maybe both.

When I heard Raf sigh in relief, I followed his eyes. The guy from the parking lot was back. He took the folding chair next to me, a Styrofoam cup of coffee in his hand. A glob of non-dairy creamer floated along the top, resisting his attempts to break it up with his plastic stirrer.

"Hey, Nate," Raf said, reaching over to me. Nate tapped

his knuckles against Raf's and silently returned to his coffee. Raf frowned, but before he could say anything else, an older woman with long silver hair in a low ponytail called the meeting to order. She held an old-fashioned plastic binder in her lap. Her fingers were stained yellow from nicotine. I wondered if there were any members of AA who *weren't* heavy smokers.

"Welcome to Up the Tubes," she rasped. "I'm Elaine, and I'm an alcoholic."

"Hi, Elaine," everyone murmured back.

Now that was more like what I'd been expecting.

"Tonight is an Open Step meeting," she went on. "We're happy to have you here, especially newcomers." She glanced down at the notebook and began to read aloud. "'Alcoholics Anonymous is a fellowship of men and women who share their experience, strength, and hope with one another that they may solve their common problem and to help others recover from alcoholism. The only requirement for membership is a desire to stop drinking.

"'There are no dues or fees for AA membership; we are self-supporting through our own contributions. AA is not allied with any sect, denomination, politics, organization, or institution; does not wish to engage in controversy; neither endorses nor opposes any causes. Our primary purpose is to stay sober and help other alcoholics achieve sobriety.'"

With that, she closed the notebook.

"Thanks Elaine," several people murmured.

She peered out at the group. "We are here because we admit that we are powerless over alcohol and other substances, and that our lives have become unmanageable.

"In step two of the program, we come to believe that a power greater than ourselves can restore us to sanity."

Most in the room recited these words along with Elaine. Raf was notably silent.

"We must make a decision to turn our will and our lives over to God and then make a searching and fearless moral inventory of ourselves. We must admit to God, to ourselves, and to another human being the exact nature of those wrongs, and we must be *entirely* ready to have God remove all those defects of character. We make a list of all the persons we have harmed and become willing to make amends and then, guess what? We make direct amends to those people."

Elaine looked around the room quickly, catching a few eyes here and there.

"We seek through prayer and meditation to improve contact with God. And having had a spiritual awakening as a direct result of these steps, we try to carry this message to alcoholics and practice these principles always."

It was clear she was reciting from memory, but her tone was passionate. She believed what she was saying. Judging from the nodding around the room, so did many others. It was impossible not to be moved.

She took a deep breath. "And with that, it's time for chips."

A younger woman handed Elaine a plastic bag full of shiny round multi-colored coins.

"Is anyone here for a twenty-four-hour chip?" she said.

The silence was punctuated by the sounds of people shuffling in their chairs. And then beside me, Nate calmly put his coffee on the floor and stood. The applause was hesitant at first and I saw shock on several faces, but then the applause swelled. He didn't smile but seemed buoyed by the support.

When Raf stood to get a six-month chip, I was surprised, but I couldn't help feeling a surge of pride. I nudged him with my elbow when he sat back down.

"Why didn't you tell me?" I whispered.

He just shrugged, but his cheeks were red. He couldn't hide the embarrassed pride.

One other person got a chip, and then Elaine started the meeting in earnest. She told a quick story about her road to sobriety. She had been sober for ten years, and she still went to a meeting every day, she said. She had learned that whenever she got cocky and thought she could do it without help, some situation always presented itself to remind her that she was not in control.

Then she asked if anyone else wanted to share. No one volunteered right off the bat.

"Nate," she said, "do you want to start?"

Nate looked chagrined, but also like he had expected this to happen. He nodded and started talking.

Nate was an alcoholic who had been sober for six years, he said. And then yesterday, he had a shitty day and he thought about drinking. And his day got shittier and he kept thinking about drinking. Until he finally found himself pulling into the liquor store parking lot and buying a pint of whiskey. And he drank it. It was that simple. He let his guard down for one moment, or a series of moments, and he regretted it, but it was too late.

Elaine praised him for coming right back to a meeting, and everyone around the room agreed. Meanwhile, I had to work to keep my mouth closed. I couldn't believe he'd thrown away six years of sobriety for one night of drinking. But I also was impressed that he'd realized his mistake and come back.

A few more people shared, telling their stories and talking about how they were feeling and what they had learned lately. People responded to or empathized with each other's complaints and concerns. It was encouraging to see all these people fighting to make their lives better.

But then I felt more than saw it when Elaine chose me. "Would you like to share . . . ?" Her voice trailed off purposefully.

I looked to Raf for help, but he shrugged. This was my choice.

"My name is Harley," I said. "And I'm not an alcoholic or an addict, but I'm here to support my friend."

A few heads turned. I worried they might object. But the faces I knew wore encouraging smiles. As did the faces of the strangers.

"Um, I hope that's okay?" I said.

Elaine nodded, and since it was silent and everyone was looking at me, I started talking. "So, a few weeks ago, my sister and another man were nearly killed by a drunk driver," I said, looking at my hands in my lap. I didn't want to see the pity anyone might be feeling for me or the challenge from those who might think I was accusing them. "The drunk driver was my boyfriend. Now ex-boyfriend."

I felt Raf drape his arm around the back of my chair. I looked at him for encouragement. He squeezed my shoulder.

"My sister was in a coma for nearly two weeks. When she woke up, she had no memory of the accident or the year leading up to it. She's learning how to talk and walk again now."

I wasn't sure what I was going to say when I started talking, but the silence in the room now told me that I was on the right track. And saying it out loud was bringing my anger to a boil, but at least allowing some to escape, like steam under the cracked lid of a pot.

"So thank you all for being here tonight," I said as I finished sharing. "I know it's not the only reason to stay sober, but if it means that someone else's sister doesn't end up with a scalp full of stitches and a body of broken bones because you didn't drive drunk, it's a pretty good one."

The room stayed quiet for a few seconds before I heard Raf say, “Thank you for sharing, Harley.” A handful of voices echoed him.

“I think that’s a great place to end tonight,” Elaine agreed. “Let’s say the Serenity Prayer.”

Four Years Ago

"Mom, I'm taking Floyd out!" I called up the stairs as I clipped Floyd's leash to his collar. He was a younger dog back then, and his boundless energy created a great excuse to get out of the house. Especially when I saw Raf and his friend heading down the street.

I hadn't seen much of him since we were kids, other than a wave out the window of the back seat of the car in passing, or when I was walking Floyd. The summer before sixth grade, he started playing basketball in his driveway. At first, I would just walk the dog past and pretend not to notice him. But I noticed. Not long after, he started calling out something funny, pretending he was talking to Floyd. I had no experience with boys, so any interaction felt important and exciting.

Eventually, he would come and pet Floyd—or, more accurately, they would wrestle—and sometimes he'd even walk with us for a little while. But after months of this, I felt it was time for an escalation.

Plus, Cassidy was at the beach with her family for a week and my other friends lived too far away for me to walk to their houses. So I was bored enough to voluntarily leave the house and enter the heat wave that July afternoon.

Raf and his friend were walking ahead slowly, and as soon as the door was open, Floyd ran as fast as he could, dragging me behind at the end of his leash until we caught up. He then immediately crammed his nose in Raf's friend's crotch.

"Sorry! God, he's the worst," I said, scolding Floyd and pulling him away. He was a strong dog, and defiant on top of it, but Raf's friend just crouched down with Floyd and scrubbed at the black Lab's soft ears while he slobbered kisses all over his neck.

Raf caught me grinning at the sight and frowned. "Hey," he said. "Your dog's accosting my friend. And frankly, I'm a little upset he snubbed me."

I smiled wider. "You can't blame him for having good taste," I said. "It's best to accept this loss and move on. You'd look better with a brunette anyway." My cheeks flushed, but I hoped it was covered by the fact that my entire body was pink from the heat.

Raf's friend and Floyd had finished their make-out session by then. The friend stood and offered a wave to me.

"Hey, I'm Paul," he said. "Your dog's awesome."

"Are you planning to make an honest man out of him after that?" I said.

Paul's mouth opened, but Raf interrupted.

"Don't even try," Raf said. "Floyd and I already have a relationship; you can't just walk in and try to steal him from me. He may be fickle, but my memory is long."

Paul laughed, but I couldn't help but wish that Raf was actually talking about me.

We walked for a few blocks, but when Floyd started panting, I told them I had to turn around.

"You should come hang out with us tonight," Raf said.

"What are you doing?" I asked.

He shrugged. "We've got some beer, and we're going to sneak out and drink them in the park once my parents are asleep."

"Sounds thrilling," I said, trying to sound calm even though I was suddenly sweating even more. "But sure, I'll come."

That night, I crept past the creaky bedroom door, down the stairs, and out the basement door. The humid night air felt like an omen as sweat gathered on the backs of my thighs and pooled on my upper lip. I fretted about the lip gloss I was wearing and eventually decided to wipe it off on the back of my hand instead of letting it melt on my lips.

I'd been early, but as the minutes sailed by without any sign of Raf and Paul, not even a whisper of the door opening, I got nervous. After more than an hour, I finally went back inside to the welcome icy blast of air-conditioning, which made the wet tracks of my tears tingle with cold.

I never heard from Raf about what had happened, even though we'd exchanged phone numbers that day. I was too proud to text him after my initial "You still coming?" message that had gone unanswered. He didn't even come outside to play basketball until the fall. I made Audrey walk Floyd after school so I could avoid seeing him.

I guess he avoided me, too.

CHAPTER THIRTEEN

We drove home in silence. I was trying to puzzle out what had happened, what I'd accomplished in that room, if anything. Maybe Raf was, too.

He slowed to a stop between our two houses. I had my hand on the car door handle when he said, "Want to come over?"

I turned back. His eyes, dark in the moonlight, were hopeful.

"Yeah," I said. "Let's go."

I concentrated on my footsteps in the grass. One step at a time. Only when his bedroom door was behind us did I trust myself to speak.

"I—"

"So, what you said tonight at the meeting," Raf started to say.

"Sorry," I said, cutting him off. "I mean, I'm sorry about that. I hope I didn't offend anyone."

He was shaking his head before I had even finished. "No, Harley, what you said was good. It was a reminder of the consequences of using. And not just for me, for everyone in the room. Elaine was really glad you shared tonight."

"She wasn't sure about me at first, was she?" I said. "She thought I might bring too much joy to the room, I bet."

Raf laughed a little. I liked making him laugh. "Nah, she's cool. Open meetings are just that: open. She just wanted to be sure you wouldn't be judgmental about what people were saying in there."

I opened my mouth to protest and then closed it. It made sense. As far as Elaine knew, I had never experienced anything even close to the problems that the people in that room had.

"It's just, addicts sometimes feel like . . . Well, the phrase is 'a gold-plated piece of shit the world revolves around.'"

Now it was my turn to laugh. "And that means?"

"Essentially, that we realize we are pieces of shit, but we think we are the shiniest, most important pieces of shit that the world has ever seen. So what *we* need, what *we* want to do, the decisions *we* make, it's all way more important than anything or anyone else. That's how an addict's mind works."

I nodded, processing.

"So having someone in there, judging us, like an outsider? It can be a little uncomfortable. It makes some people edgy. But it's important."

"You said 'us,'" I said. "Are you calling yourself an addict?"

He glanced away. "If you ask Elaine, I am."

"Is she your sponsor?" I asked. I knew that was an AA thing, but Raf had never mentioned a sponsor before.

"She was. In rehab I had to have a sponsor. They insisted on it because they really wanted me to embrace the program. But when I got out and told Elaine I wasn't sure I was an addict, she said she couldn't help me work the steps if I couldn't even accept the first one. So she's still there if I need her, but she can't be my sponsor until I'm ready."

His expression grew pained. He was wrestling with something. It almost hurt to look at him.

"What do you think would help you decide if you're an addict or not? Do you need to 'hit bottom' or something? Is that part of it?"

He shrugged. "I don't know. I don't have to hit bottom to know that I don't want to. But I think maybe it's possible to have an addictive personality without being addicted to one thing in particular . . . yet. Was I addicted to avoiding the real world by hanging out with my friends, getting drunk and high?"

I wanted to reach out. I wanted to smooth those worry wrinkles and lines. No teenage boy's face should be that world-weary and troubled.

"Are you saying that's true?" I prodded.

He laughed again. "Absolutely, yes. And I'm pissed about it."

He sat on his bed, and I sat beside him.

"I know," I said. "I mean, I get it. I'm pretty pissed at myself, too. I used to just push it down, focus on something else, and act like everything was fine. But nothing is fine now, and I have all this anger that I don't know what to do with."

Raf leaned his shoulder against mine. "Keeping it all pent up probably isn't helping," he said without looking at me. "Just saying. I've learned *that* at least from AA. And all those years of therapy."

I squirmed uncomfortably. I didn't want to talk about this. I didn't want to dig into what my anger meant. Because the last time I'd gotten angry, Audrey had almost died. I knew it wasn't a direct result, logically, but I would have to live with the fact that I'd never know what she would have done if I'd just confronted Mike at the party instead of storming off. Maybe Audrey would have spent the night at Neema's. Maybe Mike would have driven off alone.

"I've been waiting so long to be mad at her," I whispered finally. "I was waiting for her to wake up first and then we could deal with the whole Mike thing. But now . . ."

There wasn't anything left to say. There wasn't a "now." Audrey might never remember what happened that night, but I would never forget it.

"It's not your fault," Raf reminded me. "Being mad isn't going to affect whether she gets better. Whether she remembers or not, you're allowed to feel betrayed."

He was right, of course, but that didn't make it any easier. My chest felt tight with guilt and anger, and something more: a longing for the days before the party and the accident.

"I just miss her so much sometimes. Even though Audrey is still alive, she's not the same. She will never be the same," I said. "And sometimes I feel like maybe she deserves it." My voice quivered with shame.

Raf was quiet. For an instant, I worried that he was judging me, but he shifted closer and put his arm around my shoulders, hugging me against his side. I rested my head on his shoulder and drew a shivery breath.

"I wish I didn't have to see Mike on Saturday," I said. "I'm scared of what I might say."

Raf squeezed me tighter. "I'm sorry you have to do that. But I hope it helps you get some closure."

"I don't want closure," I admitted. "I want to hate him for the rest of my life. But I also feel guilty about wanting that."

"You don't have to," he said. "You recognize your feelings for what they are. That's more than most people do."

Then he was quiet, waiting for me to respond.

But I didn't want to talk about Mike anymore. I didn't

want to talk at all. I picked up Raf's hand and slowly lifted it to cup my cheek. I leaned into his palm, placing a kiss at its center. He raised his eyebrows in a silent question as his long fingers tilted my face toward his. When I answered by lifting my lips to meet his, he slipped his arm around my waist, pulling me closer against his side.

I had missed this—the comfort that came from being desired, from being able to make someone want me. Of wanting someone in return. Of that intensity. How it blotted out every other thought . . .

But then Raf stopped me.

I was reaching to unbuckle his belt. I looked up at him as he placed his hand on top of mine, stilling it. I wanted oblivion; I wanted to forget how I was feeling. I needed to think about something else. Someone else. And Raf seemed to know that.

"Just give me a second," he said. He took a deep breath in. "I really want to keep doing this, but I . . . I feel like you might regret this later. And I don't want to be something you regret."

I nodded, my heart thumping.

"I'm sorry," I said. "I just didn't want to talk anymore. And you were . . ." I let my voice trail off because the things I was thinking were not things I was prepared to tell him.

"Yeah, no, I got that," Raf said. He sounded tired now, fed up. "I assume you used to do that with Mike? Use sex to avoid talking?"

I looked at him sharply. It was none of his business. On the other hand, I knew deep down that he was right. I hated that he looked disappointed by it. A little angry, too.

"I should go," I said. I didn't look at him as I headed for the door. I couldn't. I was too humiliated.

"Wait." He bolted upright. "Am I going to hear from you, or are you going to go back to ignoring me?"

I turned back to him. "I'm sorry about that," I said. "I just didn't . . ."

"You didn't want to talk," he finished for me. "But maybe I wanted to talk to you." I glimpsed the vulnerability in his eyes, but it vanished quickly.

"I *did* want to talk to you," I admitted. "And I like hanging out with you. I was avoiding you because apparently I can't be trusted to be alone with you. But we both need to be single right now, so . . ."

He got up from the bed. When he stepped closer, I thought—hoped—that he was going to kiss me again. Instead, he walked past me to his desk and handed me the copy of *Watchmen* that I'd loaned him. My shoulders drooped a little.

"I really liked this," he said. "Thanks."

"Yeah?" I said. I tried to sound enthusiastic. "Do you still want to watch the movie?"

He paused, and I could tell that he was considering saying no. That he was still pissed. And I couldn't blame him. But after a few seconds, he nodded.

"Yeah, sure. Sunday?" he said.

I nodded.

"Can you keep your hands to yourself?" he asked with a sly smile.

I knew he'd already started to forgive me.

"I'll try," I said, returning the smile as best as I could.

"I'll walk you home," he said.

The cool night breeze felt good against my flaming cheeks. My pulse was still racing. As we neared my front door, under my window, a memory shoved its way rudely into my mind.

"Hey," I said, stopping on the bottom step. "How come

you never showed that night a few years ago? We were supposed to sneak out, remember?"

Raf blinked. He stared sheepishly at his sneakers. "I'm sorry about that."

"That's not an answer," I said. "You stood me up! Aren't you supposed to make amends in AA?"

He sighed. "Fair enough. Remember my friend? Paul?"

I nodded.

"He liked you."

"Really?" I tried not to smile. It was always nice to be liked, and I remembered thinking Paul was cute. It was part of the reason I'd agreed to sneak out with them in the first place. I waited for Raf to go on, and when he didn't, I said, "So?"

"So." His eyes met mine, full of regret. "I was jealous. I didn't want him to hook up with you."

Had I been that blind? Apparently, yes. I'd thought Paul was cute, sure, but Raf had been the one I was willing to follow down the dark streets of our neighborhood.

"We were hanging out in the basement," Raf went on, "and I made him take shots until he was too drunk to go out. And then I kept drinking so I wouldn't feel guilty about ditching you. The next day, I was too embarrassed to even apologize."

"You were drinking that much at fourteen?" I asked. I knew I sounded judgmental. I couldn't help it. But I was trying, anyway.

"Yeah. So . . . rehab was maybe a good idea after all."

"Yeah, maybe it was," I said and turned around to unlock the door. "Thanks for telling me."

"That's it?" he said. "You forgive me?"

I glanced back at him. "If that's the truth, then I do. It's sad, maybe, but understandable. You're not the same kid you were then. So, yeah."

Raf was almost disappointed, like he'd expected a bigger reaction. But we'd both had enough embarrassment for one night. Even as hope built like tiny champagne bubbles in my chest, I knew I couldn't act on it. Not again. I didn't want to go another four years without speaking to him. But then those dark eyes brightened.

"Honesty. It feels pretty good, right?"

I tried to keep a straight face. "Don't ruin a nice, awkward moment with your therapy talk," I said.

I opened the door and walked inside, closing it on his quiet chuckle.

I WENT TO the diner with Cassidy the next morning. Audrey was being moved to her new rehab facility. I could have helped—Mom had asked me to come with her to get Audrey's stuff from her hospital room—but I told her I needed to eat first and would catch up with them at the rehab center. Out of guilt, I ordered pancakes to go for Audrey. She'd appreciate that more than the pile of new nightgowns Mom was bringing.

I waited until our breakfast arrived before telling Cassidy about what had happened with Raf.

"You're telling me *he* stopped *you*?" she said.

"Yeah, it was . . . unexpected," I said. "But I'm glad he did."

She looked at me for a second, weighing what she was about to say. "You know, you don't have to be a nun just because you broke up with Mike." Apparently, she'd decided on bluntness instead of tact.

I did know that. But I had reasons. "I'd rather have Raf

as a friend than an ex-boyfriend," I said. "And with the way I've been feeling lately—full of anger and bitterness—I'd just drive him away. Or he'd start drinking again. Or he'd cheat on me."

Understanding dawned on Cassidy's face.

"It's just . . ." I squirmed a bit. Cassidy wasn't going to like what I was going to say. "I'm going to see Mike in rehab tomorrow, and I'm really not handling the anxiety very well. Making out with Raf was just one way to avoid thinking about it."

Cassidy threw her hands up. "Whoa, slow down," she said. "You're going to see Mike. In rehab."

I nodded. "His mom called. She said he needed to make amends."

"She really did that," Cassidy grumbled. "Unbelievable."

I reached across the table for her hand, and she reluctantly put it in mine. "Please, Cass, I need your support right now, okay? I know you hate him, I hate him, everyone hates him, but what if making amends with me is what he needs to keep from drinking?"

"You'd think almost killing your sister would do that."

"Yeah, you would. But I need to be sure that he remembers that almost killing Audrey wasn't the only thing that he did wrong while he was drinking. He needs to make amends for a lot more than just that. And I think maybe I need to hear him say it."

"Okay," she said with a sigh. "But if you're going into the lion's den tomorrow, the least I can do is pay for breakfast."

I gave her hand another squeeze before she went to the cashier's station to pay.

I knew I was putting myself in a position to be disappointed, but I wanted to believe Mike could be better. I always had. But giving him the chance to let me down again had my palms sweating.

Still, there was an upside. Raf was right. The uncertainty made me want to do something that I could control. It made me want to confront Audrey about what she and Mike had done to me. I might not get what I wanted from Mike, but I could at least finally get the satisfaction of an apology from my sister.

HER NEW ROOM was a smaller space than the Neuro ICU room had been, but Mom, Dad, and I all fit. There wasn't nearly as much room for Dad to pace, though.

Audrey was still weak and not moving much, though she could scoot herself into a wheelchair to go to the bathroom now at least. She was sitting up and alert when I walked in. Her eyes brightened when she saw me, clearly grateful for saving her from being alone with Mom and Dad. Currently, they were arguing in the corner over whether they should insist on a different room. She wouldn't be so happy once she knew why I was separating her from them, though.

"Hey," I said, "could I take Audy on a roll through the place?"

Mom's first thought was *no*; I could see it on her face. But she managed not to say it out loud. Instead, she and Dad went to the nurses' station to ask them if we could borrow a wheelchair. It wasn't fair to make Audrey go through all that, but I needed privacy. And in addition to some lukewarm pancakes and fake maple syrup, I had some news that was going to upend her life.

I hung the take-out bag from one of the handles of the wheelchair and pushed Audrey out the door. Behind us, Mom and Dad stood in the empty room. They looked forlorn, like they hadn't been picked for dodgeball.

"We'll be fine!" I called back over my shoulder. "Back in twenty minutes, I promise."

I wheeled Audrey to the courtyard outside. It wasn't big, but the pathways were wide, and there was room next to a bench where I could park her and sit, which I did. I pulled out the pancakes and opened the container for her. Because Audrey didn't always have complete control over her motor functions yet, I cut up the pancakes and speared a few bite-size pieces on a fork. Then I placed the fork between her fingers so she could dip it into the puddle of syrup and eat.

"This is good," she said around her first bite. "Thank you."

"Yeah, well, anything's good when you've barely eaten any solid food for weeks."

I smiled, but my stomach roiled. I'd brought her here to tell her about Mike. To tell her what she'd done. To unburden myself at last. But as I watched her struggle to eat, I realized that her life was never going to be the same. Audrey would heal, yes, but she was going to pay for her mistake every single day for the rest of her life, whether she knew why or not. Why would I want to add to that pain? Neither one of us would feel better.

Instead, I reached into the bag and pulled out a packet of butter. I peeled back the foil for her and instructed her to dip it in there first, then the syrup, before taking a bite. She needed the extra calories, and she deserved the extra flavor, but Audrey's smile was enough of a reward.

Almost Two Years Ago

In September of our sophomore year, one of Mike's friends had a party. Someone brought a bottle of rum from their parents' liquor cabinet, and though I had never seen him drink before, Mike volunteered to play bartender. His concoctions turned out to just be rum and Coke, but because he was in charge of the pouring, he served himself a little more rum than he did anyone else.

At first, he was his regular self, just a little louder. He and his friends ran around making fun of each other and tried to drink more to impress the girls while we sipped our drinks slowly. Then, he got sarcastic and the jokes got pointed and a little mean.

By then, I knew what Mike was like in middle school. I knew that he was overweight ("chubby," his mom liked to say) and that he was made fun of. I figured he was making up for lost time, but after two rum and Diet Cokes, my head was spinning and I couldn't keep watching him alienate his friends, who were not nearly as drunk as he was.

I wanted to just lie down on the kitchen floor and take a nap, but I put my head down on the table instead. I don't know how long I was asleep, but when I woke up, the house was empty, Mike and his friends were outside smoking, and it was almost my curfew.

I ran outside to demand that Mike drive me home when I saw how glassy his eyes were. How unsteady his steps. How braying his laugh. He saw me, and his grin widened.

"Harley Quinn!" he shouted, swinging his cigarette wildly as he lunged toward me. His friends laughed when he stumbled. "You missed it!"

"What?" I asked, trying not to let my annoyance show. "What did I miss?"

But Mike was on the ground now, and he was rolling with laughter. I didn't really care what I had missed, but Mike's mom was supposed to be my ride home, so I took the opportunity to grab his phone from his pocket while he was distracted. But before I could get it free, he grabbed me around the waist and pulled me down on top of him.

"I'm the drunkest," he slurred loudly.

"You don't say," I hit back, deadpan.

This was how Mike always was. His friends would have a few beers; he'd have six. They'd take a shot; he'd take four. He always had to one-up everyone. But I didn't know that yet.

"And you're not, so you're the lamest," he said while I struggled to get up. I felt someone gripping my elbows and turned to see Ryan helping me up.

"Thanks," I said to him.

Once on my feet, I looked around to find the guy whose house we were at and found an expression that mirrored my own: annoyed, with a hint of disgust.

"I'll get him out of here," I said.

Ryan and I grabbed Mike under each arm and hauled him to his feet, following the rest of the guys back into the house.

We set Mike, who was now softly murmuring to himself with his eyes closed, on the couch.

"Do you know what happened to his mom?" I asked Ryan. "She was supposed to pick us up."

"Once he started taking shots, he texted her and said he was sleeping here. Without asking Justin," Ryan answered. That explained a few things.

"Can you get him home or let him sleep over at your house? Try not to let him get in trouble?"

"What about you?" Ryan asked.

"I have to go. I'm going to be late." I was already texting Cassidy, who was one of the oldest in our grade and already had her license. "Cassidy will be here in five minutes, and she's going to need the speed of the Flash to get me home in time."

He sighed. "Yeah, okay, I'll figure it out."

"I owe you one, Ry," I said.

I made it home at 11:35 P.M. and my parents were already in bed, asleep. I was relieved, but I almost wished they were awake and had asked me some probing questions about why Cassidy had driven me home instead of Ms. Baker, or perhaps why I smelled like cheap rum. I didn't want to be punished, but I wanted someone to care.

When I got to my room, though, Audrey was there, waiting.

"What did you do tonight?" she asked. Her eyes were narrowed with suspicion. "Your eyes are red."

Rather than giving an answer, I pushed her out of my room and closed the door in her face. I wanted someone to care, but I didn't want to actually talk about it.

Mike's mom never found out, and he didn't drink again for a while, so I pushed that memory to the back of my mind. Until the next time it happened.

CHAPTER FOURTEEN

There was a name tag with my first name on it waiting for me at the door when I walked into the rehab center the next day. A table was set up just inside the doors where a woman with a silver bob and a turquoise blazer checked me in.

"Michael Baker," she repeated after me when I told her who I was there to see. "You must be Harley."

The way she said it made me wonder if he had been talking about me to her, or if she just recognized my name from some list. The thought that everyone in this place knew what happened between him and Audrey made my chest tighten. I hadn't considered that my business was going to be on display when I said yes to being here.

I was tempted to turn and walk out, but the silver-haired woman seemed to sense that. She pointed me past the front desk and into the room just beyond where chairs were arranged in a big circle. Mike and his mom stood in its center talking to a couple other people. They hadn't noticed me yet and the room was slowly filling up with people wearing name tags, so I stood to the side, not quite ready to put on a brave face.

I studied Mike to see if I could spot a change in him since I'd last seen him a month ago. He looked cleaner on a surface level—his hair was combed and tucked behind his ears, his oxford shirt was tucked into his khaki shorts, and the dark circles under his eyes were now just a light shadow. It was an improvement, that's for sure.

Mike's eyes widened when he saw me. He started toward me, so I sighed and walked to meet him halfway. Mike reached out to hug me, but when I flinched back, he dropped his arms.

"I didn't think you would actually come," he said. He was smiling, but I couldn't seem to make my mouth respond in kind.

"I'm still not sure I'm staying," I said. "I don't know why you want me here."

He seemed to shrink a little, and I could almost see his confidence take a hit. My emotions warred, satisfaction battling with guilt. I wanted to hurt him, but I still hated to see him hurting.

"I know that I may never be able to fix things with us," he said, looking down at his shoes. "But I needed you to know that I'm taking this seriously."

I raised a skeptical eyebrow. "Yeah?"

He looked up at me. "Yes," he insisted. He opened his mouth to say more, but a tall man with thick dreadlocks and a wide, bright smile clapped his hands loudly and called to everyone to take a seat.

I sat down next to Mike in a hard plastic chair, trying to keep as much distance between us as possible. Next to him, Ms. Baker smiled at me and mouthed "Thank you," and I nodded back, but when she reached her arm around the back of Mike's seat to squeeze my shoulder, I shifted out of her reach.

The man who'd called us to attention stood in the center of the circle of around thirty chairs. He spun slowly so that he could look each person in the eye as he introduced himself as Jordan, the director of the rehab center.

"Thank you all so much for being here today," he said, "even those of you who didn't have a choice."

Everyone chuckled politely.

"It is so important for addicts to have the support of their families. But families are usually the people who addicts have hurt the most, and repairing the trust that was broken can be a long, bumpy road."

If it can be repaired at all, I thought. I looked around the circle at the other family members to see if anyone was as reluctant to be here as I was. But everyone was looking attentive and nodding understandingly. I felt a little humbled. Maybe I could put my cynicism aside for a few minutes.

"That's why we're all here today," Jordan said. "To try to make amends."

My heart started racing as I worried I might have to talk in front of all these people about things like my feelings and how Mike betrayed me.

"We're not here to air dirty laundry," Jordan added and my pulse slowed slightly. "We're here to learn how to work through problems and talk to each other." He clapped his hands once and then rubbed them together, ready to get to work. "We're going to break into smaller groups and do some individual work. But I want each of you to practice something we've been working on here. We call it active listening. Pay attention, defer judgment, and respond appropriately."

A half a dozen people stood and I realized they were counselors as they started herding people into groups. Jordan walked toward Mike, his mom, and me, and stopped in front of us.

"You three are with me," he said. Then he stuck out a massive hand and enveloped mine within it. He looked me in the eye when he shook my hand, smiling broadly. "It's nice to finally meet you, Harley."

"Thanks," I said, drawn in by his bright smile. He shook Ms. Baker's hand, too, and I tried not to take it personally when he smiled at her just as widely.

Jordan pointed the way to a smaller conference room with four chairs around a table. He closed the door behind us.

"Harley, Ms. Baker," he said after we sat down, "I'm Mike's counselor here, so we've been working together, talking about what makes him drink and about what happened the night of the accident."

Ms. Baker's face colored and she looked at Mike with a frown, her chin trembling.

"I know it's difficult to talk about how Mike screwed up," Jordan said. "He's accepted that. Right, Mike?"

Mike looked up from the table and said, "Right." He took a deep breath. "I owe you both a huge apology. I'm so sorry for everything that I've put you through."

"Be more specific," Jordan instructed, and Mike's shoulders slumped. Ms. Baker's hands twitched like she wanted to reach out to comfort him, but Jordan gave her a look and she pulled them into her lap.

"I lied to you both. Mom, I lied a lot about where I was and what I was doing. And Harley . . ." He scrubbed at his face with his hands. "I don't know why I did what I did to you."

When Jordan cleared his throat, Mike shot him an icy look. "Quit pushing me, man," he said, but Jordan didn't back down.

A muscle in Mike's jaw twitched. He looked back at me. "Harley, I broke your trust more than once when I cheated on you," he said. "And I know that being drunk isn't a good excuse, but I never meant to hurt you. I'm sorry."

I glanced between the two of them, confused and distraught. "What am I supposed to say?" I said. I directed it toward Mike, but then I turned back to Jordan. "I'm 'actively listening,' but I'm not sure how to respond. I know he's sorry, but I'm still mad."

Jordan nodded. "You're allowed to be mad, and Mike has to accept that," he said, pointing at Mike. "Because he can't change it."

"What do you want from me?" Mike asked, staring at me. His eyes were pleading, but his tone was resentful.

My hands curled into fists against my thighs. "I don't want anything," I said. "I didn't even want to be here, remember?" I stood and threw the door open, marching out into the hallway. I leaned against the wall, breathing deeply and trying to get myself together. I didn't know how to get out of the building, and I didn't want to attempt it when I was blind with anger.

I could hear the muffled sound of Mike and his mom arguing behind the door, but I could also hear raised voices from behind several other doors. I bet I wouldn't be the only one storming out today.

A few minutes later, Jordan stepped out into the hallway, and I looked at my shoes as he leaned against the wall next to me.

"You okay?" he asked.

I nodded. "I just don't think he gets that we're broken up. I can't be part of his support system. I can't even be around him."

"You're right. I don't think he does understand that yet. I've tried to explain to him that sometimes the things we addicts do when we're using are too much for the people who love us. It can't always be fixed. And what he did to you . . ." He whistled. "It was big of you to come today, and I think it was important for him to have the chance to apologize. He's eaten up with guilt, but it comes out as anger."

I nodded. I knew that, but it was still hard to feel sympathetic toward him. "You said 'we,'" I said. "Are you an addict, too? Oh, wait, is that rude to ask?"

He smiled and I felt my stomach unclench a little. "I am, yes. Ten years sober last month. It means I understand where these guys are coming from, and I can relate to them."

"Well, thanks for helping him. I may not want to do it, but I do want him to get better. I worry about him."

Jordan took a deep breath and sighed. "I think you should know that addicts are liars and manipulators by necessity, so they can cover up how much they're using, and Mike is no different. I say repairing trust takes time because it *should* take time. More than half of these people in here will relapse. So you can't enable him."

I quirked an eyebrow at him. "Do I look like I plan to?"

He chuckled. "No, I guess not. But remember what I said about the manipulation."

I nodded, remembering the multiple times Mike had talked me out of being mad at him. He had even talked me out of breaking up with him.

"You should say that to his mom," I said.

"I have," he replied, "but she seems to be having more difficulty accepting that her son has a problem."

I opened my mouth to say something to the effect that she'd better learn, but Mike and his mom walked out of the room then and I shifted nervously. I just wanted to leave, but I followed them back into the larger room with the circle of chairs. Jordan thanked us for coming again and told us we could take a tour of the facility or take a walk around the facility's grounds. But I didn't want to see Mike getting comfy here at rehab. I didn't want to see the art room or the music room or whatever they did here. I wanted to go home. But before I could say goodbye and make a hasty exit, Mike pulled me aside.

"Thank you for coming today," he said. "I know you didn't want to, and I know it wasn't easy. And I'm sorry for getting defensive. That's not how I expected today to go."

I crossed my arms across my chest, trying not to let him see how much I was bothered. I wanted to be cool and distant, impervious even, but it was getting harder to keep up that façade. I just wanted to escape.

"I know you want me to just get over this and forgive you," I said. "I know that you're hoping I still love you enough to get past what you did. But that's not happening, Mike. I'm sorry to disappoint you."

His jaw clenched, a reaction I was accustomed to seeing when he was drunk and I was pissed at him. It meant he was going to be stubborn and defensive. But he didn't say anything, and I was surprised by his restraint.

"I have to get going," I said. "I'm really glad you're here and that you're committed to it. I hope you keep feeling that way. Good luck."

And then I turned and walked past the desk and out into the sun. I took a deep breath of humid air and felt my shoulders drop about an inch. I was done.

ON SUNDAY, I met Raf outside while he was finishing a cigarette and the first thing he asked me was how the visit to rehab had gone.

I sighed as I sat down next to him. "It was a weird day," I said. "They tried to teach us how to talk to each other and make amends and repair trust, and I just kept thinking, 'It's too late.'"

He nodded. "Do you think Mike knows that?"

I shrugged moodily. "I don't know how many more times I can explain it to him."

"Did he seem like he was taking it seriously?"

"Maybe," I admitted. "But sometimes he also seemed like he was performing, and I could see this anger simmering that he was just barely keeping a lid on. I guess I could have been seeing what I wanted to see, though."

Raf tilted his head in recognition. "Maybe not," he said. "I think I know how he feels."

"You do?"

"I have such mixed feelings about rehab," he said. "I recognize that it helped me, but I resent that I needed it." Raf's eyes didn't meet mine. "And I hate feeling like this."

"Like what?" I asked.

"So ungrateful and angry. I hate it even more because it's something that I'm responsible for," he said. "I can't be mad at anyone. I did this to myself."

I turned to face him, but I didn't interrupt.

"I remember that experience of having my parents in that room, feeling like I let them down so many times and not being able to promise I wouldn't do it again."

Can you blame them? I wanted to say. My jaw tightened. I wasn't sure if it was better to not believe Mike when he said he was serious about being sober, or to have the truth from Raf and be disappointed by it. Both options sucked.

"Even now, six months sober, I still don't even know if I am an addict," Raf continued. "I just know that I don't want to feel the way I did six months ago. I don't want to stay in bed all day thinking about when I can get high and be oblivious again. To avoid my parents and the emptiness of the house. Of my life." He paused, taking a shaky breath. He didn't look at me. "But I also crave that escape. That numbness. I just want to get to a point where I feel better, but I don't see it happening anytime soon. And being numb in the meantime just seems like it'd be so much easier than being patient."

My anger faded. I wasn't sure what I felt now. Sad? Curious? Both? This was the first time he'd really talked to me about his sobriety beyond a few fragments here and there. I didn't want to spook him by asking questions. On the other hand, he was the one who was always forcing me to talk. It was time for him to take his own advice.

"Are you starting to feel better than you did before rehab?" I asked hopefully.

He shook his head. "Sometimes. It's such a cliché to say 'I have good days and bad days,' but it's a cliché for a reason. Some days, I feel so good I sing with the top down. And some days, all I want is to get stoned and sleep." He dropped his face into his hands, scrubbing at his eyes.

"That does sound kind of nice," I admitted.

"My therapist says this is all a normal way to feel." He shrugged, still not looking at me. "And he thinks I'm making progress because even though I want to use, I can see the reasons behind not using and I can recognize that they're more important."

"Well, that's good, right?"

"Yeah, but I've been in therapy half of my life and I'm still depressed. Won't it ever just get better?"

"I don't think it's the kind of thing that has a timeline, you know?" I said, but my heart hurt for him.

"Yeah," he said quietly. "I guess I know that." He raised his eyes to meet mine, and there was a hint of a smile behind them. "He also pointed out that if I hadn't gotten sober, I probably never would have reconnected with you," he said. "And I wouldn't give that up."

I felt myself blushing. "Really?" I asked. "You talk about me in therapy?"

Raf nodded. His cheeks were pink, too.

"What else do you talk to your therapist about?" I asked.

He seemed surprised that I wasn't asking what else he said about me, but I wasn't sure I wanted to know.

"We mostly talk about what a piece of shit I feel like most of the time," he said. "How I question everything I say and do, every interaction I have, every move I make. How sometimes I lie in bed at night dissecting every word I said and everything anyone said to me, looking for proof that I'm stupid or boring or selfish. And usually finding several examples."

My chest tightened. I slid my hand into his, and he lifted his eyes to meet mine.

"I know how you feel," I said.

"I know," he answered. "I'm not a special snowflake." He pulled his hand from mine and put a few inches of space between us. We'd managed to avoid talking about our kiss a few nights before, but it hung between us like a spider web. I could feel it on my skin.

"Do you want to watch the movie?" I finally said after a few long moments of silence.

He nodded, so I hopped up and led him to the basement. For me, it was a space that was a minefield of memories of Mike, but for Raf, it was just where we'd played as kids. Happy memories. I was hoping it would lighten the mood.

And he did break into a grin when he saw the walls lined with bookshelves and the stacks of long boxes on the floor, all stuffed full of comics. I had to pull him away from them or I'd have lost him for the rest of the afternoon.

We sat on the couch, and I was careful to leave some space between us, even though it was tempting to cuddle up and rest my head on his chest like I had with Mike. Instead, I lay with my head at the other end and put my feet near Raf's legs.

It was a long movie. It was also not a particularly uplifting movie. But I could tell that Raf liked it, despite the changes. He wouldn't let me pause when I had to pee. Twice. And he refused lunch, which was pretty stunning since I'd seen him put down three bowls of jambalaya and two pieces of pie in one night.

But the promise of a cigarette was enough to push him out the door. I grabbed a book off the shelf on our way out. "Take *The Sandman* with you. You'll like it just as much."

We padded through the dry summer grass, and it stabbed the sensitive arches of my bare feet. When I declined the cigarette Raf held out to me, he raised his eyebrows.

"Trying to quit?" he asked.

"Yeah, I guess so," I said. "It's just . . . it's kind of a gross habit, you know?"

"Oh, I know," he said. He coughed, as if to demonstrate. "And I was actually pretty surprised the first time I saw you out here. You don't seem like a smoker."

I tried not to be offended, but I felt like he was saying he didn't think I was cool. Maybe it was the discrepancy in how we dressed. I was barefoot, wearing cutoffs and a T-shirt that read CLONE CLUB. Raf was wearing straight jeans, a fitted T-shirt, and canvas sneakers. He looked like he'd actually put a little effort into his outfit. I was feeling proud of myself for at least putting on makeup.

"Are you ever going to quit?" I asked.

"I want to, but Cajun keeps saying you shouldn't try to quit everything at once. It leads to backslides."

I snorted. "That sounds like an excuse no one would argue with. I mean, sure I'd rather an alcoholic quit drinking instead of smoking, if they could only manage one, but Cajun is a smoker, too. I don't think you can trust him to give you advice."

Raf smirked. "Yeah, I've considered that. But I'll probably smoke less if you're going to quit, at least."

"Why? I barely smoke with you."

He looked at me sheepishly. "Yeah, but I spend a lot of time out here, hoping you'll come outside."

"Wait, seriously? Well, now I feel bad..."

He nudged my shoulder with his, smiling that lopsided, mischievous grin. "You should."

I suddenly wanted to kiss him again, not caring whether he tasted of cigarettes or not, and even though I leaned into him, I knew I wouldn't. Raf seemed to know what I was thinking, and he stood, putting even more distance between us.

"So what did you really think of *Watchmen*?" I said. "The casting was pretty spot-on, right?"

He nodded. "Perfect. I was bummed they left out the comic-within-a-comic, but I get why. And I really loved the original ending—it's just so campy. But a solid adaptation. I give it a B."

I grinned, happy with his assessment, since it lined up nicely with my own.

"The book is always better," I said, and he nodded. "So, what are you doing now?" I didn't want him to leave. Because I didn't want to go visit Audrey, and Cassidy was working. I hadn't seen any of my other friends all summer, and I was perfectly happy to make that last for the next few weeks until school started up again. But I also didn't want to be alone.

"I should go get ready for work," he said. "I'll see you later."

"Yes, you will," I said.

A Year and a Half Ago

The basement of Mike's house was neutral territory for me and Ryan. We both owned it equally. Even though he had spent more time down there, I had sex with Mike there. So, like I said, equal footing. But when they played video games, I was the very obvious third wheel. That was about 70 percent of the time they were together.

I usually didn't let it bother me. I could easily entertain myself because Mike's comic collection was also housed in the basement. I didn't complain often.

But one time when I did, a year into Mike's and my relationship, Ryan tossed the controller to me as if he'd been waiting for it. I wasn't sure if it was frustration, fear, or generosity that made him do it, but I tried to give it back either way. Ryan wouldn't take it.

"Give it a shot," he said, even though Mike groaned. Ryan hit him in the chest. "Dude, give your girlfriend a chance. Knowing her, she'll probably kick both of our asses."

I didn't ask Ryan what he meant by that; I was too busy figuring out which character I was going to be. I decided I liked the female warrior with red skin and snakes for hair, à la Medusa.

"You play with her then," Mike said, handing Ryan his controller. "I've already had my ass kicked by her plenty."

"His fragile ego can't take the defeat," I said as I chose my weapon. "We decided a while back that it was best not to play each other."

"If you want to get your ass handed to you, go for it," Mike grumbled. "Let her make you look like an idiot for once."

"I don't make you look like an idiot," I said. "You do that all on your own."

He climbed over the back of the couch and headed up the stairs with a scowl on his face.

"I love you!" I called after him, feeling guilty. "And also, bring me a Diet Coke!"

Ryan shook his head at me. "You guys are weird."

I smiled. "Don't worry, Ry. Someday you'll find a girl to be weird with, too."

"I hope we're nicer to each other than you guys are." He sighed softly, and I realized he was probably lonelier than I knew.

"Listen, I'm gonna kick your ass here," I said, "and then I'm going to go home and leave you and Mike to do whatever you guys had planned before I barged in."

Ryan tried to protest, but I waved him off. "No, it's for the best," I said. "Because clearly I'm just embarrassing you." I swiftly pulled his character's digital spleen from his gut. "It's definitely for the best."

CHAPTER FIFTEEN

After a few weeks at The Flakey Pastry, I finally felt like I was getting the hang of making espresso drinks. I could steam milk while brewing shots, making several drinks at a time, and I had a couple of customers who claimed they now liked my shots of espresso better than Will's. I tried not to gloat.

So maybe it was karma (or maybe I was just getting too cocky) when I turned around too quickly and knocked the metal pitcher of steaming milk to the floor, burning my arm on the steam wand. And then my fingers, when I stupidly tried to push it away without a rag. My skin was red and blistered in seconds.

Will and Cassidy jumped into action. Cassidy took over making my drinks while Will took me into the break room to get cleaned up.

"This happens so often that most of the first aid kit is filled with burn cream," he said.

He sat me in a chair and started applying cream to my arm. I winced with pain.

"Do you just get used to getting burned?" I asked.

Will laughed. "I haven't felt my fingertips in a year."

"Oh, good, something to look forward to."

"Listen, Cassidy and I can probably close up on our own if you want to leave?" he said. "When do you work next?"

I shook my head. "I think I'm closing on Monday?"

Will squinted. "No, I don't think so. Cassidy and I work closing on Monday."

He reached back and grabbed the schedule off the desk behind him. We studied it together. He was right. I was working opening on Monday, and he and Cassidy were closing. In fact, they were working the same shifts all week.

"You and Cassidy recently started working together a lot," I said, trying to keep my voice casual.

Will nodded, his eyes on the bandage he was placing on my arm.

"And you make the schedule?"

Now he looked at me. "What are you getting at?"

"Why did you and Janine break up?"

He sat back, suddenly suspicious. "Because she was leaving for college. Why?"

"Not for another few weeks," I pointed out. "Why did you break up *now*?"

Will didn't answer.

"I know, it's none of my business, but if it's because of a certain blonde who, frankly, isn't that great of a barista, you don't have to be worried about asking her out."

Will's lips twitched into a smile. "Are you saying Cassidy likes me?"

I rolled my eyes. "Of course she does. Why haven't you just asked her out?"

He shook his head sadly. "I can't be her manager if I'm dating her. Not after Janine. Samir threatened to fire me after she quit."

"It was that bad?" I asked.

"She knew why I was breaking up with her. We couldn't work together afterward. And she wouldn't work with Cassidy, either. And there aren't enough employees to keep us all on different schedules."

"So why do you always schedule Cassidy for the worst shifts?"

"Like what?" he said defensively.

"Like closing almost every night. And Sunday opening shifts?" His cheeks flushed so red that I almost expected his glasses to fog. "Oh, it's deliberate!" I exclaimed.

"Yeah, well, she can't date someone else if she's here almost every night and has to work at six A.M. on Sundays, right?"

I shook my head in disbelief. "Wow. You really just said that out loud."

"I'm horrible, I know," he said sadly. "She should hate me."

"No, but you should stop trying to keep her locked away and just deal with the consequences of dating. Even if it means one of you has to quit." I flashed a sly smile. "Or you have to hide it from Samir."

He sighed, his shoulders slumping. "I know, I know. I'll talk to her."

"Just be careful with her, okay?" I said. "Cassidy is as tender as they come. But I am not. If you break her heart, I *will* kill you."

Will nodded, his expression solemn. "I promise," he said. "Now, why don't you leave early?"

I smiled, not sure if he was getting rid of me because I was being weird and overly protective or so he could be alone with Cassidy. Maybe both.

"Sure, boss," I said, heading out. "Good luck."

I pushed the door open and nearly hit Ryan in the back.

"Sorry, Ry!" I said, laughing. But my smile fell when he turned and I saw his face. "What's up?"

He gestured to a table nearby. His brown eyes were bloodshot, his forehead creased. For a second I worried that something had happened to Connie, his girlfriend. I sat down across from him.

"What's going on?" I asked.

"Mike came home from rehab yesterday," he said, slumping forward. "He called me this morning to invite me to a party."

My jaw dropped. "He's having a 'Welcome Home from Rehab' party?"

Ryan nodded and pounded his fist into his palm. "What the hell is wrong with him?"

"I don't suppose this is a dry party," I said, half to myself.

His lips twisted in disgust. "He asked me to use my brother's ID to get him some beer and a few bottles of liquor. He wants me to sneak it to him so his mom doesn't find out."

I wanted to punch something now, too. Not my palm, though. Mike's face. I couldn't believe he had spent so much energy convincing me that he was taking rehab seriously, and I was angry at myself for believing him. I curled my hands into fists under the table so Ryan wouldn't see.

"What did you say?" I asked carefully.

He leaned back in his chair and exhaled loudly. "I told him I shredded the ID after he almost killed himself driving drunk."

My jaw dropped. "You did?"

"Of course I did," he said. "If I hadn't brought the keg that night, Audrey and Mike wouldn't have been drinking."

My heart ached with sympathy. I knew how that guilt felt. "Come on, Ryan, you can't blame yourself for that."

"Too late." He rubbed his hands across his close-cropped hair. "Mike was actually pissed at me for shredding it."

I shook my head. "He's digging his own grave," I said. "And it's not your job to pull him out. It's certainly not mine. I learned that the hard way."

Ryan looked at me, his eyes pleading. "But what do you think I should do?"

I pulled from my memory of what I'd learned the week before at the rehab center. "By covering for him and giving into him, you're just enabling him. So just tell his mom what he asked you to do," I said. "And then stop hanging out with him."

"I can't do that," he said. "He's my best friend."

"But is he really?" I demanded. I didn't regret it. I wanted to know.

Ryan was quiet, considering. "I don't know," he said. Then he stood, clearly putting an end to our conversation. "Thanks for listening."

"Be good," I said. "And don't go to that party."

Ryan nodded, but I couldn't tell what he would do.

Not your problem, I reminded myself. And I left, feeling a little less burned, despite the blisters.

THE NEXT DAY, Mom and I sat in metal folding chairs against the wall in a room with rubber floors. Dad had to work and was missing the spectacle that was Audrey's third physical therapy appointment. Audrey was taking small, halting, but confident steps with the support of a railing and two physical therapists. The spectacle was Mom, who had her hands clasped in front of her mouth anxiously, with her elbows on her knees so that she was hunched and looked even smaller than normal. She gasped every time Audrey faltered.

Mom was pulled together, as usual, in a freshly laundered

and pressed outfit with her hair pulled back. But there were more gray hairs peeking through her dye job than before the accident. She was thinner, too; I could see her collarbones protruding beneath her twinset.

Meanwhile, Audrey, who had also lost a dangerous amount of weight, was sweating under the S.T.A.R. Laboratories sweatshirt I'd loaned her for good luck. But even without the sheen of exertion, her face showed how hard she was working. The doctors had warned her that her muscles had weakened while she was bedridden and that it would take time to regain her strength. They cautioned against doing too much too quickly. But Audrey would push herself anyway. She couldn't help it.

Audrey stumbled on a step and Mom gasped quietly beside me. Her fingers twitched as she held them against her lips, as though she were just barely holding in the concerned words she was bursting with. I squeezed her knee in support as Audrey's therapist caught her under the arm that wasn't in a sling. But Audrey shook it off as she sat down to rest for a minute. She drank some water slowly and then smiled over at us. Her grin was less lopsided now.

When Audrey started back the other direction, she was noticeably weaker. Her legs shook when she supported her weight on her own, and her steps grew less sure. Mom was practically vibrating with nerves. She would have done all this work for Audrey if she could.

I finally let her go to Audrey when her therapist ended the session. I could tell that he was congratulating her on her good work, even though I couldn't hear the words. He had the same look that all her past coaches and dance teachers had had when they looked at her.

But even though Audrey was smiling, I could see that it

was forced. She was barely holding it together, and her fingers were twitching to slap Mom's hands away from pulling her hair back into a sweaty ponytail. When she looked at me, I rolled my eyes in Mom's direction. Her plaster smile faltered and a small, real one slipped through.

I walked to them and pulled one of Mom's arms around my waist. I tried not to compare our weight, knowing I had probably gained as much as she had lost. I was an emotional eater; the proof of how stressful the last six weeks had been was sitting on my stomach. And thighs.

"You tired, Audy?" I asked. "You worked hard."

She nodded. "Can we go back to my room?"

While Mom talked to Audrey's physical therapist, I bent down to help her into her wheelchair. "I'll go out to The Cheesecake Factory while Mom feeds you dinner tonight," I said. "I'll bring you back a slice."

When Audrey laughed, Mom's head snapped back to look at us. Her eyes brightened when she saw Audrey's smile. I wished I could convince her to come with me. She could have used a slice of cheesecake, too, but Audrey needed the break from her even more.

AS MOM AND I pulled around the corner onto our street, Raf drove past. He waved, and we waved back, but I could tell it was half-hearted on both Mom's and his part.

I headed for my room when I got inside. Mom followed me upstairs.

"Do you have a minute, Harley?" she asked. She was already walking into my room, sitting next to me on the bed. It wasn't really a question.

I held in the sigh that was my innate response and paused my music.

Recognizing that as an invitation, Mom continued: "I think this conversation is long overdue." A knot of dread took up residence in my stomach. "I'm concerned about the people, the influences, in your life right now. And the choices you're making."

She held up a hand to stave off my interruption, as if she could sense that my mouth was about to open. "What happened to your sister is a wake-up call for your father and me, and we think we've been too lax with the rules in this house. We never should have let you go to the party at Cassidy's house without talking to her parents and making sure they were home."

They were pretty strict, as far as I was concerned, but she wasn't wrong that she should have checked. I'd been banking on the fact that she wouldn't because she knew Cassidy so well.

"But you should have told us," she said. "And you never should have brought your sister."

I wanted to argue that Audrey could have told her about the lack of chaperones, too, but I wanted to focus on who she thought I was seeing who was a bad influence. Aside from Cassidy and Ryan, I had barely even spoken to my friends. Or Mike's friends.

"But I broke up with Mike," I said. "I haven't even seen him since he got back from rehab."

She pursed her lips. "I'm not talking about Mike."

And finally I realized who she meant.

"You've been talking to Mrs. Juarez, haven't you?" I said. I could feel the scowl on my face.

"Yes," she said. "And she told me that you and Rafael have been spending a lot more time together than I realized. Apparently, *he* actually talks to his mother."

I knew that, but it didn't make it any less cute that he had told his mom about me. I tried not to smile, though. Mom was clearly not in the mood.

"She told me about Rafael's rehab and how he had to be cut off from his friends from his old life," she continued.

Raf had told me about his friends and they sounded a lot like my friends. We weren't good kids, but we weren't bad either. We threw parties; we snuck out of our houses; we drank and smoked the occasional cigarette, sometimes weed. But we also made curfew, made Honor Roll, made breakfast for our moms on Mother's Day.

"And you want me to do the same," I said.

She seemed to consider her next words carefully. "I want you to cut yourself off from anyone who is a bad influence on you. That's all."

I felt myself about to tip over the edge into fury. I tried to reel myself back in. "That's *all*?" I said. I could hear the tiny tremor in my voice. "What you're really asking me to do is cut ties with Raf, who, as you just pointed out, just lost all of the friends he's ever had."

"Rafael is an alcoholic and a drug addict, Harley," Mom said, her voice now teeming with anger. "I don't see how he's good for you. Especially not now, with all you went through with Mike. After all *we've* been through. I have to be sure you're making the right choices here."

And I just snapped like a brittle twig under a heavy boot. I could almost hear it.

"Mom, Raf is trying to get his life together!" I yelled. "Can you at least give him a chance to do that before you start deciding what kind of person he is? At least he's not cheating on me with my sister like my last boyfriend did!"

Mom looked like I had slapped her. And I guess I sort of had. I'd slapped her with the news that her baby daughter wasn't perfect. And that I'd failed to protect her.

"What are you talking about?" she whispered.

But my throat had closed up, burning with the tears that I was trying not to cry. I shook my head instead.

"Oh, baby duck, come here," Mom said, gathering me into her arms. We were the same height, but I had at least forty pounds on her. And yet she pulled me close and held me, rocking me like I was in her lap.

"I'm so sorry that happened," she whispered, even though I could hear her rage. "You didn't deserve that."

I wept loudly and wetly against her shoulder, ruining her silk blouse. She didn't stop me. I cried for Audrey and what she'd done to me. I cried for what I'd done to her. Because after years of feeling less important than nearly anything else in my life, Audrey had done something she knew would get my attention. And it ended up hurting her so much worse than it would ever hurt me.

When my breathing grew steadier and my tears had slowed, Mom wiped my cheeks and looked me in the eye.

"What happened?" she asked. I could tell that she was trying really hard to keep it together, and I had to give her a lot of credit for staying so calm.

So I told her. Everything. By the end, I was crying again. "I'm sorry," I said, sobbing. "I didn't want you to know. I didn't want you to think of Audrey like that."

Mom shook her head. "No, baby, no," she said. "You shouldn't have had to carry this alone for all this time."

"It's so humiliating," I said. "And I'm so *angry*."

"I'm angry, too. I just can't imagine what would have made your sister do that to you." Mom's nostrils flared as she took a deep breath. "But it doesn't change the way I think of Audrey. She made a mistake."

Anger rose in my chest again, but this time it felt good, or at least justified. "Seriously? You're not forgiving Raf for his mistakes, and you've clearly been blaming me for what happened to Audrey, but you can just *let it go* that Audrey made out with my boyfriend?"

Mom stiffened. She knew I was right. She nodded rigidly. "You make a good point," she said. "But I nearly lost one of my daughters already, and I can't stop worrying that the same thing will happen to you."

I took a deep breath before I spoke, to avoid saying something I would regret. "I *might* see where you're coming from," I said steadily. "But I need you to trust me."

Her lips pulled into a straight line, but she nodded. "I do trust you. And I'm sorry if you feel that I've been blaming you for what happened to your sister. I never liked Mike, and it doesn't shock me at all that this happened to him. I just wish that Audrey hadn't gotten caught up in his vortex of destruction."

A hot tear slid down my cheek. "But isn't that my fault?" I whispered. "That she ever even met him?"

"Don't be ridiculous," Mom said. "You can't blame yourself. But after what you've told me, I have to at least lay some of the blame on your sister." She sighed heavily. "Are you going to tell Audrey what she did?"

I slumped against her. "I don't know. I guess it's not really fair for me to tell her. If she doesn't have to live with this, if her memory never comes back, I feel like it would be selfish of me to burden her with this."

Mom suddenly burst into tears.

"God, Mom! Why are you crying?" I said, pulling away so I could look at her.

"You're just becoming such a grown-up," she said, sniffling.

"Oh, that," I said bitterly. "It turns out it's not as fun as it seems."

She laughed and wiped her eyes. "Yeah, I recommend making a quick U-turn while you still can."

I smiled and said, "Don't push it, woman. I'm growing up, like it or not."

"Don't remind me," she groaned. "We were supposed to do a college tour this summer. I promise, we'll do it this fall, when Audrey is settled at home."

"It's okay," I said. And it was. I hadn't even thought about it. Not lately. "I think I'll probably stay closer to home than I'd originally planned anyway."

Mom pulled me in for a final hug. "Thank you, baby duck. You're a good daughter."

"I know. But, um, Mom?" I said. "Do you think you could ask Aunt Tilly for a recommendation of a therapist for me?"

She pushed back to look at me, nodding. "Of course," she said simply. She surprised me again by not asking questions or asking if I wanted her to go with me. I guess we were both changing.

THAT NIGHT, I woke up to a voice calling my name outside my window. My phone beeped, alerting me to a text. And then again. And again. I picked it up, squinting at the bright screen in the dark. I had seven texts from Raf.

Wake up, read the first.

Srsly, come hang out.

WKAE UP! WAKEPU!

IMOUTSDE

They continued like that, getting less and less coherent.

I stood and opened the curtain, dreading what I would see. Raf was swaying back and forth on the front lawn, his hands cupped around his mouth, about to yell again. I waved my arms at him and he grinned. He motioned for me to come outside, nearly toppling backward with the effort.

My stomach lurched. *Oh, God, no.* He was drunk. Raf had relapsed.

I opened the window. "Shhhh," I called down to him. "You're going to wake up the entire neighborhood. Stay there. I'm coming down."

Raf cheered loudly, and I shut the window to drown him out. I sighed as I pulled on the clothes I'd worn that day and slipped my feet into flip-flops. I checked my hair in the mirror on my way out and decided to pull it into a ponytail.

He was sitting slumped on the front steps when I got downstairs, so my first task was to get him back into his own house without waking up either of our parents. I sat down next to him on the stairs.

"Hey, Harley Quinn," he said. My mind suddenly flashed to Mike, and rage flared in my chest.

"Don't call me that," I snapped.

I draped Raf's long arm around my shoulders and nudged him to his feet. He was heavy and unwieldy as he took unsteady steps toward his house. The basement door was unlocked and I pushed him inside in front of me. He tumbled to the floor. I had to step over him, pushing his legs out of the way to close the door.

I pulled him up off the floor and into his bedroom. There was torn paper all over the carpet, and as I deposited him heavily onto his bed, I glanced around and noticed that the Wall of Fame was torn down. Shredded, actually.

I sat down next to Raf on his bed, and he looked up at me with bloodshot eyes.

"You came outside," he said. "I didn't think you were gonna."

"What's going on, Raf?" I asked as gently as I could. "What made you drink tonight?"

"I'm lonely," he whispered. "I don't have any friends left. I tried to call my best friend tonight and he blew me off. I'm boring now."

I wanted to argue with him, but I couldn't. I didn't want him to hang out with his old friends anyway. And now I wasn't even sure *we* could hang out. Rage was simmering in my veins, but my heart ached for him. I understood loneliness.

Audrey had always been there, in the bedroom next to me, tapping secret messages on the wall that were unintelligible because we never agreed on a code. She'd been there every morning chattering over cereal while I mourned the fact that I had to be awake. She was the lightness in the room when things were tense, always a positive force for the family. We'd been unraveling without her.

But at least now I understood the shredded Wall of Fame.

"I'm not Cheech anymore," he mumbled sleepily.

I didn't know how to respond. But I didn't have to. He wasn't done.

Raf shook his head, his face pinched. "I'm mad at you, too, you know. And I don't like it."

It was going to be nearly impossible to have a coherent conversation with him. I needed to try, though. "Why are you mad at *me*?" I asked.

"Because!" he slurred, pointing an accusing finger in my general direction before letting his arm flop back to the bed.

"You kiss me and then you tell me you can't kiss me anymore. And then you kiss me again and then you act like nothing happened!"

"Well, that's an oversimplification," I said. "You're the one who kissed me the first time . . ."

But Raf wasn't listening. He was already talking over me. "I tried to be your friend," he said. His raspy voice caught. "But being around you and not being able to touch you, not being able to kiss you, it hurts. I can feel it in my chest." He pounded heavily on his chest with one fist.

I didn't know what to say. He wasn't wrong that I'd been confusing him. I'd been confusing myself. I reached out to push his hair off his forehead, and he caught my hand, pulling it to his cheek.

But before I could say anything, his eyes closed.

"Raf?"

Nothing. He'd passed out. Maybe that was for the best. I took a deep breath and swallowed back my anger. His chest began to rise and fall, his breathing loud and labored. I covered him with a blanket and removed his shoes. Then I took the half-empty bottle of vodka I found under his bed and set it by the door. I'd take it with me when I left. Even though I knew it was wrong, I didn't want his parents to know about this. I didn't want him to be sent back to rehab. Or to undo all the trust he had regained with them. Like he just had with me.

Raf had been my shelter these last few weeks. He pushed me to be stronger. His honesty had made *me* honest. I'd trusted him and he'd betrayed that trust. I didn't want to deal with him if he was going to be drinking again. I didn't have the patience for it anymore. Not after Mike.

Before I left, I looked for a trash can in case Raf threw up. I located one under his desk and moved to pick it up, but the sketchbook on his desk caught my eye. It was open to a page that was dated on the first night I'd seen him again—the night after Audrey's accident.

In the sketch, I was sitting on the garden wall, my face in profile as I stared into the distance. My eyes were unfocused. A cigarette burned, forgotten, between my fingers. Raf drew me as I was, with round curves, folds in my stomach, and chubby thighs—but through his eyes I was beautiful. Because those features were just small parts of the picture. My face, which undoubtedly was blotchy from crying that night, was clear and angled. Even my messy bun was more of a purposeful updo, with soft tendrils that framed my face. The shirt that I'd been wearing that I'd worried was too tight instead hugged my curves purposefully and exposed a little cleavage. Or at least, that's how Raf had drawn it.

My breath caught in my throat. Raf had drawn this weeks ago and had brought it out tonight. While he'd gotten drunk. Because he was mad at me. Because I'd broken his heart.

I left the drawing on his desk, set his trash can on the floor next to him, and ran from the basement with the bottle in my hand.

THE NEXT MORNING, I waited for Raf to text me. I checked the backyard a few times to see if he was out there smoking, but he wasn't. It was almost noon when I finally caved and sent him a message asking if he was okay. It was possible, I realized, that he didn't even remember what he had done.

I'm okay, he wrote back a few minutes later. Sorry about last night.

So he did remember. The anger that had burned in my veins last night now froze to ice.

Can we talk? I asked. I didn't want to do this over a text message.

He didn't respond for a full fifteen minutes while I stared at my phone like it was an egg getting ready to hatch. But I could have waited longer to hear what he said.

No, he wrote. And then a minute later: I think I need to not see you for a while. I need to just focus on my recovery. I guess that's pretty obvious after last night.

I was almost relieved that he couldn't see me, because I didn't know how to react. I'd been trying not to ruin our friendship with romance, and then he screwed it up by getting drunk. So now I didn't get to have the friendship. Plus, I never even got to enjoy the physical part.

My throat burned, and my hands were trembling. I wanted to call him or storm over to his house, but that would be directly defying what he had just asked of me.

With shaking fingers, I wrote just two letters: OK. And I hated myself when I hit send. Because I should have stood up to him. I should have told him how angry I was. How betrayed I felt by his drinking. And how wrong it felt that he'd come to me, of all people, when he knew what I'd been through with Mike. And with Audrey.

I had relied on him so much for the last few weeks. More than I had realized. And now that trust was shattered, and I didn't think we could put it back together. Apparently, he didn't want to, anyway.

Three Years Ago

The highway streaked by outside the car as I stared at my reflection in the window. There wasn't much to see outside anyway; everything was dark beyond the dim light the lampposts cast on the shoulder. Mom and Dad had been singing along to one of the four playlists Dad had on his phone. We'd basically been listening to the same fifty songs for the last ten years.

Audrey was watching a TV show on Dad's iPad, and Mom was using hers. My phone wasn't getting enough service to do anything that required data, and Cassidy wasn't responding to my text messages.

I couldn't stand the sound of Mom's and Dad's slightly off-key voices for one minute longer.

I poked Audrey in the side and she pulled out one earbud.

"What?" she said.

"Can I watch that with you?"

She frowned. "No," she said. Whined, really. "I don't want to listen with one ear. Mom and Dad are singing too loud. Read a book or something. Isn't that, like, your favorite thing to do?"

"It's dark, genius," I spat back. "Just let me watch with you."

She stuck the earbud back in her ear. "No."

So I ripped the tablet from her fingers, yanking her earbuds out in the process. It didn't hurt, but she wailed like a baby anyway.

"Goddammit!" Dad yelled from the driver's seat. "Stop fighting! You're sisters; you should try harder to get along. I'm tired of this shit."

"Henry," Mom said, admonishing him. For the cursing, not for yelling at us.

It didn't take much to set Dad off in those days. We were high-energy kids—or Audrey was, anyway—and he'd been driving for almost six hours. I would have yelled at us, too. But his solution was to take the iPad from both of us, leaving us in the dark back seat seething as we tried to ignore each other.

When he and Mom started singing again, though, I couldn't help glancing at Audrey. There was a point in one song where Dad always tried to hit the high note. Always. And he sounded like Beaker from The Muppets. *We hadn't ever made it through that song without at least a shared eye roll. So when it came on, I had to look at her. And she had to look at me. And we had to laugh.*

We didn't get the iPad back after we stopped fighting, but Audrey and I eventually started singing along with Mom and Dad. Not too loudly, though. We couldn't let them know we were enjoying it. But we made it to Charleston a couple of hours later without fighting again, at least.

CHAPTER SIXTEEN

The therapist's office was in a residential neighborhood, in a two-story Tudor home with a separate entrance around the side. I couldn't help thinking how nice it must be to have your commute consist of a walk down some stairs and I added it to my short list of career goals.

The inside was as quaint as the outside. There was a tiny reception area, without a receptionist. Just a light switch that I flicked on to say I'd arrived. Dr. Talia opened the door almost immediately, as if she had been waiting for me. She ushered me into her office and pointed at a chair to sit in.

She was young, maybe midthirties, but with enough small worry lines and stray gray hairs to make me believe she'd been doing this a while. She gave me a soft smile and picked up a legal pad and a pen.

"So, Harley, what brings you to me today?" she asked.

I physically slumped at the weight of what I'd have to tell her. There was so much, I wasn't sure where to begin. And I wasn't exactly excited about discussing all my issues. But Raf was right: I'd been avoiding talking for too long.

"I guess the biggest reason is my sister," I said. "She's

recovering from a traumatic brain injury because my boyfriend drove drunk and got into a car accident. And Audrey was in the car with him." I shrugged uncomfortably. "So there's that."

Dr. Talia nodded while she jotted notes and then glanced up at me. "That's quite a lot to deal with," she said.

"You could say that." I shifted in my chair. "But that night of the accident, they were both drinking. And my boyfriend cheated on me with her."

"With your sister?" Dr. Talia said. Her dark eyebrows were raised in surprise.

"Yep, my little sister."

"That must have really hurt," she said.

I snorted. "Yeah, to put it mildly."

She was quiet for a minute, waiting for me to continue.

"I think I've forgiven Audrey," I said. "She doesn't even remember doing it."

Dr. Talia's eyebrows raised again. "Interesting."

"But a lot of guilt has built up. And I can't seem to stop being mad at Mike. He's the one who cheated on me, and he's the one who drove drunk, but I can't stop feeling like I have to shoulder some of the blame. If I had just broken up with him, or if I had taken Audrey home with me even though I was mad, she would be fine."

My throat ached with the building tears.

"It sounds like you're feeling pulled in a lot of different directions, emotionally speaking," Dr. Talia said.

I nodded, but all of that wasn't what was really bugging me right at that moment.

"But, um, there's something else," I said.

"More than all that?" she asked.

"Yeah," I said, slowly. "See, I've been hanging out with

my next-door neighbor, Rafael, a lot lately. We were friends as kids, but we only recently reconnected."

"Okay," she said, drawing the word out so it sounded like a question.

"He's a recovering addict or alcoholic, or maybe both," I said. "And then last night, he got drunk after six months of sobriety."

"How did that make you feel?" she asked.

"I feel betrayed. I can't believe he would drink again after seeing what Audrey has been through. What *I've* been through," I added, my voice quieter.

"That's understandable," she said.

I sighed. "I know it's not my fault or anything. But he was, like, proof that people can change. That things can get better. And now . . ." I paused. "I don't know what happens now."

Dr. Talia nodded and jotted more notes, as if realizing something about me. "You can't control what other people do, Harley. That's something you should learn as early as possible."

"No, I know that," I said. "But Raf blamed me. For being ambivalent about what I want, I guess. About whether I want to date him or not."

"He's feeling confused because you're confused," she said.

I nodded. "I do really like him," I continued. "But how can I date an alcoholic when my boyfriend's drinking is the reason my sister is lying in a hospital bed?"

She spread her hands on her desk. "I can't answer that question for you," she said.

"I feel like an idiot for trusting him," I said, "and for believing that he wouldn't drink again."

"So you're angry?"

I thought about that for a few seconds. "Yes. I understand

why he would want to drink. I get why he's lonely and why he's sad. But yeah. I'm pissed."

"And have you told him that?"

I shook my head. "No. I have this tendency to compartmentalize things. Like, with Raf, I was more concerned with making sure he was safely home and that he didn't get in trouble. Then once I knew he was safe, I got mad, but I didn't tell him I was." I didn't want to admit the next part, but I figured therapy was about figuring out your patterns and I just had a lightbulb moment. "I used to do that with Mike, too. I'd be so pissed at him for drinking or doing something stupid, but I'd just fume about it internally and rarely would actually say anything to him. Not until it built up, and then it would seem like I was overreacting because my anger wasn't about one situation; it was about all of them."

My chest hurt with the realization. This wasn't me. Or not the me I thought I was. Or wanted to be.

"Why are you getting upset?" Dr. Talia asked.

I brought my fingers to my cheeks, brushing away the tears. "Because I don't like that about myself."

She nodded. "So do you think maybe you can change that? Start standing up for yourself?"

I twisted my lips to one side while I considered that. "I think so, yes. I stood up to Mike finally, but only after he cheated on me, almost killing Audrey in the process." I took a shaky breath in. "I used to be way more confident. Raf reminds me of that all the time."

"Interesting," she said again. "We like to say that people don't change, but that's not true; they do. They grow up and they mature, their interests change, and they learn. Rafael has a lot more growing to do at this age and so do you. You're still figuring out who you are and how to handle yourself in tough situations. So take it a little easier on both him and on yourself, okay?"

I nodded as relief and guilt collided.

Dr. Talia crossed her legs and leaned toward me. "Rafael may be an addict, and he may relapse again, but the real test will be to see what he does with it. He may have changed in the short-term, but the proof will be if he can go back to the program, stick with it, work the twelve steps, and make long-term changes."

I saw now why Raf liked going to therapy. It gave a person permission to feel exactly the way they were feeling. There was nothing wrong with having doubts about how I'd handled things with Raf and Mike and Audrey, nothing wrong about the fear that I might want to change who I was but didn't know how, nothing wrong with wanting to believe Raf could change, too.

"What is it that you want to change about yourself?" Dr. Talia asked.

Right, I thought. *This is where it gets difficult.* I wasn't even sure where to begin.

"I guess . . . I don't even know. I just want to be more . . . me. I want to stand up for myself and say what I'm feeling when I'm feeling it."

Dr. Talia nodded. "Sometimes it's hard to identify those feelings in the moment, though. So I have an exercise I want you to try."

Oh, good, homework. I was good at homework.

"I want you to think back on situations where you had strong feelings, good or bad, and write down those memories. Identify what you felt then and what you might realize now. I think you'll see that it's not always easy to react to a situation while you're in it. Sometimes sisters are mean to each other for no reason. Sometimes things take time to sink in. Sometimes we have to build up the courage to do what's right or stand up for ourselves."

I nodded. Raf would be happy to know that I'd be writing. Except . . . he didn't want to talk to me.

I bit my lip to keep from crying, but Dr. Talia wasn't buying it and pushed a tissue box across her desk to me.

"We've got a lot to unpack here," she said. "Are you free to come back next week at the same time?"

I was, of course, and I was willing, but I wasn't exactly looking forward to it. I knew I had issues, but hearing it, crying about it, talking about all the things I'd been bottling up—it took a lot out of me. I was exhausted as I left the cozy comfort of Dr. Talia's office. And I spent the rest of the afternoon in bed.

MOM AND I were visiting Audrey the next day to pick up her dirty laundry and deliver clean clothes. I'd snuck in some junk food, which wasn't prohibited by the rehab center, but by Mom. She spent about an hour tidying up around the room, stacking books and putting clothes away. She didn't seem to know what to do with herself now that Audrey was improving and didn't need her as much.

Finally, she ran out of pretend projects. Audrey and I had barely glanced up from the movie we were watching while she shuffled around, so Mom made the right call when she physically shut it off in order to talk to us.

"I have to go do some work. Your dad will be by before dinner," she said. "Harley, do you plan to leave soon, too?"

I shook my head. "No, if it's okay with Audrey, I'll stick around for a little while."

Audrey nodded, so Mom kissed us both and left.

"I have a confession," I said, pausing the movie. It was a superhero movie I had been begging her to watch, and though she was trying, she didn't seem as interested as I'd hoped she would be.

"What?" she said warily.

"I watched some of your favorite movies while you were in the coma." I named a few of the ones we'd watched "together" and Audrey's smile turned to a round O of surprise.

"You?" she said. "The girl who won't even watch *Love Actually* with me at Christmas?"

I rolled my eyes. "Half of that movie sucks," I said. "And I'm not watching the crappy parts just so I can get to the scene with 'All I Want for Christmas Is You.'"

She shook her head. "You're just so wrong," she said.

"My point is," I said, "that you were right. Some of them are really good. And I'm sorry I made fun of you for watching them."

She barked a sharp laugh and then insisted I tell her which ones I liked the most. I listed off a few of my favorites, and she made me tell her which scenes I liked.

"Is that why you decided to go out with Raf?" she asked after grilling me. She had a knowing smile. "Because you were inspired by all the love stories?"

"How did you know about Raf?" I said.

She looked guilty. "Mom," she said. "She told me you guys were 'spending time together.'"

I tried to hide the smile that crept onto my face, but she saw it and pointed at me with a knowing grin. "You like him," she said.

"I do," I said. "But we're not together."

"Why not?" she said.

I held in the sigh that I wanted to release and debated how much to tell her. I didn't want to burden her, but I also couldn't explain why his relapse hurt so much without telling her about Mike and his cheating.

"It's too soon," I said instead.

"You mean after Mike?" she said. I nodded. "Harley, can I ask you something?"

"Of course," I answered.

"Was it because of me?" she asked, her voice small. "You and Mike breaking up, I mean."

My heart beat loudly in my chest while I wondered if she had finally remembered what had really happened the night of the accident. Mom and Dad had been honest with her about the fact that she'd been in a car with Mike and that he was drunk. The doctors said that it was best to tell her as much as we thought she could handle, in case it triggered memories. It hadn't—Audrey still couldn't remember any of the events of that night—but at least if she did ever remember what she did, maybe it wouldn't be as much of a shock.

But then she added, "Did you break up because of the accident?"

"No," I said. "We broke up because of *him*. He was an asshole. And I was planning to dump him for a while before he ever got into that accident. And he probably knew that when he got drunk that night."

"Right," Audrey said. "I forgot." She shook her head slowly, sadness engulfing her like a fog. "I've lost a whole year. And I'm losing more every day that I'm in here." She hit the railing on her bed with a clenched fist.

I moved to sit on her bed, facing her. "I know this sucks. So much," I said. "But you will work to get your life back. You're too stubborn not to."

Audrey nodded. She was silent, but I could tell she was feeling a little better. She reached her arms out and I fell into them, hugging her until I felt like I might break her ribs.

"You're the stubborn one," she said finally.

I laughed as I released her. Just then, there was a knock on the door and Neema walked in. She saw Audrey's tears and turned on me.

"What's going on?" she said. She leaned in to give Audrey a hug and whispered something to her. Audrey shook her head, but Neema clearly didn't believe her.

"I think I'm going to go," I said. "You guys hang out. Finish the movie if you want."

Audrey protested, but I waved her off.

"It's fine. I've had you to myself all day. Make some new memories with Neema."

Audrey reached for a bag of M&M's. "Take these," she said. "It may be good to get angry, like you said, but even after being in a coma, I still remember that chocolate makes everything seem better."

I laughed and kissed her goodbye.

I nodded at Neema. She looked away.

"Okay then," I said. "Be that way."

But outside, as I reached my car, Neema was suddenly behind me. Her face was streaked with tears. She was breathing rapidly, as if her grief was so heavy that it was fighting for space with air inside her lungs. "Neema? What is it? What's wrong? Is Audrey okay?"

She nodded, swallowing hard. "It's not Mike's fault, what happened between him and Audrey," she blurted out. "It's mine."

I ignored the leaden feeling in my gut. "What are you talking about?"

Fresh tears streamed down Neema's face. "I can't believe she did that to me," she choked out. "I thought her crush on him was just because he was your boyfriend and she always wanted everything you have."

I shook my head, bewildered. "What does this have to do with you?"

Neema was trembling; she wouldn't make eye contact. "I told Audrey that night that I loved her. Like, wanted to be with her. And instead of dealing with it, instead of telling me she didn't feel the same way, she made out with *your* boyfriend."

I reeled back. I felt as if I'd been slapped. Of all the possible confessions, this was the last I expected to hear.

"She was supposed to be with *me*," Neema said quietly. "I thought she was finally falling for me. And then she hooked up with him instead."

"I didn't realize," I said lamely.

"That I'm gay?" She rubbed her eyes and finally met my gaze. "Yeah, well, I am. And your sister never made me feel weird about it. But now she can't remember shit because your asshole boyfriend almost got her killed."

"I'm really sorry, Neema," I said. "I know you must feel betrayed. I do, too."

She bit her lip. It was clear she was fighting back anger and sadness. "I just wanted to say that I was sorry, for not telling you sooner," she said. "And for leaving that night without doing anything to stop Audrey." Her eyes filled with tears again. "I saw her drinking with him and then I saw them go upstairs and I followed . . . I saw her kiss him and I just lost it. I had to get out of there."

"I'm sorry," I repeated. "I know how much it hurts, believe me. But Audrey loves you—maybe not in the way you want her to, but she does love you. And I appreciate that you still want to be her friend. She needs you."

Neema nodded. She drew a shaky breath and wiped the tears from her cheeks. "I know," she said. "I'm not going anywhere. At least I know the truth about how she feels. And if she never remembers, the only way it can ruin our friendship is if *I* let it."

Right. My mind went to Raf, as usual.

"I just wanted you to know that it wasn't Mike who initiated what happened between him and Audrey," Neema added. "It was Audrey. And it was because of me."

It dawned on me, finally, what she was really telling me. I'd been angry at Mike for so long, and I had forgiven Audrey. But now . . .

"I'm not saying you should forgive Mike," Neema clarified. Her voice was even. She pushed her thick hair off her shoulders while she spoke. She seemed lighter already, now that this secret was off her chest. "But I can tell how much it's been weighing on you. You look more exhausted every time I see you. I just thought you should know the truth."

I tried to nod. My head felt like it was full of cotton.

She smiled grimly and shrugged. "Anyway, thanks for listening. And I'm sorry again for . . . well, for everything."

"Me too," I said quietly as she walked away.

I LAY IN bed that evening thinking of Neema. It was hard enough being in love with someone you could never have. Audrey's betrayal must have made it hurt so much more. But Neema was strong. She'd get through it. She already had the ability to say how she felt, out loud, to the person she loved. That night, she hadn't let the fear of what Audrey might say or how she might react stop her. And she didn't run away from the possibility of being hurt—whether it was now or in the future.

I should have told Raf how I felt. But I didn't have the same strength that Neema did.

At least Mike hadn't been the one who initiated their kiss. On the other hand, he hadn't told me about Audrey pursuing him. I thought he would have at least tried to use that to get me to forgive him . . .

I was exhausted from running laps in my mind. I didn't want to be alone, and I couldn't stop thinking about Raf, and I couldn't call him. This was an emergency. Which meant I knew exactly who to call.

It was time for Cassidy.

Five Years Ago

We sat under an umbrella at a table near the snack bar, sitting next to each other so we could both be in the shade. My skin was dry from the chlorine, and my bathing suit was damp because I wouldn't walk around without my towel covering me. The shouts of other kids in the pool rang in my ears.

Cassidy gave me one of her Reese's Cups, cold from the snack bar freezer, and I poured half of my Coke into a cup for her.

"Who was working at the snack bar?" I asked. I had been saving our seats while she got the snacks, and now I craned my neck to see the snack bar behind her. Because I knew who was working. We both did.

Cassidy and I had spent the majority of the summer in these seats watching the same guy: Matthew Sanders. He wasn't a lifeguard, not chiseled and tan from days in the sun. He was more attainable. Tall, thin, with glasses. When there wasn't a line, he'd read behind the counter. And not summer reading books for school. Actual novels by authors I'd never heard of.

"He was there," she said.

"How did he look?"

"So hot." She grinned. "Go and get another cup or some napkins," she said. "Tell him I said hi."

I rolled my eyes, but only to hide my nerves as I stood and walked toward the snack bar. The condiment station was right next to the counter and I timed my arrival at the moment that he returned to the register with a customer's soda.

"Can I have a cup, please?" I said, hating the way my voice sounded high and squeaky.

Matt smiled, said, "Sure," and handed me a cup. I grabbed a stack of napkins, spun around, and walked as quickly as possible back to the table. I collapsed into a pile of giggles next to Cassidy, and she prodded me until I told her what had happened.

"He smiled at me!" I squealed, and her mouth dropped open jealously.

Neither of us had ever said more to him than giving our orders. But if we had, if he had ever liked either one of us, we would have had no idea what to do. Aside from my kiss with Raf years before, neither of us had any experience with boys.

But our crush on Matt brought us closer. We spent all day together, all summer, at a time when we were quickly becoming different people. When she was growing tired of hearing me talk about comics, and I was growing tired of hearing about her friends on the yearbook. We should have been growing apart, but Cassidy and I clung to each other, refusing to drift apart, like sleeping otters.

And we made it through high school without losing sight of each other. It was practically a miracle.

CHAPTER SEVENTEEN

I texted Cassidy in the middle of the night, asking her to come by before her opening shift. She let herself into the house using the hide-a-key we kept on the porch and walked upstairs without waking anyone. I'd finally fallen asleep near dawn, so I only stirred when she slipped her shoes off and curled up next to me in bed, taking my hand under the comforter.

"What happened?" she asked softly.

My eyes were dry and cloudy from being awake late into the night. And now, they were blurry with tears, too.

"Neema told me something about that night of the accident," I said. I tried not to breathe on her since I hadn't brushed my teeth yet. My mouth tasted like I'd licked a dirty sandbox. "She told Audrey she loved her."

Cassidy sat up. "Wait, really?" she asked.

"Do you think Audrey initiated what happened between her and Mike as a way to make it clear that she wasn't interested in Neema?"

Cassidy shook her head slowly, sifting through the information. "It's possible," she said. "Would it be easier for you to forgive Audrey if that's what happened?"

I sighed. "I don't know. I thought I had forgiven her. But now . . ."

"I get it," she said. "It was one thing when *he* kissed *her*, but knowing it was the other way around? That has to hurt."

And it did. But I also felt myself understanding why she might have done it. Audrey knew nothing about relationships. She only knew grand romantic gestures like the ones she saw in the romantic comedies she watched. And she knew the massive mistakes the characters made that led to those big moments of reconciliation.

We were quiet for a minute, sitting side by side.

"So, knowing all of this," Cassidy asked, "do you forgive Mike now?"

The heat that flared in my chest gave me my answer. "No," I said, my voice cold. "I'm tired of trying to forgive him. I've spent years forgiving him, over and over again. Even if Audrey threw herself at him, how could he have cheated on me with her? She's my *sister*. What kind of monster does that?"

"The insecure kind, I think," Cassidy said. "I mean, it sounds like he had a really hard time being alone. Like he needed someone to constantly reassure him. And you weren't doing that anymore."

I knew she wasn't blaming me, that she was trying to help, but I still felt guilty. God, I was so tired of feeling guilty.

"You know, he was always self-conscious about his weight." I sighed. I hated talking about weight, even when it wasn't my own. "I always assumed that was why he could overlook my flaws."

Cassidy squeezed my hand, but she'd learned not to argue with me when I talked about things I hated about myself.

"He told me that he had low self-esteem, so I guess he wanted the attention. But he was always doing something stupid, always making an ass of himself, without seeming to care. He seemed like he had plenty of confidence."

Cassidy fell silent for a moment. "You may not be one to throw stones here, Harley," she said gently. "You have the same mix of low self-esteem and blinding confidence that Mike had. Except instead of making an ass out of yourself by getting drunk like he did, you just kind of tuck into yourself. You get lost in comics and movies and TV and you ignore the world, telling yourself you don't need it."

I knew she didn't mean that as an insult. But knowing that didn't make me feel any better about it.

"It's just that sometimes . . . you can be a little intimidating," Cassidy added. "You don't always seem like you need people. And people like to be needed."

"Maybe that's why Raf drank again," I said, almost to myself. "He said it was my fault."

Cassidy's eyebrows shot up. "He drank? And blamed you?" she said. "That's bullshit!"

Her sudden anger somehow lessened mine, as if she took it and held it inside of her, shielding me from it.

"It's not entirely bullshit though," I said. "He knows that the only reason I won't let myself fall for him is because I don't trust him. And that's making him feel bad about himself, so he drank. It's like a self-fulfilling prophecy."

She thought quietly for a minute and then asked, "Would you rather just try to forget about him?"

The pain in my gut told me what I needed to know. "I don't think so."

"You told Will the same thing," she said. "That we had to choose between not being together and quitting our jobs. So I told Samir that I quit The Flakey Pastry."

"Wait, so it's official? You and Will are together?"

She nodded with a dreamy smile on her face.

"That's the best news!" I said, smiling back, genuinely happy for her, but a piece of me now dreaded going to work the next day. "Oh, man, Samir is going to be so pissed at me."

"Nah, it's okay," she said with a dismissive wave. "The second I said I was leaving, he decided I could stay as long as Will and I are together. But if I dump him, I have to find my own replacement. Same goes for Will."

"Oh, thank God," I said. "I was worried I'd gotten my first strike."

She laughed, but her expression quickly turned serious again. "Harley, I don't want you to miss out on something that could be great because you're scared."

I put my hands over my face. "What if I'm *too* scared?"

Cassidy tugged one of my hands away until she could see an open eye. Then she scooted down until she was inches away from my face. "You can't keep hiding, sweetie. You've spent all of high school hiding behind Mike. But *you* have to have a life, too. You have to get out of bed and see people and do things."

"You sound like my mom," I mumbled, but she was right. "And before . . . well, Raf was encouraging me to write again. And Dr. Talia, my new shrink, told me to keep a journal." I was embarrassed to admit that I'd missed writing, that I felt passionate about it. It felt too personal to let people see me want something. Especially when it seemed so easy to fail. Especially since the last thing I'd wanted—Mike—had crushed me. But if anyone understood passion, it was Cassidy, joiner of a hundred after-school clubs.

"Maybe you should try then," she said softly. "If so many people think it's a good idea. Maybe even ask Connie if you can join the literary club."

"Now you're pushing it," I said, but I was smiling.

"Don't make me ask her for you."

"You'd do that?"

She rested her head on my shoulder. "I'd do anything for you, stupid."

I WENT BACK to sleep after Cassidy went to work, not waking until just before noon. Even though it was Sunday, the house was quiet, and I could tell that Mom and Dad were out. Mom, I assumed, was playing golf or visiting Audrey. Dad was almost certainly at the hospital doing rounds. Those visits to his patients usually took up most of his weekend mornings. So when the garage door opened, sheer curiosity pulled me out of bed. Floyd had barked, so I knew it had to be one of my parents since he paid little to no attention to strangers. He wasn't a great guard dog.

Dad's heavy footsteps gave him away before he'd even come through the door, so I was waiting for him when he walked in.

"Hey, kid," he said, glancing at my pajamas with disdain. "You know it's officially afternoon, right? You're burning daylight!"

"Burning it how?" I asked. "Sleeping feels like a perfect way to spend the summer."

Dad's happy expression dropped for a second, and I could see the worry in his eyes. "How about lunch?" he said. "I know you won't turn down a pastrami sandwich for breakfast." He could tell by my pause that he had me, and his face broke into a smile. "That's what I thought. Go get dressed."

Dad drove with the top down on his convertible, and the wind tossed my hair into my face. I could feel my shoulders starting to burn within minutes but didn't ask him to put the top up. After spending months indoors, I could use the tan. And probably the vitamin D.

At the deli, Dad pointed toward two seats at the counter despite the multiple open tables. He usually ate here alone on workdays, so maybe it was habit. Or maybe it was so he wouldn't have to look at me when we had the awkward discussion I knew was coming. At least he was feeding me while he lectured.

After we ordered, he got right to business.

"So your mom told me about what Audrey and Mike did."

I wasn't surprised. Mom told Dad everything, like when Audrey and I got our periods or when she found out I was having sex and she took me to the doctor for birth control pills. He just usually didn't let on that he knew. It was easier on us all that way.

"Pretty shitty thing to do, huh?" I said.

I saw him nod out of the corner of my eye, but I kept my gaze on the milkshake blender across the counter in front of us.

"I just wanted to make sure you know that not all relationships, not all *men*, are like Mike." He cleared his throat. "Are you sure you don't want to tell Audrey about it?"

My head snapped sideways so I could look at him. "Do *you* think I should?"

He sighed. "I don't know, kid. It's your choice, but you have a tendency to bottle everything up and ignore it. And I just want you to know that you don't have to do that. Not with this one. I don't want a Hulk situation happening. I like you the size and color you are."

I couldn't help smiling. "She-Hulk is quite respectable, despite her green skin. Don't be racist."

Now Dad laughed. "Did I ever tell you who I would be if I could be a superhero?"

I shook my head.

"Aluminum Man. So I could foil crime."

I groaned. "That was bad. One of your worst, I think."

He smiled proudly to himself.

Luckily, our sandwiches arrived then, so he was too busy eating for a few minutes to tell any more jokes.

"So, how's our friend Rafael?" Dad asked. "Has he figured anything out yet?"

"What do you mean?" I said, stealing an onion ring off his plate. He reciprocated by stealing a fry off mine.

"I mean, last you told me, he was trying to figure things out. And you two were just friends. So, how's that going?"

"I don't know," I mumbled. "He doesn't want to see me anymore."

"What?" he said. "Why?"

I took a bite of my sandwich so I had time to think. I didn't know how much I could actually share with him without him getting uncomfortable with it. Or telling Raf's parents. But I decided to chance it.

"Don't tell Mom," I said, pointing a French fry at him.

He nodded solemnly. Unlike Mom, he actually would keep a secret.

"Raf and I kissed, as you know, and I told him it was too soon for me after Mike," I said, my eyes glued to my sandwich. "And then he got drunk. And now he says it's too soon for *him*."

Dad was quiet, so I chanced a look at him. His face was completely neutral, and I could see how hard he was working to keep it that way.

"So?" I said. "You *must* have an opinion."

He thought for a few more seconds. "My opinion is that you're a smart cookie. You're thoughtful, and you don't often jump into things. So a little time to figure things out can't hurt."

My heart sank. I'd been hoping he would tell me just to go for it with Raf. I wanted permission to forget about his faults, to forget about the possibility that he might drink again. That he might break my heart.

"But Raf is a good kid," he added. "I've always thought so. And from what I see, he and Mike are two very different people. But maybe Raf isn't so sure that *you* know that."

I glanced at him, surprised, but maybe Dad was right, and he needed to hear me say that. I opened my mouth to tell him how smart he was, but Dad had already moved on.

"So did you hear about the time the old man and his wife were pulled over by a state trooper?" he said.

"Nope," I said, even though I had heard this joke at least four thousand times. "What happened?"

I TEXTED RAF a few times throughout the afternoon, even going so far as to call him once, but he didn't answer. And even though I knew that I should probably give him space, I didn't want to. I was tired of pulling away and tired of not saying how I felt or doing things the way I wanted to.

So as the sun finally began to set, I walked through the backyard, up to his basement door, and knocked. My stomach tied itself into a crisp bow while I waited for him to answer. After a minute, the blinds twitched and he peered out at me. I could see his shadow shaking its head before he opened the door.

"Hey," he said. He was in loose sweatpants and a T-shirt. There was paint smeared across his chest and along his arms.

"Hi." I tried to take a step farther inside, but he didn't back up. I got the message. "How are you?" I said cautiously.

He looked a little sheepish. "Okay. I spent a full day in bed. And then I went to a meeting. Picked up a twenty-four-hour chip. And I told Elaine that I was ready to work the steps. She's going to be my sponsor again."

I smiled, relieved. "That's great, Raf. I'm really glad."

"I'm sorry," he said. "About the other night. I shouldn't have woken you up. I shouldn't have gotten drunk. Or blamed you for it. There were a dozen reasons I got drunk, and this thing with us, it's just a drop in the bucket." He looked at me, then looked away. "I hate that you saw me like that."

"I've seen worse," I told him. Raf hadn't been a mean drunk, or even a loud drunk. He was just a sad drunk.

"I know it bothered you when Mike drank. More than bothered you. And I never wanted you to worry about that with me. But I can't guarantee that I won't relapse again."

I wouldn't have believed him if he'd tried to make that promise anyway.

"I know," I said, choosing my words carefully. "And I'm trying really hard to accept that. I'm pissed off that you blamed me. That was a shitty thing to do. But I know you feel bad about getting drunk. And I know you regret it. And even though I'm angry . . . I miss you, Raf. Even after just a couple of days, I miss you. This space thing sucks."

He shifted uncomfortably, staring down at the carpet. "I miss you, too," he said. His eyes flicked up to meet mine again before they were back on the floor. "But I can't promise that I won't disappoint you again. That sort of seems to be my thing."

I rested my hand on the doorframe below where he was gripping it. Not touching, but close enough.

"You have trust issues, Harley. After what Mike did, why wouldn't you?" Raf said. He crossed his arms across his chest.

"And I have problems with breaking people's trust. Doesn't this seem like a disaster waiting to happen?"

I didn't know what to say. He was right, but that didn't stop me from wanting to kiss him.

"I have to get ready to go to a meeting," Raf said, stepping back so he could close the door. It was an excuse that he knew I wouldn't argue with.

"Let me come with you," I said. I didn't phrase it as a question.

He thought for a moment, and then he nodded, just once, and opened the door wider.

"I'm going to take a shower," he said. "Why don't you stay out here?" He pointed to the couches in front of the big flat-screen TV. I got the message that he didn't trust me in his bedroom when he was about to be naked. I got a small tingle in my belly just thinking about him in a towel.

But Raf didn't take long, and he didn't walk past in a towel either. I called him a prude when he came out of the bathroom fully dressed. That, at least, got a smile.

He drove us to the meeting, but he didn't speak much on the way, aside from asking if I was okay with the music. I nodded, trying to be agreeable, even though I didn't recognize the band.

Raf didn't stop to smoke with the gang gathered outside, though they exchanged quick hellos and head nods of recognition as we walked through. I got a knowing look from Cajun that meant he knew about Raf's relapse. I saw Elaine across the room, and she crossed quickly to embrace Raf and pull him aside. While they talked, I made myself a cup of coffee with non-dairy creamer. I had to pour it out after one sip. Working at the coffee shop had turned me into a snob.

Gradually the room quieted. After Elaine read the preamble,

Arjun opened the meeting reading the twelve steps and then asking if anyone wanted to share.

Raf's hand went up immediately.

"My name is Rafael, and I'm an alcoholic and an addict," he said.

I held my breath. It was the first time I'd heard him say those words.

"About seven months ago, my parents came home from a nice night out and found me facedown in a puddle of my own vomit. I'd taken enough Oxy to make me completely unresponsive after the fifth of Jack Daniel's I washed it down with, and I could have choked if I had been on my back."

My chest squeezed like a fist. But I forced myself to breathe. My eyes began to sting. That was not the story I had heard about how he got sent to rehab.

"While I was in the hospital, they went through my room and found my stashes: bottles of liquor hidden in my sock drawer, Oxy and weed and all its paraphernalia in my closet, plus a few of my mom's Xanax pills that I'd been stealing for the last six years, ever since my sister died." He paused for a moment. "I denied that I was an alcoholic when my parents put me in rehab. Truthfully, I've been denying it for the last seven months, even though I was sober. But the other night, I drank again, and I realized something when I woke up the next day and felt like shit."

The crowd around us chuckled knowingly.

"Seriously, not worth it," Raf reiterated. "But worse than the hangover was the feeling of knowing that I had betrayed the trust of someone who had no obligation to, but seemed to like me anyway." He finally looked at me then, as if he wanted me to really hear what he was saying. "I'm the one screwing up my life. I am the only one. No one is making me drink. It's no one else's fault that I want oblivion so much that I sometimes just want to drink until I can't function, because it's easier than being sober. And no one is going to make it better for me."

A few people in the room murmured in agreement.

"Being an alcoholic can be lonely," he said, "but being sober can be so much lonelier. Giving up everyone I used with meant I had no one."

I almost objected, but then he turned to me again and reached for my hand.

"Except that's not really true," he added. "Not if I don't want it to be. All of you being here tonight means we're not alone. As long as we can find one of these rooms, we will never be alone. And I just wanted to thank you all for that." He squeezed my hand and then let it go. "Thanks for letting me share."

Seven Years Ago

Raf was eleven when his sister, Allie, was diagnosed with cancer. Leukemia. She made it barely a year past her diagnosis.

I remember the days after her death like a dream sequence in a movie, its edges blurry and indistinct. I remember neighbors parading down the street to the Juarezes' house, each with a casserole dish or a Tupperware container. After dropping it off and expressing their condolences, they would come to our house and gather in our kitchen. Mom had a pot of coffee brewing constantly, even though most of them drank wine. At night, when they'd finally gone, Mom would polish off what was left in the bottles.

The day of the funeral, after the service (about which I only remember hating the itchy tights I was wearing), Mom and Dad hosted the reception at our house. We kids played outside in our black and navy finery, kicking off our shoes and ties and tights in the bright afternoon sun. It was spring, and the grass was wet in the backyard. We got yelled at afterward when we came inside with grass stains on our knees, tracking mud on the carpet.

But Mrs. Juarez pulled me into a too-tight hug. Her eyes

were wet and her nose was red, and I didn't know what to say to her. I liked hugging her, though. I missed Allie and I was sorry that she was dead, but I didn't know how to say that. So I tightened my arms around her middle.

"Take care of Rafael, okay?" she said. "I think he'll need his friends."

I hadn't seen much of him over the last year or so, and I wasn't sure how to be his friend anymore. Boys were a weird breed that I was only just beginning to take an interest in after years of keeping my distance. But I nodded at her anyway.

That night, when it was just Mom, Dad, and Audrey left at the house, I watched out the window as Raf stood in the cul-de-sac throwing a tennis ball in the air and catching it. Over and over again. I wanted to go out there and talk to him, or at least catch the ball for him and throw it back. But instead, I went back to the couch where Mom was cuddled with Audrey, and I climbed in, forcing myself between them.

"Don't ever die on me," I said. Mom and Audrey nodded solemnly.

Then I looked at Dad, who said, "Have you heard the one about the three-legged pig?"

I nodded and smiled. "Too good to eat all at once."

He winked and went back to reading his newspaper.

CHAPTER EIGHTEEN

I sat through the rest of the meeting, but I barely heard a word of what anyone said. I kept replaying in my mind the story Raf had told about being found passed out, drunk and high, nearly dead. I didn't know that version of him, and it scared me that *that* part of his life was so recent. It was still, and always would be, a part of who he was. And if I was his girlfriend, if we stayed together, it would always be a part of mine, too.

I had no plans to start drinking heavily or doing drugs, but hadn't I always imagined a champagne toast at my wedding? Hadn't I planned to go to parties and drink at college? Would I be giving up too much of my early adulthood if I stayed home or went to meetings with Raf instead of having drinks with my friends at happy hour? What would we do on New Year's Eve?

I was spinning out, completely panicking, by the time the hour came to a close. I could see Raf sneaking glances at me as we walked outside and while he stopped to smoke a cigarette. I kept my hands in my pockets and my mouth closed as Raf smoked and as he led me to the car. I climbed in silently.

"Are you okay?" he asked me as we pulled out of the church parking lot.

I nodded. "Yeah, I'm just . . . processing."

"You look like you have a thousand questions and they're piling up so fast that they're choking you."

I managed a tight-lipped smile, and Raf looked relieved.

"I just . . . didn't know all of that. About you," I said. "I knew you went to rehab, but honestly? I thought you were more like Mike, drinking on weekends and smoking weed sometimes. I feel stupid that I didn't put it together."

Raf was quiet for a minute and I could see his jaw working anxiously while he thought. "Are you disappointed?" he asked softly.

"No!" I said automatically, but I wasn't really so certain. "I was just surprised."

He scoffed. "That's convincing," he said. He turned to me as we pulled up to a red light just outside our neighborhood. "Harley, that's why I agreed to bring you tonight. I needed you to know that this sobriety thing isn't a fun new group of people to hang out with; it's not about the parties or the all-nighters at the diner, and it's not just smoking cigarettes outside at meetings and goofing off. It's going to be a struggle for the rest of my life."

We pulled up in front of his house, but he didn't look at me as he turned the car off. "I want to be with you, but I don't blame you for pulling away and not being sure about me. I need you to really think about what being with me could do to your life. I'm not always a happy person. I get depressed and surly, and sometimes it's really hard to get out of those moods. I could be a ticking time bomb."

His words rolled over us like a fog. Finally, I opened the door and walked around to his side.

"I understand," I said. And I leaned in and kissed him, just in case it was the last time, breathing in his familiar smell that reminded me of home-cooked meals and movie nights on the couch. "Just give me a little time to process."

Raf nodded with a solemn, single tilt of his head. "Okay," he said.

I walked back to the house in a daze and proceeded to pace its silent rooms restlessly. Floyd followed me for a while, from kitchen to basement to bedroom, before he grew tired and curled up at the bottom of the stairs. I didn't know what to do with myself. I wanted to fix things, to *do* something, but I didn't know what or how.

I wished Audrey were home. Mom and Dad were early-to-bed types, but I could always count on Audrey to be awake late into the night if I was ever bored or couldn't sleep. Now, almost two months into her hospital stay, it still felt weird not to hear the low murmur of the TV show or movie she was watching or the creak of the floorboards beneath her feet while she roamed the house at night. Without thinking, I picked up the phone and called her.

She answered right away, sounding wide awake. "Hello?"

"Hey, Audy," I said. "How are you?"

"Pretty good, considering," she said. "You?"

I sighed into the phone so she could hear it.

"That bad?" she said. "What's wrong?"

"I'm a mess," I confessed. And I told her about Raf's relapse and going to the meeting with him. What I had learned, and realized, about what a relationship with him could be like.

"Wow," she murmured.

"This is why I don't take chances. I just know disappointment will follow."

She scoffed dismissively. "That's a ridiculous philosophy."

"I know that," I said. "But it was working for me."

"Really?" she asked. She knew the answer as well as I did.

"I don't want to get hurt again," I confessed.

"Of course you don't."

"Fine, but what do I do? I mean, you watch all those movies about love and finding The One, and now I've watched them, too, and . . . I just don't get it. It all just seems so hard. There's always so much heartbreak that goes into finding the happy ending."

She laughed softly. "Maybe it's naïve," she said, "but I just feel like it has to be worth the pain or there wouldn't be so many movies made about love, you know?"

"But when do you know it's worth taking that risk?"

"I wish that I knew," Audrey said, sounding wise beyond her years. "But I think there are too many people in this world for it to be impossible to find someone you want to be with for the rest of your life. I mean, people are friends for years, right? Some people are friends their whole lives. And that's not an obligation. There's no marriage certificate or ceremony."

I thought of Neema and wondered if she and Audrey really could remain friends. I'd hate to see their friendship end when it clearly meant so much to them both.

And I thought of Cassidy, who I loved like a sister, who I probably wouldn't be friends with if we had met later in our lives, but who I would do anything for.

Audrey kept talking, amazingly at length and with very little slurring. "I also think it's better to have loved and lost, you know? I just think everyone should get to experience that happiness, even if there's a chance it might lead to heartbreak." She was silent for a second, but when I didn't answer, she went on. "Do you want to be with Raf badly enough to take the chance that it might not end well? That you might go through what you've been through with Mike all over again?"

I was quiet. It was the same question that Cassidy had asked, but now it held much more weight.

"You still there?" she whispered.

"I'm here," I answered. "I'm just wondering how you ever got so much smarter than me."

"Ha! I've always been smarter than you. You just refused to see it."

"Maybe," I said, allowing her to get away with it.

"You didn't answer my question," Audrey said.

"I know. Because I don't think I can. And not because I don't love Raf, I do. It's because I don't think I'd let myself get treated the way Mike treated me again. If Raf wants to keep drinking, then I'm out. And it'll hurt, but not like it would if I kept letting him break my heart over and over again the way Mike did."

This time it was Audrey's turn to be quiet.

"I love you," she said finally.

"I love you, too," I answered, swallowing the lump in my throat. "Come home soon, okay?"

"I'm working on it."

We said good night and hung up. But I wasn't ready for bed yet. I dug around under my bed until I found a half-empty notebook and turned to a blank page. But this time I wasn't writing angry poetry to submit to the literary magazine. It was a script for a comic. I illustrated it crudely with the worst stick-figure drawings in history, but I hoped it would make Raf laugh, at least.

I wrote a note and clipped it to the front page of the "comic." It read:

Dear Raf,

I don't remember the first time I saw you. It felt like you had always been there, at my side. I would have followed you anywhere as long as my hand was in yours.

You were my first friend. My first kiss. My first broken heart.

You are *my first love. I just didn't know what love was when I was three.*

I don't know how to tell if I'm ready, or if you are, or what our future might be. I don't know if we'll be happy or if I'll be enough to pull you from those dark moods. But I know that I don't want to take the chance of losing you. Of not loving you. I don't want to dream of a future without you in it.

Love,
Harley

Then I snuck outside, my heart racing, almost hoping that I would run into him. But I put the pages of my scrawlings in the mailbox and dashed back inside on bare feet without encountering so much as a hint of smoke in the air.

I texted Raf before I could second-guess myself, telling him to check his mailbox.

And then I waited.

I DIDN'T SLEEP much that night. I couldn't close my eyes because they were glued to my phone. But Raf didn't text me back. I hoped he'd called Elaine or Cajun or gone to another meeting. He'd told me there were places, sober clubs, where you could go to a meeting even in the middle of the night.

I spent the night writing, doing what Dr. Talia suggested,

and reliving memories painful and happy, embarrassing and hopeful. And remembering things a little differently, or at least putting some of those memories into perspective.

Eventually, though, I must have fallen asleep because when I woke up early the next morning and immediately checked my phone for a text from Raf, the screen was black. I nearly sobbed when I realized I'd forgotten to charge it. While I waited for it to charge enough to turn on, I opened the door to my bedroom to go to the bathroom, and on the carpet in the hallway was a manila envelope. A sticky note, in my mom's handwriting, read:

Baby duck—

Found this in the door when I walked Floyd. Didn't read it. See? We're both growing.

The seal was in place, and my name was written on the outside in block letters with several outlines and 3-D effects. It looked like it should have been spray-painted onto a brick wall. I pried it open carefully, trying not to shred the envelope.

Inside was a small book, ten pages long, crudely made with sketch paper and staples. The title was *Addicted to You.*

Raf had illustrated my comic.

The cover was an image of a hand holding a liquor bottle, but inside, instead of alcohol, was a tiny version of Raf, a perfect illustrated replica—from the crooked smile to the Chuck Taylors.

The first page of panels showed me and Raf as kids; we were standing under the willow tree in the nature preserve behind our houses. In a close-up, I was holding a My Little Pony in one hand and Raf's hand in the other. The caption read: IT STARTED WITH A PLASTIC HORSE. Raf was telling me that we were going to live there forever. I answered that I was going to need a bed because I wouldn't sleep on dirt. When Raf asked if I'd sleep on a bed made of dirt, I hit him with a long willow branch, leaving a welt across his arm.

The next page of panels showed our first kiss, on the street in front of our houses. Me, being dared by Allie, followed by me kissing him. The caption above read: WE'VE ALWAYS HAD BAD TIMING.

I felt my lips curl into a smile.

The next page was about us when we were around twelve and thirteen. One panel showed him playing basketball while I walked Floyd in the background. He was missing the shot because he was looking at me. I hadn't written that part. My script picked back up when I was following him and Paul down the street, flirting. And then I was sitting on the front steps of the house, waiting for him. He was inside with a beer bottle in one hand, a pill bottle in the other.

Following that was a page of panels about us now. Us sitting together on the garden wall between our houses, smoking. Lying next to each other as fireworks exploded overhead. Sitting in an AA meeting. Fighting outside his back door. I narrated them, as if I was speaking to him from the pages of the comic in each scene.

"Maybe I don't understand addiction," I said. Raf had drawn my ski-slope nose a little too upturned, my ponytail a little too curled, but I looked adorable illustrated in his hand. "I never even got addicted to cigarettes," I continued. "But I know that I can't picture my life without you now that you're back in it. So maybe I'm addicted to you."

The last two pages weren't from my script. The first showed Raf holding my letter, a small lopsided smile on his face, followed by a close-up. The smile had widened. A caption below narrated: I'VE BEEN TOLD THAT DATING COULD BE BAD FOR MY RECOVERY. I'M NOT SUPPOSED TO REPLACE DRUGS AND ALCOHOL WITH A PERSON. Above his head, a thought bubble read: "Too late." Hearts floated in the air around him like butterflies.

And on the back page of the book was the drawing of me I'd seen in Raf's book. It took up the entire last page. A note at the bottom said,

I'll be here when you're ready. –R

My heart was beating so fast, I could hear it like thunder echoing in my head. The rush of relief that we hadn't screwed everything up, that we were going to really do this, made me dizzy. I put on a bra and threw my hair into a ponytail. I considered changing into something cuter and then remembered Raf had seen me in this exact outfit of yoga pants and a T-shirt so often that he had drawn me wearing it. So I ran down the stairs and out the back door.

Raf was sitting on the wall, just as he'd said he would be. There were smears of ink on his jeans, his forearms, and across his cheek. When he saw me, my eyes widened like a startled deer and his lips twitched into a small, tentative smile. If this were a romantic comedy, I'd have run into his arms and he'd swing me up gracefully as we kissed. But I wasn't exactly an agile runner. I would bowl him over trying to leap into his arms.

"Hi," I said as I came to a stop in front of him.

"Hey," he answered. He had a small smile on his face. He looked like he was trying to keep it from widening. That's when I realized I didn't smell smoke.

"You're not smoking?" I asked.

He lifted his sleeve and showed me a nicotine patch.

"Trying this out," he said with practiced nonchalance. All I could think about was how much nicer it would be to kiss him now.

"I'm sorry," I said as I sat down next to him. The stone wall was warm under my thighs, but the sun wasn't completely up yet, so it wasn't hot enough to burn me.

He shook his head. "Why would *you* be sorry?"

"I'm sorry I've kept you guessing. I'm sorry if I made you feel like I didn't trust you," I said. "But thank you for putting up with it so I could figure out what I want."

"You're worth it," he said as he shifted sideways to face me.

I turned, too, meeting his dark eyes. Trying not to focus on his full lips.

"I feel like I don't deserve you," he said. "You've already been through so much with Mike. I don't want to put you through that again."

I reached out my hand and rested it on his. "You're not Mike," I said. "You're sweet, thoughtful, polite, sexy, and about a thousand other things that he's not. But more than any of that, you're working on making yourself better. You actually beat yourself up about not working hard enough at being happy. And that's why I love you. You make me want to be better, too."

Raf blushed, deep enough that it was visible even under his tan skin. And before I could worry that I'd blurted out that I loved him, he said, "I love you, too, you know."

My heart lifted in my chest and a smile stretched my lips. "You do?"

He nodded. "Like you said, I didn't know what it was when I was four; I just knew I wanted to be around you all the time." The blush spread to the tips of his ears. "I used to invent reasons to be around you. Remember when I told you it was International Hug-A-Friend Day and you had to hug me once an hour?"

"No!" I said, reaching out to smack him in the arm. "You little perv."

He grinned sheepishly. "I'll discuss it with my therapist."

"Maybe I'll talk about it with mine, too," I said.

I laughed when Raf's eyebrows shot up. "You have a shrink?" he said.

I nodded. "Yeah. I may not have all the insight you do yet, but she's been helping."

"I'm just so proud," he said, his hands clasped against his heart. His smile turned mischievous. "What do you say about me in therapy?"

"Well . . ." I blinked a few times, caught off guard. "I said that I want to be with you, to help you. And my therapist said I shouldn't try to change you or fix you. She said that I can love you without taking responsibility for your actions."

"Mmm," he said. Then he was quiet for a second. "Do you know the Serenity Prayer?"

"I sort of remember it," I said, not sure where this was going.

"*God, grant me the serenity to accept the things I cannot change, the courage to change the things I can, and the wisdom to know the difference,*" Raf recited. "I still have trouble with the 'God' part, but the rest makes a lot of sense."

"Yeah," I said. "I see that."

"There are a lot of things we can't change. Including what might happen in the future. But change can be a good thing. And I want to change for you. And for me."

I nodded, but there was still an anxious knot in my stomach. "Do you think it's a good idea to ignore what the program says about dating, though?" I asked.

He looked down, away from my face, and picked at his nails. “I can see how getting my heart broken would be bad, and tough to deal with. But I don’t think staying away from you, being miserable and alone, is *good* for my sobriety,” he said.

I reached for his hand and took it in mine. “I’m not criticizing you, Raf. I just don’t want you to be with me if it’s going to be bad for you . . .” I let my voice trail off because I didn’t really want him to agree with me.

“I know,” he murmured. “What both my therapist and Elaine have said is that I have to create a life that doesn’t include drinking or my old friends. That that’s the only way to stay sober. To build a network and a support system, and to create a life that’s better than the life I had when I was using. And I’m one hundred percent sure that life includes you.”

I could feel my face flush. “I’m glad,” I said. “I want to be a part of your life.”

We sat quietly, his thumb tracing circles on my palm.

“You know, aside from Dr. Manhattan, none of the Watchmen had superpowers,” I said. I glanced at him out of the corner of my eye. He wore a curious smile. “They’re just regular people who decided to be superheroes.”

“And?”

“And it seems like an apt metaphor for sobriety. People find strength and confidence to do all kinds of extraordinary things every day. And getting sober takes remarkable strength. You don’t have to have superpowers. You just have to believe in yourself. And assemble your team.”

His smile widened. “So you’re part of my superhero team?”

“I’m definitely on Team Raf,” I said. “I know our timing sucks, but I don’t want to wait for it to be better.”

Raf squeezed my hand. "Right now, I don't want to be anywhere except here, with you."

"Me too," I said, leaning into his side.

"Actually, I'd rather be inside, in bed," he said. I turned to look up at him. He was blushing again. "I mean, with you, but also because I didn't sleep last night."

"Oh, right," I said, gesturing to the comic I still held in my free hand. "What inspired you to do this last night? I wasn't asking you to illustrate it. You didn't have to do anything except text me back and I would have come running."

Raf shook his head. "Don't you get it?" he said with a note of exasperation in his voice. "You're worth more than a text. One declaration of love deserves something equally heartfelt in return."

I got it now. His gesture was small. Less expensive than Mike's gestures were. Less embarrassing. More Harley-sized. Because he knew me. He knew when to push me and when to leave me be, even if he couldn't do it for himself. But I could do it for him. We could push each other to be better.

"How did it feel to write again?" he said with a small, knowing smile.

I rolled my eyes. "Are you just trying to get me to tell you that you were right?"

"Maybe," he admitted. "But I was, wasn't I? You liked it?"

"Fine, yes," I said with a sigh. "You were right, okay?"

His face brightened. "I love hearing you say that."

I scooted closer to him, until we were inches apart, and leaned forward to place a soft kiss on his chin. And then his cheek, and right next to his mouth. "You. Were. Right," I said to punctuate each kiss.

And when he turned, ravenously covering my lips with his, I responded with equal hunger.

LATER, I TRIED my hardest not to feel embarrassed or awkward as I lay next to him. I didn't try to cover myself up, to shield my stomach with my arms or put my shirt on. I left the lights on and tried to enjoy the appreciative look in his eyes when he looked at me. And I looked at him, at his perfections and imperfections both, and I loved every inch.

Raf fell asleep pretty quickly. I couldn't blame him. And yet despite my late-night and early-morning activities, I was too keyed up to sleep. I smoothed the hair from Raf's forehead and kissed him softly as I decided to head home, but I realized I was trapped against the wall and would have to climb over him to get out.

"Hey, Raf," I whispered. I poked him softly in the ribs. "I need to get up. Wake up."

He groaned and turned on his side, facing away from me like a petulant kid who doesn't want to go to school. I curled against his back, big spoon to his little, and kissed his neck. I ran my hand down his stomach, and by the time I reached his pelvic bone, he was awake again.

"What are you doing?" he asked. He was suddenly very still as I let my hand rest on his hip.

"I needed you to wake up," I said. I used his body to pull myself up and over him to the other side of the bed. But he caught me around the waist before I could stand up and held me against his chest.

"Don't go," he said, his breath soft on my ear. I melted into him, letting his lips on my shoulder hold me like a magnet.

"Okay," I said. I settled against his side, tucked under his arm. "Hey, I thought of a new name for you to write. Super-Raf. But you can write it like Super-AF."

His laugh rumbled through his chest. "That's ridiculous,"

he said, kissing the top of my head. "Maybe you can write the comics, but leave the naming of characters to someone else."

I couldn't help laughing. "Okay, I'll keep working on it."

I smiled against his chest as I listened to his breathing deepen. And this time when he fell asleep, I was on the edge of the bed and was able to get dressed and escape out the door without waking him. I left a quick note on his bedside table (*You don't snore. Bonus points! Love, H*) and closed the door softly behind me. I headed toward my house, deciding to take my good mood to the people. I'd been such a massive downer for the last few months, since long before the accident, and I figured the best way to remove some of that guilt and redeem myself was through food.

My first destination was Cassidy's house, but I stopped by The Flakey Pastry on my way. Samir and Will were working behind the counter, and I had to wait for them to stop bickering before I could order.

"Relationships are a marathon, not a sprint," Samir was saying. "You must be good to Cassidy and make an honest woman out of her."

Will's face went red. "Samir, man, I'm nineteen. I'm not ready to get married."

Samir shook his head sadly. "You can't keep dating forever," he said. "Before long, you'll be an old man like me."

I laughed, because Samir was only in his forties, and they both turned to look at me. Will's face went even redder.

"Don't worry, Will," I said. "I don't think Cassidy's got the marriage itch yet, either."

He nodded and gave me a small wave before making an excuse and ducking into the break room.

I ordered two iced coffees and a few pastries from Samir, who seemed to have warmed up to me and accepted that I was a decent barista. That didn't mean he let me have them for free, though. I got a 20 percent discount and any leftover pastries at the end of the night when I was working. It was better than nothing.

As I was backing out the door with my mind focused on not spilling the coffees, the door suddenly swung open and I nearly fell over. Strong hands on my back kept me upright and I turned to see who they belonged to.

"Oh, hi!" I said to Ryan. He released me, and I set the coffees down on the wrought-iron table next to the door.

"Hey!" he said. "I was hoping you were working today. I guess not, huh?"

"No, not until this afternoon. I just came by for some discounted caffeine."

Ryan gestured to the guy who was standing behind him. "Do you know Jason?"

I tried not to look guilty as I waved at Jason Raymond, my sister's freshman-year crush.

"Not really, no, but Audrey's always said good things about you," I told him.

Jason blushed. "How is she?" he asked.

"She's better," I said. "Her memory of the last year is still spotty and she may never remember the accident, but she's getting stronger and she's talking pretty well now. She's surprising us all by how quickly she's improving."

In the summer light, Jason looked younger than his seventeen years. I could see what Audrey saw in him. He was pretty cute. And I could read in his eyes the concern he had for her. I suddenly regretted getting between them.

"She should be coming home in a couple of weeks," I said. "You guys should stop by to see her."

Jason's face lit up. "We will," he said.

Ryan looked at him and then back at me, a question clearly sitting on his lips, but he just raised an eyebrow at me. I shrugged.

"Go ahead in," Ryan said to Jason. "I'll be right there."

Once Jason was gone, Ryan sat at the table and I sat next to him.

"I thought you didn't want Audrey to go out with him," he said. He and Jason were on the same Ultimate Frisbee team, so he'd been my main source of information when Jason and Audrey were flirting. He'd chastised me, saying that Jason wasn't actually stupid; he just had ADHD and learning disabilities. But I'd thought Audrey deserved someone better, smarter, who her friends wouldn't make fun of.

I was wrong. What I'd been telling her, I realized, was that *she* wasn't good enough. She and Jason shared those difficulties, so every time I implied he was stupid it also meant so was she.

So even though I felt like crying, I shrugged. "I've changed my mind. If Jason will make her happy, then I want them to have a chance. Without my interference."

Ryan smiled. "I'm glad you're still willing to do something nice for Audrey. I was worried about how things would be between you guys now."

I tried to keep my tone light when I said, "Ry, how much did you know? About Mike's . . . dalliances?"

His dark complexion hid any blush, but he looked away and I had my answer.

"Did you know about Audrey, too?"

Ryan nodded. "Yeah, he told me. After the accident."

"Do you . . . um, do you think he planned to hook up with her?" I said quietly.

He shook his head vigorously. "No! He never would have planned that. He just liked the attention she gave him. The more girls wanted him, the more he liked himself."

I knew that, but the rationale didn't make me feel better.

"After he cheated on you with Sofia, I told him you deserved better," Ryan said. "And even though he knew that—he really did—he just wasn't good enough for you. He was never going to be good enough for you."

I reached out to Ryan and wrapped my arms around him. He stiffened with surprise. We weren't the type of friends who hugged.

"Thank you," I said. I meant it. He said all the things I needed to hear, even though none of them changed anything.

"So, did you go to the party?" I asked as I pulled away from him.

Ryan's expression hardened. "Yes," he said. "Mike was wasted."

I shook my head. "How?"

"Does it matter?" he asked. "His mom was so mad. But she won't do anything about it. She never has. I think his being in rehab was harder on her than on him."

I nodded. "Yeah, that sounds about right. But remember, Ry, he's not your responsibility."

He tilted his head. "I like this new version of you," he said.

"Me too," I said. I couldn't help smiling. "It was good to see you. Let's hang out soon."

Ryan stood and I followed suit. "It was good to see you, too," he said. "I'll come by with Jason when Audrey's home, but call me before then. Connie misses you, too."

Connie and I were friends mainly due to proximity, like Ryan and I had been, but I liked her. She was the editor of the literary magazine and had bugged me to join last year. Maybe this year I finally would. Mom would love that. Cassidy and Raf, too.

I said goodbye to Ryan and headed for my car, but I was distracted by a text from Raf.

So . . . does this mean I can change my relationship status on Facebook? he wrote. My lips tilted into a smile as my stomach announced its approval by doing a backflip. I bet he wasn't even on Facebook, but I liked that what he was really asking was, "Can I call you my girlfriend?"

Let me at least tell my mom first, I wrote back. She'll want to friend you.

Nice, he answered. Moms love me. I post a lot of inspirational cat memes.

Armed with coffee and chocolate croissants, I drove to Cassidy's with a smile on my face. She was outside before I'd even opened my car door. She wasn't wearing shoes, but she got in the car anyway, pushing her curly hair out of her face.

"I have to stay in here until I'm calm," she said, "or I'll be going to jail for murder. You might want to lock the doors."

"Nuisance?" I asked.

"Nuisance," she confirmed. "She's just begging to be killed, slowly and deliberately." Only her sister could turn Cassidy into a murderer.

I pointed at her coffee and handed her a croissant.

"I think I'll just drive you around the block until you're caffeinated and full of flakey pastry. Get some distance between you and Morgan."

She smiled grimly. "Good idea." Then she tapped her plastic cup against mine. "Cheers, to sisters who make them hard to love and who we are saints to put up with."

"Cheers," I echoed, thinking how lucky I was to have Audrey instead of Morgan as my sister. All Audrey seemed to want was to spend more time with me, not deliberately hurt me. Even cheating with Mike was a cry for my attention.

I was no saint. I never would be. But I could try to be my best self. I would do the work.

Three Months Ago

The sun was high in the clear sky, baking the tops of my thighs to a raw chicken pink, while a cool breeze lifted the hair from my neck. It was an unsettling combination of warm and cool as I sat on the hot wooden planks of the pier with my toes skimming the chilly Chesapeake Bay.

It was April, the week of spring break, and Mike and his friends were swimming despite the frigidity of the water. And, being typical boys, they were splashing and yelling, and threatening to pull us girls into the water.

I sat with the rest of the girls who had been invited: a couple who were girlfriends of Mike's friends, like me, and a couple who were just friends. I was reading the most recent issue of a comic, and though the other girls would sometimes try to include me in their conversation, which was generous of them, I just didn't know how to answer. It wasn't that I had little interest in discussing their friends' problems or what they were planning to wear to dinner that night. (It hadn't even occurred to me that I would need to bring multiple outfits; I had brought exactly enough clothes for the two days we were staying at Ryan's family's cabin.)

It was more that I couldn't figure out a response that didn't make it obvious that I had no idea what I was talking about and that I was more interested in reading. So I just read instead. It got the message across, maybe more blatantly than I had intended.

I stood, having decided to go back up to the house and read on the porch in the shade, but Mike grabbed my ankle harder than I think he meant to, and I lost my balance. I slid into the freezing water, clothes and all. When I came up sputtering for air, I could see on his face that he was worried, that he had been drinking, and that he was sorry.

"Come on, Michael," I whined, shoving him.

Some people might have been pissed about their clothes or their hair getting wet. I was pissed about my book, which was now floating soggily along the top of the water. Ryan fished it out and tossed it back onto the dock, where it landed with a wet thwack *next to Connie. He flashed a mischievous smile at her and grabbed her by the ankle. Connie's grin told me she knew what was coming as he pulled her off the dock.*

Around us, the rest of the girls screamed as they splashed into the water.

Mike put his arms around my waist and pulled me toward his bare chest. I pushed back against him briefly, but he held strong. And he was warm, despite being in the water, so I let him hold me, slipping my arms up around his neck. He kissed me with wet lips and the guys in the water around us whooped.

"Sorry, baby," he said. "I didn't mean to ruin your book; I just wanted you to stay here with me."

I tried not to roll my eyes and failed. "Then next time, use your words," I said. "You're officially the worst, and you owe me a new copy of Squirrel Girl.*"*

My instinct told me to get out of the water and run back to the house to get out of the now see-through white shirt I was wearing. But Mike kissed me again, deeper this time, and I wrapped my legs around his waist, enjoying the moment. Around us, his friends splashed one another and played chicken, trying to knock the girls off the guys' shoulders. I declined their invitation to play, but I stayed in the water until my teeth were chattering.

When I finally climbed back up onto the dock, the rest of the girls followed me, heading to the house to change. And suddenly I understood how they all knew to bring extra clothes.

That night, we were all in the living room of the cabin while a fire roared in the fireplace. Most of us were drinking, including me, and since no one had to be worried about going home to their parents or driving anywhere, everyone was drunker than I'd ever seen them. The night had descended into a contest between some of the guys as they tried to outdrink one another. Mike, unfortunately, was one of them.

As we got older, alcohol became increasingly available at parties. And when it did, at first, it was special, and we were secretive about it. As the availability increased, so did the number of embarrassing incidents involving Mike. But this was only the second time I'd seen him truly blackout drunk.

Six shots and three beers in, when his eyes lost focus, I decided it was time for me to go to bed. I stood, but Mike reached for me. As I skirted his outstretched fingers, he grabbed the hem of my shirt, stretching it. I twisted away futilely until my shirt had risen farther up my stomach than I was comfortable with. I pushed at his hands, but Mike slid them up my bare skin instead, squeezing my breasts while his friends laughed.

"Doesn't Harley have the best boobs?" he said. "It's because she's not skinny. My girl has meat on her bones."

I felt my cheeks burn with embarrassment. "Stop it," I hissed, slapping his hands away.

But his large hand gripped me tightly around the wrist, and I squeaked in pain. "Don't be like that, baby," he slurred, sliding his free hand up my stomach again.

"Stop it!" I said as I twisted out of his grasp. "You didn't think my boobs were the best when you were kissing Sofia."

Mike's friends shouted things like "Damn!" and "Burn!" and laughed at us, the drunk couple fighting at the party. I didn't want to be part of that couple. I wasn't even that drunk, but the alcohol was fueling the fire of my anger.

I headed for the kitchen. Mike followed me, but we didn't get far enough away from everyone else before he accused me of being "no fun" and "focusing on the past."

"I don't give a shit if you think I'm fun, *" I said through clenched teeth, knowing everyone was listening. "You're wasted, you've been embarrassing me all night, and now you're acting like an idiot."*

"I'm not an idiot," he slurred. I hated the way he sounded when he was drunk. His mouth would get all twisted when he talked, as if there were silent syllables in the words, and he was tripping over each one.

"You are right now," I said, turning to go to the bedroom we were sharing.

Mike wanted to keep arguing, but Ryan walked up behind him and distracted him long enough for me to make my escape. I shot Ryan a grateful look and he nodded, apology reflecting in his dark brown eyes.

Later that night, Mike knocked on the locked bedroom door and then started pounding on it when I ignored him. There was no point in talking to him when he was that drunk. He wouldn't remember what he'd done the next day anyway. But I would.

Eventually, I heard Ryan convince him to sleep on the couch, and I made a mental note to buy Ryan all the iced coffee he could drink for the next year.

Something changed after that weekend. Mike grew less interested in hanging out in my parents' basement watching movies, especially when he could be somewhere else, drinking. And I wasn't at all interested in being where he was when he was drunk.

It was a widening chasm that would have soon been too wide to bridge. But not soon enough.

CHAPTER NINETEEN

I drove the familiar route to Mike's house with a knot in my stomach. He'd sent me a text in the middle of the night, just a Hi, but it was enough to make me act. I needed to tell him that I wasn't fooled, that I knew he wasn't sober and didn't plan to be, and that I didn't want to be a part of his life. I wasn't looking forward to his reaction.

"Oh, Harley," Ms. Baker said as she opened the door. "I was worried I might never see you again. How are you?"

"Okay," I said. Ms. Baker held the door open for me and tried to pull me in for a hug on my way in, but I pulled away, apologizing.

"Don't be sorry," she said, closing the door and sealing in the cool air. "I know my anger can't possibly compare to yours, but honestly, sometimes I can't bear to even look at him."

I tried not to look as taken aback as I felt. This was her perfect son she was talking about. I'd never heard her have anything but praise for him.

"I'm sorry, I shouldn't be telling you this," she said. Her eyes misted with tears, and I finally opened my arms and gave her a quick hug. She sighed gratefully.

My throat was clogged, full of anger and sadness and pain. I was practically choking on it. But she didn't wait for me to answer. She wiped her eyes and ushered me inside.

"I'm sure you're not here to see me. Michael is downstairs playing video games."

There was so much I wanted to say to her. To yell at her, really. But instead, I just watched her back as she headed toward the couch, settling in to watch TV.

From the top of the stairs, I could hear the sounds of the first-person shooter game Mike was playing in the basement. He was shouting at someone somewhere else in the world, something about "flanking his left." I'm not sure even he knew what he was talking about.

I stepped around the couch until he could see me in his peripheral vision, but he did a double take anyway.

"Harley!" he said, dropping his controller. His eyes flew back to the TV as his character was violently shot, multiple times, in the head. I heard several groans through the earpiece. "Sorry, guys," he said to the team he was playing with. "I gotta go."

"Wow," I said as he pulled off the headset and stood. "It used to take hours to get you to quit playing."

He shrugged. "Maybe I've changed." He smiled then, that glib, knowing smile that meant he knew he was doing something I wouldn't like but was going to let him do anyway. I almost shuddered. How I had ever fallen for his charm, I couldn't understand.

I sat down on the couch, and he sat next to me. I shifted to put a few more inches between us and his forehead creased, but he didn't say anything.

"So how are you?" I asked.

"I'm glad to be home," he said. A careful response to a

loaded question. "The people I was in there with . . . Well, you saw them. Let's just say they weren't the type of people I wanted to be friends with. It wasn't summer camp."

He was smiling, but I wasn't. "It wasn't supposed to be."

Mike rolled his eyes. "Have a sense of humor, Harley Quinn."

"This isn't funny, Mike. I know that you're drinking again. You just got out of rehab and you're already drinking."

"I just need to escape sometimes," he said. "I need to forget. Just for a while. Drinking is the only thing that makes the guilt fade."

I wanted to slap him. "You don't get to forget!" I said, nearly shouting. "Audrey never will. I never will. Your mom, my parents, Cassidy, Ryan. None of us will ever forget. Because of you."

He wouldn't look at me.

"I know you don't want to hear this," I said. "And I know you have no intention of being sober. But you need to stop hiding your insecurities by getting drunk. You are better than this, Mike. If anyone knows that, it's me. I didn't stay with you for so long for no reason."

The muscle twitched in his jaw again, but at least he wasn't telling me to shut up.

"But that person you are when you're drunk? He's dangerous. He's mean. And there were times when I was afraid of you."

"I never laid a hand on you," Mike said in a low, angry voice.

He had never physically hurt me or forced himself on me when he was drunk, but I refused to touch him once his eyes became glassy and his personality morphed. It was like kissing a stranger. He hadn't appreciated that.

I shook my head. "You hurt me *constantly*," I said. My throat tightened. "You chose alcohol over me all the time. And I know I didn't stand up for myself or yell at you, and I'm sorry for that because that wasn't fair to either of us. I should have told you I wouldn't put up with it. But I'm not afraid of losing you anymore. The worst has already happened."

I swallowed and steadied my resolve. "So now I'm saying it. You are *unbelievably* lucky that you, Audrey, and the man who hit you are still alive. You are even luckier that you aren't in jail right now. I don't think you appreciate that you were sent to rehab instead. Most addicts can't afford it, and you need to recognize that privilege instead of mocking the people there."

He looked away guiltily.

"At the very least, I need you to swear to me that you will never drive drunk again." I stood and looked down at him until he looked back. "Swear it."

To my surprise, he nodded. "I swear," he whispered.

"Thank you," I said. "And I need you to know that we are done. I can't be around you, especially if you're going to be drinking. It's really over, Mike."

"I know," he said.

I stood, ready to get away from him, but I realized I had one more question. "Why didn't you tell me about what really happened at the party? That Audrey kissed you?"

He glanced down and his hair fell into his eyes. "It wouldn't have mattered," he said. "And it's not like you gave me a chance." Bitter wasn't a good look for him. But he was right.

"I guess not," I said. "But did you even remember? Do you remember anything about that night?"

His gaze hardened. "I remember. Every. Second."

I was so surprised, I actually flinched. "Oh," I said. I turned to go, but he grabbed my hand.

"That accident was one of the most terrifying experiences of my life," he said. "I'll never forget what it felt like when I saw that car coming at us or the sound it made when he hit us." He blinked rapidly. "I get that it's over, I do, and I get that you're angry. But I just really need you to forgive me." His glacial blue eyes were glassy with tears.

I bit my lip. I wasn't sure if I forgave him or not, but I knew it wouldn't be good for either of us if I just kept holding on to this anger. I needed to move past it. Past him. And maybe he needed my forgiveness to stop drinking, or at least to stop drinking to forget his guilt. And maybe I needed to believe that, if only just for a second.

"I do. I forgive you," I said.

His shoulders slumped with relief and a tear slipped out.

"Bye, Mike."

"Bye, Harley Quinn," he answered with just a hint of a smile.

When I got to the top of the stairs, I headed for the front door. But as I reached for the knob, I heard Ms. Baker in the kitchen. Adrenaline was still racing through my veins and it turned my feet around and pushed me toward the kitchen. Ms. Baker turned to look at me, and I stepped toward her.

"I know it's probably not my place to say this," I said, "but you need to do better. You need to be a better parent to him."

Ms. Baker's face grew pinched with anger, but I could see that I'd struck a nerve.

"You know that, don't you?" I continued. "I know Jordan told you the same thing he told me: you can't enable him."

She nodded silently.

"He's drinking again."

"I know," she said, her voice a strained whisper. A tear slipped down her cheek.

"You need to be stronger for him. He's only a kid for one more year—you only have control for *one more year*—and then he goes to college." She nodded again, her chin trembling. "You can't let him go to college and drink like he does right now. He'll hurt himself. Or someone else."

"I know," she said.

"Do better," I repeated. "Help him be better."

"I'll try," she answered.

Two Months Ago

I wanted to go home.

Cassidy should have known better than to ask me to sleep over. The chances of me making it to the end of any party were minimal, even if it was hers.

I started the search for Audrey, hoping she might be willing to leave early, and Mike, who had probably continued drinking until he had passed out on a couch somewhere.

I could hear shouts from the garage, where a raucous game of beer pong was being played on a pink plastic ping-pong table. At the other end of the house, in the kitchen, wobbly Jell-O shots were being passed out by Cassidy's fourteen-year-old sister, Morgan. Her mouth was red at the corners, and she was laughing at something a guy said as she passed by.

I took a picture of her and sent it to Cassidy. Keep an eye on The Nuisance, *I wrote.* She's sampling the merchandise.

I wandered around for a while looking for Mike. I didn't need him; I drove myself to the party. But I didn't want to leave without saying goodbye. And I had to track down Audrey anyway. I needed to make sure she had a way to get home, even if it wasn't with me.

I threaded my way through the crowd and headed upstairs. It was the only place I hadn't checked, but I also needed to get my bag from Cassidy's room. It had been optimistic of me to bring my pajamas in the first place, and now I had to carry them through the party as I left.

The door to Cassidy's bedroom was closed, but that wasn't a surprise. She'd told me she was going to lock it so no one could have sex on her bed, in front of her stuffed animals. But I'd spent many nights sleeping in that room, so I didn't think twice when I reached above the doorjamb, grabbed the hidden key, and opened the door.

I waited for my eyes to adjust in the dim light, so it took me a moment to realize that I was face-to-face with my little sister.

"Harley?" she whispered.

"Jesus Christ, you scared the shit out of me!" I said, jumping back a foot.

Audrey's chestnut brown hair, normally pin straight with tidy bangs, was messy and her light blue eyes were wide with shock. No doubt it was a mirror of my own, both in features and expression.

My anger melted, reshaping into embarrassment when I saw that her shirt was half-buttoned and her shoes were in her hands. The bed behind her was mussed. This was unexpected, sure, but I hadn't meant to interrupt my sister's make-out session. I was more curious who it was with.

I mouthed "Sorry" and started to back through the door, but Audrey didn't scream at me to get out or smile with embarrassment. Instead, her eyes flitted to the floor where a familiar Hellboy T-shirt lay on the rug. I had seen it in that very position many times before. I leaned down and reached for the shirt, holding it out accusingly toward her, but I couldn't speak.

"Who is that?" Mike's voice called out through the bathroom door. A second later, he appeared, bare-chested and with his fly half-zipped. His mouth dropped open when he saw me silhouetted in the doorway to the bedroom. His eyes were glassy and unfocused. "Harley. Shit."

I could see he was searching for a plausible lie for why he was shirtless in a bedroom with my little sister, but he was so drunk that he had to lean against the doorframe just to stay upright. I held up a hand to stop him.

"Don't," I said. My voice was a hoarse whisper as my throat closed around a golf-ball-sized lump. "I don't want to hear it."

I turned and ran for the stairs, dropping Mike's shirt on my way. Audrey called after me, but I ignored her.

As I ducked through the living room to the front door, I felt bile rising in my throat. The door to the bathroom opened and I dashed into it, cutting off a line half a dozen people long. I ignored their mutinous cries as I slammed the door behind me.

I'm pretty sure I threw up everything I'd ever eaten in my whole life. I kept picturing Mike, his belly full of beer protruding over his unbuttoned shorts, putting his hands on my sister. Kissing her. On top of her.

My throat was raw, and my lips were stinging when the door opened a crack. Audrey poked her head in.

"Harley? Are you okay?" she said. Her words were slurred, and she had to put one hand on the counter to keep her balance.

I leaned back against the wall and breathed in through my nose slowly. "Get out," I moaned. "I don't want to look at you right now."

Her chin trembled, and her eyes filled with tears. "But

nothing happened! Just let me explain." A tear glanced off her nose and hit the floor near my knee.

"If nothing happened, then why are you crying?" I said as I pushed myself up from the tile. I rinsed my mouth out with water and washed my hands. Bloodshot and red-rimmed, my eyes in the mirror reflected a glassy blue. My face was flushed from crying. From throwing up. From the sting of betrayal.

Audrey bit her lip until my hand was on the doorknob.

"I was jealous," she whispered finally. "You spend all your time with Mike, and you don't even seem to like him. And then tonight, he let me be his beer pong partner. And after we lost, I spilled beer on myself. He took me upstairs to clean up and borrow a shirt from Cassidy and . . . we kissed."

"Did you sleep with him?" I asked, though I wasn't sure I wanted to know.

"No! We just kissed . . . and stuff. I didn't plan it; it just happened."

"But you let it," I said.

I left her crying in the bathroom. She could find her own ride home. She could walk for all I cared.

CHAPTER TWENTY

When I visited Audrey the next day, she was curled up in bed with her back to the door. She didn't roll over when I walked in, and she barely looked at me when I sat down next to her.

"Hey, kid," I said.

She pushed her knees away from her chest and rolled onto her back to stare up at the ceiling. "Hey," she murmured.

"Want to watch a movie?" I asked. "Dad really wants us to see *The African Queen*."

She groaned. "I've been saying no to seeing that movie for years. Why now?"

"Your wide-eyed, naïve optimism seems to be rubbing off on me," I said. "I figure we can give Dad the benefit of the doubt."

She tilted her head, another question on her lips, so I told her what had happened the day before with Raf. "So I might be buying into the Audrey Langston school of thought that love is worth taking chances for," I said as I sat down next to her. "Scoot over." I cuddled in on her hospital bed as she slid over slowly and rested her head on my shoulder.

"I'm happy for you," she said. But her tone was seriou
much more so than I'd expected.

"You don't sound happy," I said. "What's wrong?"

She wouldn't look at me, but I could tell she was working on an answer, so I didn't ask again.

"I've been remembering some things lately," she said finally.

My heart was suddenly beating loudly in my ears. I could feel the blood rushing to my face. I hoped my expression was neutral, just in case she glanced at me.

"Did something happen between me and Mike?" she asked. "Because . . ." Her chin trembled. "I just keep having this memory of fighting with Neema and then all of a sudden I'm with Mike. And we're . . . kissing." Her entire face turned red, all the way to the tips of her ears, but she rolled over to face me when she asked, "Is it real?"

"Yes," I said, once I'd swallowed the lump in my throat. Audrey's eyes widened. "It was at the party the night of the accident. You kissed him after Neema told you she was in love with you."

Audrey stared at me, her eyes filling with tears. "Oh God," she whispered. She looked down at her hands, and the tears spilled over, splashing onto the blanket. "I kept thinking it had to be a nightmare. I never . . . How could I have done that? How could I have hurt both of you like that? How are you both still here, anywhere near me, after I did that to you?"

Her breathing was shallow and fast, and her hands squeezed into fists. I wrapped my hands around the fist closest to me.

"I was so angry," I said. "At first. But seeing you here, in the hospital, struggling to breathe, to walk, to live? Eventually, I was able to put things into perspective."

"Why didn't you tell me?" she asked. She looked so hurt

that a spark of anger coursed through me. She shouldn't get to be hurt when I was the one who had been betrayed. But I couldn't sustain the anger. Having almost lost her, and having had enough distance to see that I could survive the aftermath of it, I just wanted to forgive her and move on.

"I hated you for a while, but when you didn't remember, I felt like you were given a do-over. You could go back to being the Audrey who had never betrayed me. Because you aren't the same person you were when you came with me to that party. And neither am I."

Audrey's forehead creased, and she swallowed hard. "I'm so sorry," she said, her eyes pleading. "Harley, I'm so, so sorry."

I gathered her into my arms, pulling her thin body to mine. I could feel her ribs even through the hoodie she was wearing.

"I know you are," I said. "I'm sorry, too."

She pulled back enough to look at me. "For what?"

"For all the times I was mean, or ignored you, or made you feel like I didn't want you around. I wasn't always the most supportive sister."

"You were, too," she said, hugging me again. "You slept next to me for years, and you could have smothered me with a pillow a thousand times, but you never did."

I laughed, pushing her playfully. "You're right," I said. "I really *am* a saint."

Audrey laughed, too, wiping away the remaining tears on her cheeks. "Thanks," she said. "I love you."

"I love you, too, kid," I said. Then I gasped and sat up. "Oh my God, I almost forgot to tell you. I saw Jason today."

Audrey's smile grew shy. "Jason Raymond?"

I nodded. "He asked about you."

She glanced away, but her smile grew. "How did he look?"

"He looked good, I guess," I said. "He and Ryan were coming from Frisbee, so they were a little sweaty. Do you want me to invite him to come see you here?"

She considered it for a moment before shaking her head. "No, I'm not ready to see him yet. I want to wait until I can shower and dry my own hair. I want to be wearing something besides sweatpants."

I argued that I didn't think he'd care, but she was adamant. And I knew better than to try to convince her otherwise.

"So," I said instead, "do you feel like watching *The African Queen*?"

She grinned. "Yeah. But if we like it, let's not tell Dad. It'll just make him insufferable."

I stuck out my pinkie, and she linked hers with mine. "Deal."

A LETTER FROM THE AUTHOR

One night when I was sixteen, I came home drunk and high after a party and found my parents waiting for me. I was drug tested and, soon after, put in a rehab program. In the hours of group therapy that followed, the counselors tried to help me and other kids my age understand why we used drugs and alcohol, but I already knew.

I used because it was the only thing that eased the anxiety and depression that led me to cut myself. My fear that no one would ever understand or accept me wasn't unique, but I often thought about taking my life because of it. My parents were afraid that the next time I got drunk or high, I would actually do it. And though I wouldn't admit it, so was I.

Part of rehab required going to Alcoholics or Narcotics Anonymous meetings, getting a sponsor, and working the twelve steps. I was resistant, but I went. I listened to the stories of the people in those rooms and, over time, I found a community of young, sober people. We were all a little off, a little weird, a little broken. We all carried around something inside ourselves that told us we were worthless. But together, we learned that with the support of the program and each other, we were strong. We were fun. We were capable of being happy. While sober.

But I was also exposed to a world outside of my privileged, suburban bubble. I saw the trauma that brought other kids into the rooms with me. Kids who had killed their best friends because they drove drunk, who had lost their parents to addiction and were following in their steps, who drank or used drugs because they were abused or neglected as children. Who found the strength to quit—without expensive rehab programs—and turn their lives around. And I was given perspective on whether my life really was too difficult to keep living.

The young people's program in Alcoholics Anonymous saved my life, but my heart aches for the teens who won't get there. Alcohol is an incredibly dangerous drug and the accepted abuse of it in our society is alarming. Teaching teens responsible drinking is important, but so is teaching them to take responsibility for the things that happen because of alcohol abuse, which is a message I tried to weave into this novel.

But I also wanted to share the stories of the people I met in the rooms who were so warm and welcoming when I needed a safe place. People whose nicknames were often holdovers from their using days, who were entirely comfortable with their weirdness, and who embraced my peculiarities and insecurities and helped me learn who I was and who I wanted to be.

The Art of Losing is about making mistakes, accepting things you can't change, and figuring out when to forgive and when to walk away. But mostly, it's about loss, especially the loss of the life you expected to have and the terror of realizing you have to reimagine your future.

I hope this book will help make the possibilities of the future a little clearer for someone who needs it.

All my best,
Lizzy Mason

ACKNOWLEDGMENTS

I've spent my life surrounded by the most inspiring book lovers. I have dreamed of someday seeing my own name on the shelves of the bookstores in which I've spent hundreds of hours. But seeing the dream come true has taken the help of an army of people, to whom I owe enormous thanks.

This book is dedicated to my sister, Anna Woodward, because I could—and did—write pages about how wonderful she is. Bugso, you've always had confidence, whether you're dancing or singing or learning or teaching. I believe in myself because you never seem scared to try something new and I've always wanted to be like you.

But this book wouldn't exist without the constant support of my mom. Thank you for telling me so many times "You are a writer," for showing me that creativity is important and teaching me to write, for insisting that I always keep a journal, and for asking "What happens next?" until I finish my stories. But mostly, thank you for talking me down off all those ledges and being there to catch me when I jumped anyway.

Dad, thank you for all the jokes, the puns, and the one-liners. You've taught me that work and fun don't have to be mutually exclusive, and that fun sometimes takes work. Sorry for all that burned daylight. Thanks for checking my medical facts, and for loving this book and making me believe in it too. I swear, someday I will watch *The African Queen*. And I'll keep working on that Ferrari.

Thank you both for putting me in rehab, and for loving me enough to not be afraid of letting me hate you. I am strong because you supported me.

To my agent, Stephen Barbara, who signed me for what was

clearly an imperfect book based on the number of revisions we did: thank you for seeing the good and for helping me fill in what was missing. Thank for you holding my hand and answering questions I should probably know the answer to after this long in publishing. Thank you for making my dream come true.

To my editor, the incomparable Daniel Ehrenhaft: thank you for believing that Harley and I had an important story to share. Thank you for working through the corrupted files and feverish epiphanies that made this a better book and me a better writer, and for somehow knowing what I was trying to say, but not quite saying, and making it better. (Could you edit that sentence?) I am lucky to count myself among the many members of the Dan Ehrenhaft Fan Club.

"Thank you" may not cover what the team at Soho Teen deserves, especially Bronwen Hruska, Rachel Kowal, Paul Oliver, Steven Tran, Monica White, and Janine Agro. As a publishing veteran, I know how much work goes into making a book, and I know that it can't happen without an incredible team behind it. Thank you for believing in this story, for making it look pretty, for making sure people know it exists, and for a hundred other things that I didn't even know were happening.

To my family—especially Patricia Hinn, Della Hinn, Andrew King, Jane Palmer, Maury Palmer, Robert Palmer, Steven Woodward, and Sara Taylor—thank you for proving that family can be friends. I'm sure people all over the world think this, but I have the BEST family.

To my mother-in-law, Betty Gold, thank you for believing I would finish this book long before I did. Your notes were invaluable and your encouragement kept me writing. Thanks also to my father-in-law, Alan Gold, for your support and writing wisdom, and for giving Karl the comics that eventually inspired my main character.

I wouldn't know what friendship was without my best, oldest friends Meredith Bracco, Kara O'Donnell, and Erin Riley. Thank you for getting me through high school and for sometimes acting like we're still teenagers.

Marcio, thank you for being my first best friend and for appearing out of the dark that night all those years later. Thank you for inspiring Rafael.

My amazing earliest readers: Ksenia Winnicki, thank you for being there any time for a book signing or writing date or movie or nachos. Jamie Pacton, proof that Internet friends are real friends, thank you for always being willing to talk me through plot problems and read my messy drafts. Gaby Salpeter, thank you for so many nights of tots at Big Daddy and for your invaluable thoughts on this book when it really needed it. And to Stephanie Brown and Hannah McBride, thank you for being my first blogger friends, for being so supportive for so many years, and for being the first to ever give me an "author" badge at an event and making me cry.

To all the authors who believed we'd one day share shelf space: thank you. Special thanks to Robin Benway, Alexandra Bracken, Susan Dennard, Elizabeth Eulberg, Jeff Giles, Brigid Kemmerer, and Danielle Paige for all the pep talks, hand-holding, advice, and writing wisdom.

To the Bloomsbury team, my work family, thank you for the support when I took days off to write and for not mentioning it if you saw me crying at my desk. I feel incredibly lucky to have found a place among such creative, enthusiastic, and brilliant people.

And finally, to my husband, Karl, thank you for sitting next to me while I wrote every word of this book, and for never once complaining when I was so distracted by my stories that I forgot to make dinner, or left my keys in the front door, or left the bathmat in the laundry room. You are my love, my puppy, my bee bee, my sweet. Thank you for your unfaltering support and for holding me while I cried, and especially for not letting me give up on myself. (You know I tried.) You are everything I could have ever hoped for.

AUTHOR'S NOTE

If you're struggling with substance abuse, there are several places you can turn to. You can find an Alcoholics Anonymous meeting near you at www.AA.org or a Narcotics Anonymous meeting at www.NA.org. Or if you know someone who is struggling, check out Al-Anon at https://al-anon.org.

For more information about addiction, you may wish to visit the resources below:

Hazelden Betty Ford Foundation:
http://www.hazeldenbettyford.org/addiction/what-is-addiction

National Institute on Drug Abuse: https://www.drugabuse.gov

Substance Abuse and Mental Health Services Administration's National Helpline:
https://www.samhsa.gov/find-help/national-helpline

If you're dealing with mental illness or thinking of suicide, help is available:

American Psychiatric Association: https://www.psychiatry.org

National Alliance on Mental Illness: https://www.nami.org

National Suicide Prevention Hotline:
https://suicidepreventionlifeline.org
Or call 1-800-273-8255

Continue reading for a preview of Lizzy Mason's next novel,

Between the Bliss and Me

CHAPTER ONE

Graduation day definitely wasn't the right time to tell Mom I'd lied to her about my college plans. But it's not like I could have kept it a secret much longer.

I just wish the reveal hadn't been at my grandparents' country club. My dad's parents. Ever since he left when I was a toddler, we've been the Holman quartet, gathering awkwardly at major holidays and life events.

We were having lunch after the graduation ceremony, the quiet so thick I could hear Grandpa's nose whistle while he chewed his prime rib. Mom squirmed next to me, impatient to leave, but we were in this for the long haul. My grandparents would be ordering dessert. They always did. And insisted everyone else order it too, because they'd be paying.

How can you not love someone who insists you eat cake? Somehow Mom managed.

When our desserts arrived, Grandma handed me an envelope. Inside was a schmaltzy FOR MY GRANDDAUGHTER ON HER GRADUATION DAY card, and when I opened it, a check fluttered to the linen tablecloth. Mom looked at the amount and choked on her cheesecake. That was a lot of zeros.

"Grandma, Grandpa, this—this is . . ." I stammered.

I didn't look at Mom. I could feel her disapproval without needing to see it on her face. My stomach churned.

"I know you said you'd pay for school, but you can't just give me thirty thousand dollars in a check, can you?"

"Why not?" Grandma asked, truly puzzled. "It's our money, Sydney. We want you to have it. But this isn't for tuition. I've set up a trust for that. This is just for books or groceries or clothes. For rent, if you want to get an apartment with some friends. Or if you want to go to Mexico for spring break."

I felt something loosen in my chest, like a spool of thread unwinding. I'd been saving for college since I was old enough to work. I knew how expensive all of the things Grandma had just mentioned were. And even though Grandma and Grandpa had agreed to pay my tuition, I'd been expecting to pay for everything else. My bank account just hadn't grown quite enough to actually cover it. I'd been planning to work all summer to try to catch up.

Visions of sitting poolside all summer flashed in my mind.

"Thank you, guys!" I jumped up and squeezed Grandma in thanks, maybe with a little more enthusiasm than she would have liked. She smoothed her neatly pressed dress and smiled at me with tight lips. She hated it when I called them "guys."

I hugged Grandpa, too.

"I wish your father were here to see you," he said quietly.

My smile slipped. I tried not to think of my dad. My memories of him were hazy. And not just because he'd been surrounded by a near-constant cloud of smoke, cigarette and otherwise.

When I returned to my seat, Mom was still glaring at the check that sat on the table between us.

"Why would Sydney need this much money when she's got a full scholarship to Rutgers and is living at home?" she said. Her voice was icy.

Grandma and Grandpa both looked at me expectantly. My stomach turned to lead.

"I'm, um . . ." I took a deep breath and started over. "I'm not going to Rutgers, Mom. I'm going to NYU."

Her eyes narrowed. "What do you mean? Rutgers gave you a full academic scholarship. NYU didn't offer a dime!"

I nodded, swallowing hard against the lump of fear in my throat. "I know. That's why Grandma and Grandpa offered to pay. So I didn't have to settle. So I could go to my dream school and not have to work overtime for the rest of my life to pay off loans like you did."

I didn't add that I was also counting down the days until I could move out of our apartment. Out from under her watchful eye and her overprotective wing.

Mom threw her napkin on the table. "You went behind my back?"

There was nothing to say. Obviously I had. But Mom turned her fury on Grandma and Grandpa instead.

"You two are unbelievable," she said through clenched teeth. "Don't you think it's irresponsible to give that much money to a child? With her . . . history?"

I stiffened. My dad might have been a drunk and an addict, but I was way more responsible than that. I'd spent my life proving to her that I wasn't like him. It was insulting that the thought would even cross her mind.

But Grandma and Grandpa brushed off her concerns. Grandma literally waved a hand in Mom's direction.

"Let's not discuss that today," she said. "This is a celebration."

Mom stood, grabbing my elbow to haul me up beside her. "Not anymore. We're leaving."

I pulled my arm from her grasp. The country club members around us were looking on curiously, no doubt judging my Forever 21 dress and Mom's fake pearls. But Grandma seemed impervious to their judgment as she stood to kiss me goodbye.

"Congratulations, Sydney," she said. "You'll do wonderfully at NYU." She leveled her gaze at Mom.

I stepped between them to kiss Grandpa's papery cheek.

"I love you, sweetheart," he said.

"Thank you again!" I called over my shoulder while Mom pulled me toward the door.

Her anger crested as she marched to the car. Fury practically radiated off of her.

"I just don't understand, Sydney," Mom said. She slammed the door. "We've worked toward Rutgers for so long and now you just want to forget it? What about all our planning?"

Mom and I had never made any decision without a pro/con list and a lot of discussion. We were organized to an obsessive degree. Our budget spreadsheet was taped to our refrigerator. We kept a shared online calendar detailing where we'd be at every moment. Every one of her binders and notebooks for nursing school had been meticulously organized. Setting up my bullet journal every month was my happy place.

"I planned for NYU too," I said calmly, even though my heart was racing. "I picked my classes and housing. I figured out how to pay for it. I just didn't do it with *you*."

She opened her mouth and then closed it, blinking back tears. That had come out harsher than I'd intended. But her sadness hardened quickly and shifted to anger.

"You just want to take the Holman's money like it doesn't

matter that you didn't have to work for it?" she said. "That you didn't *earn* it?"

I rolled my eyes. "So many people's parents or grandparents pay for them to go to college. Why do I have to struggle just because you did?"

Mom pinched the bridge of her nose. This was a familiar argument. We'd had it when I first got my acceptance letters and she decided where I'd be going.

"I'm not saying you should struggle," she said. "I'm saying it's important to take ownership over your successes. If you let the Holmans pay for college, then it's not yours, Syd. It's theirs too. And after spending the last eighteen years allowing them be a part of your life, of them constantly giving me advice and judging the way I was raising you, I was . . ." She paused. "I was really looking forward to having some autonomy."

"So this isn't really about me at all," I said with a smirk, finally understanding. "You just want Grandma and Grandpa out of *your* life."

She turned to face me. "No, sweet. I want you to go to school and live your life. Now you have to be accountable to *them*."

I shook my head. "I was always going to be a part of their lives. I'm sorry you don't like them, that you don't love them like I do, but they paid for me to go to private school for thirteen years so that I could even dream of going to a school like NYU. Not going feels like a slap in the face to all of us."

I sounded confident, but my throat was tight. She couldn't take this away from me. Not after all the planning I'd done. All the dreaming.

"Sometimes it's better to struggle to reach your dreams," Mom said. "You appreciate it more when you work for it."

"I've worked every summer since I was twelve," I grumbled. "I appreciate it, believe me."

She was quiet, but her eyes were watery. "I'm sorry you had to do that," she finally whispered.

"I'm not asking you to apologize," I said. "*I'm* sorry. For not telling you about NYU. And that Grandma and Grandpa are difficult, and that they're in your life because of me."

Mom reached out for me, awkwardly hugging me across the armrest. "I wouldn't change that for anything in the world," she sniffed.

"Remember that at Thanksgiving," I said with a laugh. It got a smile.

"Let's go home," Mom said, turning the car on. "I have to be at the hospital at six tonight."

She wasn't over it, that much was clear. Moving to New York instead of living at home was going to take some convincing. But it had been a long day and there was an entire summer ahead to work on that. It would probably take me that long.

WHILE MOM CHANGED into scrubs, I texted my best friend, Elliot, to tell him I was finished with lunch.

Come to band practice, he wrote back. I need your help with something.

I cringed. Elliot was an incredible musician, but his bandmates were usually mediocre at best. He'd had a revolving door when it came to bass players, especially. So unless he needed me to sing lead while he trained a new member, I avoided his basement band practices.

But Elliot was a year younger than me and this was our last summer together before I left for school. I could make an exception this time.

I changed out of my graduation dress and looked for my favorite pair of jeans. I knew I'd put them on top of my dresser with the T-shirt and bra I'd planned to change into. But the shirt and bra were on the floor and my jeans were nowhere to be found.

I knew where to look. Under my bed, my cat, Turkey, had created a nest. This was a habit of hers—and the reason I usually kept my door closed when she was home alone.

Turkey meowed angrily as I scooped her up and pulled my jeans out. They were warm. And covered in fur.

"You little thief," I said. I kissed the soft fur between her ears before setting her on my bed. "You have, like, six cat beds. Why do you have to steal my clothes?"

Turkey ignored me as she curled up on my pillow.

Once I was dressed, I put in my earbuds and pressed play on The Playlist—my dad's favorite music. Hundreds of hours' worth. I'd found it on a flash drive buried in the junk drawer when I was twelve. It was the only remnant of him in the house, and that's only because Mom seemed to not know it existed.

When I listened to it, there were fleeting moments where I thought I knew what kind of guy my dad was. He was a kid in the eighties who loved pop music by male singers but wasn't afraid to put Whitney Houston and Bonnie Raitt on a mixtape. He was an angst-ridden teenager in the nineties who listened to Pearl Jam and Nirvana and, later, My Chemical Romance and The Killers. He embraced old school hip-hop from the eighties and R&B from the turn of the millennium. He loved soul and Motown, swing and big band. There was at least two hours' worth of New Orleans blues and jazz. And, of course, there was the occasional nod to his New Jersey heritage with Bruce Springsteen and Bon Jovi. But just as I thought I'd put a finger on him during a long run of Stevie Wonder, Ray Charles, Al Green, and Otis Redding, he'd switch to The Cure and Blondie and Talking Heads.

The current song in my ears was Sam Cooke's "Bring It on Home to Me," which always brought back flashes of what was either a memory or a dream. I couldn't really be sure which.

I pictured my dad in front of an upright piano, his back to me as I sat on the floor. I could feel the vibration of the music when I pressed my hands against the hardwood. Dad was no Sam Cooke, but his voice was soft and soothing as I swayed along with the music.

A moment later, Dad was sitting next to me on the edge of my bed.

"Hey, kid," he said. His brown eyes were kind, not glassy or clouded with intoxication. I didn't have many photos of him, and they were all more than fifteen years old, but the image I had of him in my head was clear, accurate or not. He was average height, not much taller than me, and thin, almost scrawny, with dark blond hair that he kept short to control the curl. He had an easy smile and a square jaw that looked like mine.

I wasn't surprised to see him. When I was a kid, after my real dad left us, this version of him was my imaginary friend. Plenty of only children have imaginary friends, so that's not weird. (Right?) We had tea parties and played board games. I'd put on recitals, singing my heart out for an audience of him and my stuffed animals.

But as I got older, I kept imagining him. I kept talking to him. Because talking to this imaginary version of my dad was as close as I'd ever get to the real thing.

Sometimes the pain of missing him felt like an actual hole

through my chest. How was it possible to miss someone I didn't even know?

"She's being impossible again," I said. I didn't bother to remove the earbud. Imaginary Dad could hear me just fine.

His smile was sympathetic. "I know your mom is tough sometimes, but she does it out of love."

Even my imagination couldn't help trying to forgive Mom.

But even with Dad's music in my ears and his invented sympathy tempering my anger and guilt, I could practically feel the tension through the wall between Mom's bedroom and mine.

It was a small apartment; there wasn't really space for arguments. It was too likely Mom and I would run into each other on our way to the bathroom. Our tight quarters forced reconciliation.

But this time, even though we'd both apologized, the matter wasn't settled. And there was no way to change that when we were both convinced that we were right.

So instead of pretending everything was fine, I headed to Elliott's house.

I COULD HEAR the music before I even reached the front porch. It wasn't good.

I didn't bother knocking because no one would be able to hear me over the noise anyway. Elliot's mom was sitting at the kitchen table, noise-cancelling headphones over her ears, a book in front of her. When I tapped her on the shoulder, she jumped.

"Sorry, Mrs. K," I said loudly as she removed the headphones and pulled a foam earplug from one ear. Doubling up today. That wasn't a good sign. "How long has this been going on?"

"Feels like forever," she said wearily. "But really just the last hour. They still have an hour to go before our neighbors are allowed to complain. Thank God for the Home Owners Association."

I waved as she put her headphones back on and steeled myself to enter the basement. Elliot had padded the walls with foam, and carpet covered the floor and ceiling, but that didn't make the music sound any better.

Elliot was keeping pretty good time on bass. Even though he'd only been playing for a few weeks, he seemed to have a decent feel for the instrument. It looked like his fingers might be a little weak for the strings, though. His face was red with the effort. His neon-pink hair stuck to his forehead with sweat.

The guy on drums, Arlo, was sweating through his T-shirt and still not keeping up. He winced every time he messed up, too, so it was obvious. As if Elliot's glare wasn't enough of an indicator. Or the lack of an actual beat.

And the lead guitarist, Maddie, wasn't keeping up with anyone. The chords she was playing, even to someone who had never so much as plucked a string, were audibly off-key. She could sing, though, and leant a credible air to their attempt at covering an early Beatles song, one of the up-tempo peppy ones, at an alarmingly slow pace. I couldn't figure out which song it was until the new guitarist turned around from where he was modeling how Maddie *should* be playing and she started singing the refrain.

Mid-century pop music was never meant to be played that slowly. It highlighted the flaws in the songwriting.

The new guitarist, a tall, dark-haired guy with a hint of shadow along his sharp jaw, was admirably attempting to keep up with the off-sync time of Elliot and the drummer.

I perched on the arm of the couch and pretended to be looking at my phone while discreetly admiring the new guy.

Don't bother, I heard in my head. *Musicians aren't worth the trouble.* Inner-conscience Sydney was right. My dad was a musician and look how he'd ended up: broke and alone. I imagined him playing trumpet on street corners, the only people hearing his music on their way to somewhere better.

That hadn't stopped me from dating musicians at first. When Elliot started the band my sophomore year, his drummer and I started dating. I joined the band in order to be around him more, which he found "clingy," and quit. And broke up with me.

After that, Elliot made me swear not to fall for any of the other guys who joined. I quit the band, but none of the new guys had wanted to go out with me anyway. Or even make out with me.

But this one . . . I'd have trouble keeping my promise for him. He looked so happy while he was playing, grinning like a kid at recess. When Arlo and Maddie screwed up, he just played louder to cover their incompetence. At one point, he closed his eyes as if he was focused so intently on the music, he had to block out everything else. Or maybe he was just trying not to laugh at how terrible they sounded. With his eyes closed, though, I had free reign to ogle the hell out of him, and, God, was he ogle-worthy.

When I finally tore my gaze away, Elliot was shaking his head at me. I stuck my tongue out at him.

Mercifully, the song ended and Elliot announced that they would take a break while he massaged his fingers. I could see the blisters on them from across the room.

Elliot waved the new guy over to me while Arlo and Maddie headed outside to vape. And probably to make out.

"Syd, this is Grayson, our new guitarist," Elliot said. "He's filling in this summer until we find a real replacement. And he's attempting to save us from ourselves."

As I caught Grayson's eye, we shared a conspiratorial smile that made butterflies take flight in my stomach.

"Great!" I managed to say without laughing. "How's he going to do that?"

"You may have noticed Grayson can actually play?" Elliot said.

I nodded slowly, trying not to appear overly enthusiastic. "Yeah, but anyone's better than Rhythmless Nation out there." I jerked a thumb toward the back door where Maddie and Arlo stood.

Grayson turned a laugh into a cough, but I caught it. My chest swelled with pride.

Elliot ignored it. "And it gives me the chance to play bass," he continued, "which, apparently, is my destiny since no bassist in all of New Jersey wants to be in my band."

"I don't understand," I said, tearing my eyes from Grayson's chiseled cheekbones to Elliot's rounded, baby face. "You actually play drums and guitar well—like, professional-level well. Why do you have to play bass and let those two destroy whatever chance you had at being a band people might actually want to listen to?"

"Because," he said, pausing as if that were explanation enough. "Maddie and Arlo only know how to play guitar and drums, so I had to fill the missing spot. Why *not* me?"

Calling what they did "knowing how to play" was being generous, but that wasn't the point I wanted to make at the moment.

"Because you already play, like, five other instruments! And annoyingly well!" I said.

It was exhausting having this argument for the twentieth time, but I didn't understand how it could be so easy for him. Just like it was for my dad, who played piano, trumpet, and guitar. Professionally. It should have been in my genes, but I'd never had the patience to learn even one instrument. I took piano lessons for two years and barely made any progress. I worried too much about being perfect, which just made me impatient and angry. My piano teacher quit after I threw one too many temper tantrums.

There would have been years of playing terribly in my future if I wanted to be as good as my dad or Elliot. So I gave up and stuck to singing.

But that didn't stop me from being jealous of people who could play an instrument—or multiple. And sometimes my jealousy came out as anger.

Elliot just shook his head sadly. "Never mind."

I looked to Grayson for help, focusing on his deep-blue eyes. "Do you play five instruments too? Do I need to go join Maddie and Arlo in the dunce's corner?"

Grayson chuckled and shook his head. "Not really. Just guitar."

Elliot snorted.

"Don't let him fool you," he said. "Grayson's going to—" But he stopped and waved a hand as if he was in agony. "No, you tell her. I can't. It hurts too much to even say the words out loud. I'm too jealous."

I looked back at Grayson. "Tell me what?"

"I'm going to Juilliard," he said, ducking his head shyly.

My mouth dropped open. I searched his face for a hint that he was lying, but his expression stayed neutral. He didn't start laughing or even let his lips twitch.

"No! People don't actually *go* to Juilliard," I said.

He tilted his head. "What do you mean? Of course they do. About eight hundred of them every year."

I was incredibly gullible, but I wasn't going to let myself look like an idiot in front of this guy. Except he still wasn't laughing.

"Are you serious?"

He didn't answer. He just pulled out his phone and started scrolling through his emails until he found the one he wanted. And then he held out the phone to me.

Dear Mr. Grayson Armstrong, the email read. *It is the admission committee's pleasure to welcome you to the Music Program at The Juilliard School for admission in the fall semester of 2021. Welcome to the class of 2025!*

I stopped reading after that. "Oh," I managed, trying not to focus on the heat that had risen to my cheeks. "Um, congratulations?"

Grayson suddenly burst out laughing, a deep, resonant sound that made the flush in my cheeks spread downward.

His laugh trailed off as he reached out and put his hand on my shoulder. "Don't worry about it," he said. "I'm still having trouble believing it myself."

He dropped his hand after only a second, but I could still feel its weight and warmth as he asked me where I was going to school.

"NYU," I answered. I couldn't keep the grin from my face.

"Oh, awesome! We could hang out when school starts," Grayson said.

Somehow, I managed to squeak out, "Or before then, even."

He nodded normally, as if I hadn't just sort of asked him out. Or maybe that kind of thing happened to him every day. When you're that hot, it must be at least a weekly occurrence.

But just then, Maddie and Arlo walked back in, saving me from making a bigger fool of myself. The band, if you can call them that, went back to practicing with Elliot and Grayson gently coaching the couple through the songs. I curled up in one corner of the couch, pretending to look at my phone as I snuck glances at Grayson. I only caught him looking back once, but he also could have been looking past me, trying to read the clock on the cable box.

"I better get going before El's mom comes down and turns the hose on us," Grayson said when I pointed at my wrist to signal that it was six o'clock. "You laugh, but that's what she threatened to do last week."

I watched him head for the basement stairs. He waved at me before turning the corner. I turned back to Elliot with a dreamy smile.

"Don't," he said, flipping his neon hair from his eyes. "He's got a girlfriend. They've been together for like two years, so it's not gonna happen."

My heart burst into flames. "Why?" I beseeched the basement ceiling. "But we had a connection, I'm sure of it."

Elliot grinned. "Yeah, I'm sure you did," he said.

He'd heard me say that too many times since we'd met in his freshman year. Initially, I even thought Elliot was hitting on me because he kept complimenting my outfits, but when I tactfully tried to turn him down, he less tactfully told me he was "as gay as a flamingo on Fire Island." In my defense, his hair was a very normal dull brown back then.

"Grayson," I sighed. "What a great name."

Elliot just rolled his eyes.

"Hey, why did you even ask me to come over, if not to introduce me to my future husband?" I asked as I flopped onto the couch.

His face brightened. “I want you to sing for Maddie so she can focus on playing first. Do you think you can step in for a little while she improves?” My grimace betrayed my reluctance, so he added a “Please?”

Singing was fun, an escape, but I never let it be a passion. I joined the choir and the Madrigals for my college applications, not to practice. I also joined the yearbook and film clubs, so my interests would seem diverse. I turned the lyrics I wrote into poems so they served a practical purpose: I could submit them to the literary magazine. A few of them even got published.

For four years, my focus was on crafting my résumé to be the perfect candidate for a school like NYU. So I could study something that would get me a job outside of Plainville, New Jersey, that paid enough money so I wouldn’t struggle like my mom did.

Singing was not a career. Music was not a future. My dad’s fall from promising musician to deadbeat (or so I’d been told) was proof of that.

I wanted a future. I wanted a good job, health insurance, marriage, kids, pets—I wanted all of it. And music wasn’t going to get me there. But I could help Elliot out . . . if it meant being in close proximity to Grayson.

“Okay,” I said.

“Thank you!” he cried, throwing his arms around me. “Let’s try something now.”

I nodded. “Acoustically, though,” I whispered. “So your mom doesn’t murder us.”

He strummed the first few chords. I tried to ignore the rush of adrenaline. But I couldn’t help smiling as I started to sing. I could try to lie to myself, but the truth was: I loved it.

WAYS TO CONVINCE MOM TO LET ME GO TO NYU:

* Lie and say I got a scholarship
* Problem: she'll want to see proof

* Agree to live at home
* Problem: I have to live at home

* Agree to come home every weekend
* Problem: I have to come home every weekend

* Tell her I'll pay back Grandma and Grandpa once I have a job
* Problem: I may never make enough money to pay them back

. . . ?